To Malcolm
Xmas '96
with love
A...

Tanith Lee, born in Lond... the age of nine, and was first published in her early twenties. Since then she has produced over sixty novels and several radio plays, and has twice won the World Fantasy Award for her short stories. She now has a world-wide following

She lives in the South-East of England with her husband (the writer John Kaiine) and a black-and-white cat.

Tanith Lee's novels *Heart-Beast*, *Elephantasm*, *Eva Fairdeath*, *A Heroine of the World* and *Reigning Cats and Dogs*, as well as a short story collection, *Nightshades*, are also available from Headline Feature.

When The Lights Go Out

Tanith Lee

HEADLINE
FEATURE

First published in 1996 by
HEADLINE BOOK PUBLISHING

First published in paperback in 1996 by
HEADLINE BOOK PUBLISHING

A HEADLINE FEATURE paperback

10 9 8 7 6 5 4 3 2 1

ISBN 0 7472 5216 5

Typeset by Avon Dataset Ltd, Bidford-on-Avon, Warks

Printed and bound in Great Britain by
Mackays of Chatham PLC, Chatham, Kent

HEADLINE BOOK PUBLISHING
A division of Hodder Headline PLC
338 Euston Road
London NW1 3BH

How many goodly creatures are there here!
How beauteous mankind is! O brave new world,
That has such people in't.

Miranda: **The Tempest**
Shakespeare

Foretaste

Near winter's end, the man walked by the sea's edge. The sky was pale and low and calm, the water almost still, like silvered mirror, and meeting the pebbled beach, slow like cream. The horizon, with its world-curve, seemed very near. It indicated how large the planet earth must be, how small. But the other way, the old town ran along above the promenade, faded by the light, the colour of a pen-and-wash drawing. Nothing moved there but for the gulls. And then the gulls settled, and nothing moved at all.

A wave came in, another.

The man looked back at the mobile sea. It would be easy to pretend there was no other human creature on the earth but for himself. But Hassinger did not do that. He was too old to do it, perhaps, it had lost its savour, such a game. Or else, he did not need the game.

Tall, heavy over-large bones, about fifty. With a gaunt, battered handsome face, hooked nose, large, long-lidded eyes, faded blue like some of the plasters of the town. All his life often taken for a German. He had not argued. His thick hair, part grey and part blond, sprang back from his forehead, hung round his cheeks, his neck, ended in the collar of the bulky leather jacket. Below, paint-spattered trousers, equally bulky boots.

He looked as if he had come from laying a road or redecorating a house, but on the way, he had done cunning murder, and perhaps read the Bible, or the Koran, from cover to cover, and could quote it at you. Brutal and clever, intellectual, sensual, spiritual, and too strong. And the thin mouth always on the lip of amusement. Just.

Hassinger watched the waves.

Something was coming in, a dull brown thing, crusted by pieces of the sea. A corked bottle dressed in tiny barnacles.

It swam to his feet and knocked against a boot. The wave withdrew, and left it there.

Hassinger bent. In the movement was all the power of his strength, an unusual coordination – and too the stiffness of half a century.

He picked the bottle up and, turning, held it to the weak, cold sun. There was something inside. A paper. A message.

Not surprised, you could see he was not, not at all, Hassinger took the jeweller's glass from his pocket and set it to his right eye. He looked through it at the paper in the bottle.

A name, not to be made out even with the glass. Fine writing rather, but not mostly, eroded.

We are going down, it said.

We are going down. We are lost. God have mercy upon us.

Under that was a note which read:

Night. April 14th. 1912.

And then:

White Star Line.

Beneath this, the words, very clear, the most clear of all: *You who find us, leave us in peace.*

Hassinger took the glass from his eye, put it away. He put the bottle in the other pocket, and when the light left it, its life seemed to drain out.

As he walked up the pebbles to the promenade, he passed a black and white gull, tearing at something small and red with its savage beak. The beak had stored all the colour of last summer in its yellow. So had the bloody meat. Hassinger glanced, and saw that the meat hung from a long white bone. The gull watched him, but when Hassinger spoke to it, a single word, it flew up and settled massively on his arm.

Hassinger smoothed the gull's feathers with one finger.

Above in the town nothing moved, but again the other gulls lifted.

In two months the Season would start. The shops would put out their awnings, the funfair would open with its scream of rides, the lights switch on all along the bleak grey poles that rimmed the promenade. Red and brown, the makers of holiday, in crowds, coming and going.

'April, the fourteenth,' said Hassinger, to the gull, 'White Star. The *Titanic*.'

The gull laughed, a noise like a devilish sheep. And flew away.

PART ONE

One

'Stand up.'

Hesta looked at the woman.

'Are you talking to me?'

'*Ms Simpson*. Yes, Heather, I'm talking to you.'

Hesta said, 'Hesta.'

Ms Simpson, the supply teacher, was turning a deep purplish pink, that would have been pretty in a flower. But not in her. Her pale eyes bulged behind her glasses.

'All right, *Hester*. Stand up.'

Hesta Web stood, without hurry or fuss, fear or fury. With . . . distaste?

'Now, I know you've been messing about with your hair. It's ridiculously obvious, isn't it. Only a fool couldn't see it. And you must know the rules here.'

A little whisper of sound went around the classroom, a compendium of surprise, hilarity and suspense.

Twenty girls between fifteen and sixteen, in the uniform of the Aspens, the dark dull green skirts, that some had raised a little above the knee and some let down a little below, the white blouses, the green ties pulled as loose as possible in the late October heat. The heat too brought out the heady smell, over the school-cage aroma of dust and wood and books, the hint of the lime trees outside, of very young, very clean female flesh, sprayed with deodorants and essences, imbued with secret need and thoughts.

'Well, Hester, what do you have to say?'

Hesta knew Ms Simpson, the supply teacher, would spell her name this way – H.E.S.T.E.R. That is, if she did not spell it *Heather*.

'What do I say to what, Ms Simpson?'

Ms Simpson turned darker, more malevolent. She raised her voice. 'Your hair, girl. Dyeing your hair.'

'It isn't dyed.'

'Don't be stupid. It very definitely is.'

Hesta did not point out that Ms Simpson, the supply English teacher, had just qualified an absolute. She said, mildly, 'This is my own colour.'

Ms Simpson uttered a melodramatic laugh. 'How can it be? That bright *red*. It's out of a bottle.'

Someone else laughed. Possibly because dyes no longer came from bottles, did they, and Ms Simpson, though she was a hag of thirty-two, should still be young enough to know this. Ms Simpson glared at her.

'No,' said Hesta.

She could now see in Ms Simpson's bulbous eyes, that Ms Simpson would like to run at her, attack her, perhaps pull out clumps of the offending hair. Hesta had seen this look swell out at and for herself in many women's faces. It had started with her mother.

'Well, Hester, I expect you to go home tonight, and either wash it out, or re-dye your hair your own natural colour. Your

8

hair is any way too long and extremely untidy. Do something about that too. How old are you? Seventeen?'

'Sixteen,' said Hesta.

'Then for the time being you'll have to abide by your school rules, and not do yourself up like a clown.'

The normal English teacher, quiet, clever Mrs Pryne, was away, learning to use a computer. Ms Simpson could manage computers perfectly well, although once a week their use resulted in a blinding headache, beginning on a Friday night, and ending sometimes as late as Sunday evening. Hesta could see all that, in some form, in the woman's bunched brow, her resentment and her desire, which must be partly checked, to wound. But Hesta was not compassionate. She did not have the space.

'This is my own natural hair colour,' said Hesta. 'Look.'

The class of Aspens girls had all been waiting, for something, although they had not known for what. Now they gave collective gasps and sat forward avidly, some pretending to be shocked, one or two very embarrassed, yet anxious not to appear so.

Hesta had pulled up her skirt, made into one of the much longer varieties, and holding it at her waist with one hand, with the other she pulled down her sheer tights and the white cotton pants beneath. There then, exposed to the gaze of them all, and to the glasses of headachy vicious absolute-qualifying Ms Simpson, was Hesta's bush of pubic hair, the exact same fiery scarlet as on her head.

Hesta said nothing. She stood there, showing her hidden centre. Without shame or exhibitionism, not even defiant. Then she drew up her pants and tights and let the skirt fall easily down again over her narrow hips.

A silence commenced, threatening to overwhelm.

Ms Simpson bravely said, 'What do you think you're doing?' Her voice was a strengthless croak. The ugly petals of her face were quite purple. Out of synch, the headache was coming on her too early.

Another girl spoke. 'You can't dye down there, Ms Simpson. It's dangerous.'

And one more, 'Hesta's always had red hair.'

Ms Simpson touched the edge of her desk, as one touches an amulet. She said, 'Go straight outside, Hesta. And sit in the corridor. I'll decide presently what to do about you.'

Hesta picked up her Biro, and the fountain pen her father had given her. She put them into her bag with her notebook, and left the room.

Outside, the heartless corridor ran through a hot afternoon shadow. The big clock above the stairs recorded the time as a quarter past three. In fifteen minutes the school week ended. Hesta went down the corridor and down the wide stone steps, where, yesterday, a twelve-year-old had fallen and cut her lip quite badly. When Hesta had told Janey of this, Janey had said, 'Poor little bitch. Scarred for life 'cos of going to bloody school.'

All about, sounds came from classrooms, the buzz of the computers and the tang of sudden voices. The futility of this dreary, lawful little hive, caught in the green amber of an autumn afternoon, was emphasized when the outer door beyond the cloakroom was opened.

Lavish lawns spread away to the distant gate, the formal flowerbeds, with last golden wallflowers and red begonias, the lush lime trees dribbling their sticky droppings on the shale of the drive.

Hesta, with her blazer over her shoulder and the terrible school hat squashed into her bag, walked along the drive, past the tennis court, towards the ironwork gates.

She had come here first when she was twelve.

It was a 'good' school, you had to pay for it. Stephanie said it would iron out Hesta's speech and she would make 'proper' friends. But Hesta did not make friends, and kept the original friend (Janey), from whom Stephanie had hoped Hesta would become detached. As for her speech, Hesta had a musical voice. Her diction was clear, her grammar mostly immaculate, and she had retained her South London accent, as Stephanie never ceased to lament.

Relays of birds flew off the drive, and back, as Hesta left it. In the tree-shaded road beyond the gate, the houses basked in the last sun of the year.

Despite the hectic summer, Hesta was white as alabaster. Stephanie's tactic of sun-creams, garden and beach sunbathing, preferably abroad, and sun-beds in winter, had never interested her daughter. Years of this, however, had matured Stephanie to a curious yellowish-brown, a jaundiced eternal tan. Stephanie coaxed it, petted it, shaving and depilating and creaming her thirty-six-year-old body, smothering it in lotion and endlessly turning herself under the sun as if on a spit.

Stephanie was older than Ms Simpson, and looked ten years younger. Except for the lines around her eyes and mouth, the sharp corners of her neck, her loose breasts that seemed to have no filling, save when cantilevered upwards by wire and lace. 'I take care of myself,' said Stephanie, who, apart from now and then, limited herself to salad and crispbread, and one bottle of dry white wine a day. When she spoke of herself like this, she sounded to Hesta like a woman of fifty. And to Hesta, actually, Stephanie, her sharp-edged mother, *looked* fifty.

It was too early for Janey at the bus-stop in the High Street. Hesta walked to the Asian shop and bought a Diet Coke. It was not permitted to eat and drink publicly while wearing school uniform.

'Are you well, Hesta?' asked the woman from Bengal. She spoke Hesta's name in a perfect way – *Heths-stuh*. Hesta said she was. She asked after the woman's husband, son and cat. All were apparently flourishing.

Once Hesta had seen the woman's hair come undone from its bun. It had fallen drenchingly to her knees, black as cobras. Was India like that?

Leaning on the wall near the bus-stop drinking the Coke, Hesta watched cars, people, the metropolis as it passed. She knew it had little, or nothing, to do with her. Sometimes one of the loud boys from the Milton School cycled alongside and shouted at her. Once one had come directly over and put a hand on her breast. She had smacked him in the mouth and he backed off, jeering, but there were peculiar tears in his eyes.

Janey was running down the street, waving. It was an odd if only momentary thing, this recognition. Did you feel for a sister like this? Maybe not. The sisters Hesta had come across seemed to hate each other.

Janey was thin, almost as she had been at ten, her long

dark hair cut now in the same wild spiky way as Hesta's – they had scissor-slashed and combed the style for each other one Saturday morning in September, before the mirror in Janey's bedroom, on a carpet of shed red and black.

'What a bloody afternoon,' said Janey. She laughed, and drew in a deep breath of heat and acid car fumes. 'That bastard Snotgas gave us two hours extra homework.' Snodgrass, the maths teacher, was often a problem. 'Do you want the bus? I'm dying to *walk*. I've been wriggling like a little kid, and that Leonard said, Look at Janey, she wants to go to the bog. We can go through the park,' she added, 'I've saved a sandwich for the ducks.'

'So have I,' said Hesta.

Martin Peecey stood under the fake flowering tree, the telephone receiver tucked between jaw and shoulder.

'Steph, I'd love to. You know I'd love to. But, baby, the way they've got it stacked up here, it's a shambles.'

A female waiter went by, in her ultra-short black skirt, sheer black tights and glimpse of white knickers. She had good legs, though her shoes were flat – it was a long day's work – he and Kevin always checked their legs. If he had had a free hand, Martin Peecey might have patted her bottom, but he was occupied with pad and pen, writing down a list of wines missing from the wine bar's menu, and those that needed to be left off in future.

The girl may have appreciated her luck.

Peecey was tall and skinny and very tanned. His Brylcreemed hair was receding only a little at the front, but stopped short behind, an inch above his collar. He wore a trendy, floppy suit that was a few weeks out of date. His Rolex was too expensive.

'No, baby, listen. Tomorrow. OK?'

At the other end of the line Stephanie said, 'I hate Fridays, Marty. You know I do.'

'Yes, Steph, but it's one of our busiest—'

'*She* comes in, and then she's there and I don't get a word out of her. Iain takes me out, you know. He always does.'

'Yeah, yeah, Iain,' said Peecey nastily. 'But he's off on his little drilling rig, isn't he?'

The female waiter bent to a table of eager four o'clock drunks. Peecey saw right up her skirt. Very nice. With the clean white blouse buttoned to her throat, it was all rather like a naughty school uniform.

Not like Hesta's uniform, however.

What would Hesta look like in this gear? He had put it to her. Make a few bob waitressing on a Saturday. He would take care of her. Hesta had looked right through him. Well, that was a sort of come-on. Of course, she was too young for him. But Steph was a bit too old, wasn't she?

'Your Hesta's a pain,' said Martin Peecey, dutifully. 'Yeah, all right, Stephie. Yeah. OK. I'll come. About seven . . . eight. When Kev gets here, the cunt.'

Just after five, Hesta let herself into her mother's house. This was how she thought of the house, in essence if not words. Her *mother's*.

Her father of course, Iain Web, had bought the house eleven years ago. It was a large semi in a long quiet street. Two wide storeys, and an attic that, when she was a child, had been done up as Hesta's playroom. Stephanie had raised a wallpaper with pictures of dolls, and hung the inset windows with chintz curtains. There had been child-sized furniture which perhaps, as a child, Hesta had found accommodating, but quickly she grew too tall for it. Now the room lay abandoned, and Stephanie moaned about it – a room that was not employed.

Hesta's bedroom was on the second floor, and next to the 'family' bathroom, which she used. Far off along the upper hall, lay the huge bedroom which was Stephanie's, Iain and Stephanie's when he was at home, and the en suite bathroom where Stephanie and Martin Peecey took Dolphin showers together after their noisy sex in the king-size bed.

If she had thought back, Hesta might have noticed she had never heard the sounds of the sexual act between her mother and father. Probably this was because, as Stephanie had sometimes hinted, with Iain it was not much use. Out of this unusefulness, Hesta had been fashioned.

All the house was furnished and decorated to Stephanie's design. That is, in mixed ideas from magazines. Every thing was very modern, even luxurious, and quite awful. Stephanie had no idea of colour, and believed that if a room were made only in shades of blue, or green, or red, it would work. But certain shades of the same colour can clash; they did so all over the house. There was also nothing comfortable in the house, in the sense of relaxing. It was not . . . what was it that it was not? A home.

Hesta went into a large, all-white kitchen (troubling to the eyes of any but the very young and strong-sighted), and opened the fridge.

Through the double-glazed glass of the kitchen door, she could see Stephanie lying on a bright mauve lounger, naked but for a small yellow bikini-bottom. The Victorian garden had been pared back to its verdant rim, to leave yards and yards of scalped lawn. Den, the cleaner, did the lawn too, kept it free of everything but scorched grass, like partly-greenish tobacco.

This, the immemorial image of her mother, flat on a sunbed, a lounger, a beach. In Spain, in Italy, in France – and long ago, at Clacton. (All countries alike. A beach, a few restaurants.) Stephanie basting and cooking herself in the savage damaging sun.

Hesta took a piece of lite cheese from the fridge, and ate it with three crispbreads buttered by diet mayonnaise. Bread was not kept in the house normally. Later, there would be a salad dinner with a small grilled steak or wafer of grilled fish.

As a child, Hesta was always hungry. Stephanie told her this was quite right. She always would and should be. A girl had to watch her figure. In fact Hesta had never needed to attempt this curious feat. She could eat anything, everything, and did not gain an ounce. But Stephanie had to be careful, and thus, so did everyone. No wonder Iain took her out to dinner when he was at home. It was the only way he could get any food.

As Hesta finished her snack, Stephanie rolled over, looked at her gold watch which gave a sun-flash like lightning, rose, stretched in a balletic way described to her in a magazine, and walked into the house by the French doors.

After a moment, she entered the kitchen.

'Oh, you're back.'

'Yes,' said Hesta.

'What have you been eating?'

'Crispbread.'

'Well don't stuff yourself. We're having a big meal tonight.' Hesta smiled a little. Stephanie's ideas of a big meal were sometimes amusing. 'Den's going to drop some stuff by from the supermarket. I'd like you to help me with it. Martin's coming over.'

'I'll go to Janey's, then,' said Hesta.

'You're always over there. That common girl. And that awful fat mother of hers. Why do you go there?' Stephanie did not wait for the answer, which was obvious: Janey's was evidently preferable. 'Why won't you stay? I really need you to keep an eye on the food. It's a chicken and I don't want to splash my dress.'

Hesta said, 'No.' She did not speak rudely or harshly. It was a statement, empty of offence. Save for all its implication.

'Don't speak to me like that, you little beast.' Hesta took her plate to the sink, rinsed it, set it in the rack. '*Look* at me when I'm speaking.' Hesta turned, looked at her mother. Stephanie stood quivering, her naked empty breasts trembling at her annoyed heart. 'I want you to stay. You only come back here one night in seven.'

'I need to do homework,' said Hesta, 'apparently.'

'Of course you need to. It's supposed to be two or three hours a night. You skimp it. Your father pays enormous fees for you to go to that school. And you've got GCSEs next year. If you want to go on and do art—'

'I don't,' said Hesta.

'You've got to do *something*!' Stephanie's voice desired to ascend into a scream. She shut it off. She said, straining at her rage, 'My God, if I'd had your chances—'

'You wouldn't have ended up married with a kid,' said Hesta.

'No, I bloody well wouldn't.'

When Stephanie swore, unlike Janey, it was unpleasant, vitriolic, even with the word 'bloody'. When Janey said fuck, it was funny, innocent, and wise. But, on the rare occasions 'fuck' burst from Stephanie, it was gut-churning. A bawdy basic word for an extraordinary human activity, became what it often had, on the lips of the cruel and the violent – not gratuitous, but *foul*. You *could* take exception to it. You wanted to write and complain.

Stephanie pushed her way to the fridge, opened it, and took out a bottle of Diet Coke. She poured herself a glass, not offering it to Hesta. Of course, Hesta drank Diet Coke not because she needed to, but because she preferred the taste.

'Listen, Hesta. I can't cope with you. You don't do a thing to help me or yourself.'

'I do one thing,' said Hesta.

'Oh *yes*? Well, madam. What's that?'

'I don't tell Iain you're screwing that disgusting little prick.'

Stephanie swelled, all her thin dieted body, dry with sun, greased with lotion. A fiery scented horrible smell came from her, the odour of *hate*.

'I'm *lonely*. You don't understand, you little bitch. Martin's my friend.'

18

'Martin tries to put his hand up my skirt.'

'You filthy little fucking *liar*.' There, it was said. 'All right – get out – get *out*!'

Hesta walked by her mother. And as she did so, Stephanie swung at her and slapped her hard as a stick across her arm. Hesta paid no attention. She went from the kitchen, along the hall, past the clash-blue sitting room, and through the front door. She took nothing with her, as they say, but her *self*.

Two

This kitchen, very small, with indigo walls and red and pale cobalt crockery, smelled of pork sausages and apple.

'I'll do another batch,' said Lulu.

She got up, a woman in her forties, five feet four inches tall and weighing fourteen stone. Despite this diagnosed handicap, she moved with utter grace and sureness in the tiny room. And the sun through the high windows blazed on her magpie hair, half black, white and silver coming through, magnificent hair that gave off, in winter, blue sparks.

Janey and Hesta munched on, now and then referring to their glasses of hot black tea where orange slices floated like goldfish.

The grill re-awoke with a pop.

Tea today was Christmas Sandwiches. Lulu's invention. White bread crisped under the grill, margarine, layers of thin packet turkey breast, slices of hot pork sausage, cranberry and apple sauce. Wedges on the side of apple and thyme stuffing, baked in the oven, and to hand, a large red bowl of fried potatoes.

Janey lifted a red chicken tea cosy off the teapot. Then she got up and added boiling water from the simmering kettle.

Over the closed pot she reinstated the glamorous chicken.

The chicken was quite old. When Hesta had been eleven, and taken it in for the first time, she had asked what it was. Lulu told her it was a tea cosy, and Hesta had said, quietly, 'My mummy says tea cosies are lower class.'

She had not meant this impertinently, nor naively. She was searching for answers – she had already somehow realized Lulu was a sort of dictionary – or for questions. And Lulu, Janey's mum – '*Never* say mum. I'm Mummy' (and later) 'Call me Stephanie, now' – responded. She explained that tea cosies kept tea hot, and tea strainers – which, too, Stephanie would never have allowed in her house – were better for leaf tea, as they kept the leaves from falling in your cup.

Through the chicken and the tea strainer had come a precise demonstration of real truth. That being alive is not about classes, objects, or correct behaviour, but about what works best.

Hesta, when she arrived today at the block of flats, had glanced at the lift – as generally, not working – and walked up the six flights to Lulu's home. Knocking on the door she had been answered by Janey. '*Hallo* – Mum – it's Hesta!' And Lulu's unflurried reply, 'Good.'

Lulu was never surprised by Hesta's sudden extra arrivals. In the course of five years it had ceased to be a matter of Hesta, taught from an early age that one was unwanted unless expected (invited), calling first from the phone box in Fulton Road.

As Stephanie had railed, Hesta was often here in the small two-bedroomed box on the sixth floor of Manor House, an evilly neglected block, one of ten, that overlooked the park

22

one way, and the railway the other. Although urine was regularly sprayed in the concrete foyer, and the lift did not work, and snarling dogs patrolled the bleak grass verges below, up here you could see to the Thames, dirty silver as an ancient spoon, and the sun sank, amber to bronze to red, and Venus starred the dusk like a diamond.

The new sausages were chuckling under the grill. Lulu was cutting bread, singing softly under her breath a song about golden fields. At other times roars of Shostakovich and Rachmaninov burst from the music centre. She took an hour or two each evening for her music. Otherwise Janey might do with the music centre whatever the Stranglers, Faith No More or Elvis Costello desired.

They sometimes shared each other's tapes and CDs. Janey might fall asleep with Ravel, or Lulu be found with Janey's cassettes of Numan. 'This composer has broken his heart,' said Lulu, 'over and over again, so now he has at least twenty hearts, all of which work.' 'He flies planes,' had said Janey. Lulu said, 'He can fly without them, too.'

This interchange had interested Hesta. She did not lean on music as Janey did, as Lulu seemed to. Besides, in the beginning, she had been surprised to find how Janey and Lulu could live in each other's countries, honoured guests, not spies, invaders.

Hesta had met Janey at the junior school. They became friends in some way Hesta could never recall. When she had told Stephanie she had been invited to tea that Saturday, Stephanie had immediately asked the child's address. Hearing it, Stephanie announced, 'You must thank her politely, and say no.'

But Iain was coming home that weekend. He found them in a white silence. He laughed, and drove Hesta over to Manor House and walked her up the stairs himself.

What did it matter, said Iain, that Lulu had no husband or partner and that she lived in a slum? She was great.

In those days, so long ago, so far away, Iain had retained a life force. But now, thin and hollow as if from Stephanie's regime of starving, which he mostly missed, his red hair fading drearily, Iain had become a ghost.

'You know what I'd like to do,' said Janey, 'tomorrow? I'd like to get a train down to the seaside. Mum, can I?'

'Yes,' said Lulu. She added, careless, 'I'll do that maths thing for you, if you like.'

'Oh yes, Mum, please. 'Cos otherwise old Snotty starts squawking. Mind you,' she added, 'he knows it's you.'

Lulu smiled. Her round face was peach-skinned, and her green eyes sexy as deep pools where nymphs, firm and fleshy, with wet loins and hair, lay waiting.

In her thirteenth year, Janey had been cornered and given a lecture by some teacher at the Milton School. If Janey did not work, put her back into it, pull up her socks, Janey would be a failure. And Janey had cried. Hesta had found Janey crying at the bus-stop.

They had walked to Manor House that day in the rain, Janey crying like the rain, Hesta not saying anything – what could she say? Janey was not academically clever. Instead, she was a genius. She wrote short doggerel poems that played with language, or painted mouth-watering pictures in gouache, castles, cats, flowers, hills under moons, and doorways with pillars.

24

When Lulu opened the door of the box which was a home, she drew Janey straight into the grey and pink front room, and there delivered her own lecture, which was brief, ringing, oratorical. School was a legal requirement but in this case immaterial. Janey should know by now tests and exams did not matter. She should work as hard as she could only at what inspired her to work hard. The rest could be got over. And after school, Janey would perhaps find something, but if not, still they would manage.

'I didn't have you to support me in my old age,' said Lulu. 'As long as you can crank me up on the seat of my Harley now and then, that's fine.'

Then Lulu had provided a tea – not dinner, dinners were different – of grilled cheese with mustard on toast, and a luscious gooseberry tart – a treat, as if she had known something would happen. That was the initial occasion when Hesta stayed without an invitation.

Stephanie had seen Lulu it seemed, out shopping. Although Stephanie had then got into the hire car and Lulu had walked on to the bus-stop. 'That woman is like a hippopotamus. She really needs to lose some weight before she has a stroke. I suppose she fries everything in lard, and you eat it, you stupid child.'

'Olive oil,' said Hesta.

At which Stephanie shook her short layered highlighted hair, as if she knew Lulu's hair, when undone, was as long as the cobras of the Indian woman, the hair of a sorceress.

Most days, until three, Lulu worked in a charity shop.

'We can go to that seaside place you talk about,' said Janey to Lulu. 'That place – you know.'

'Oh, yes,' said Lulu. 'Why not.'

'It only takes an hour or so,' said Janey, 'from London.'

Hesta said, 'I'd better not.'

Lulu had her back to them. She was spreading the bread, cutting the sausages.

Janey said, 'Oh go on.'

'I have to do a whole week's homework.'

'Why?' asked Janey. 'Is it *her*?'

Hesta said, 'My father gets upset.'

'Oh,' said Janey.

Iain had written one of his letters to Hesta. He only did this when Stephanie had been on at him by phone. Usually his method of communication with Hesta was by a selected postcard, one of many he had collected years before, postcards from wild and distant zones, or areas in history now altered. The message would be, *Dear Hesta, Today I caught a whale but let it go.* Or, *Had an ice-cream here but dropped it down a lady's front. Hospital bill to follow.* Or, *My window marked with an X* – this on the nineteenth-century palmed villa-palace of a king in Sumatra.

Hesta had loved these cards for years. And then the aching sadness of it, his own small, momentarily desperate fantasy that he was not where he was, on a few metres of chemical platform in the midst of the cruel sea, the drilling rig, came in to Hesta on a wave of thought.

After that, the postcards disturbed her.

She felt protective of him. Who else would be? She had not told him of Stephanie's recurring lovers – not from fear of or loyalty to her mother. It was from her pity for him.

And Iain thought Hesta should go to 'art school'. She had

26

tried to explain to him it was rather more complex, this procedure, than it had been when he – had he? – had maybe wished to do it.

Yet she had kept up the pretence. She had, and it weighed on her. It was a blot of darkness that lay somewhere in the clarity of her sixteen-year-old brain. To protect him. To do what he thought she wanted and did not, so he could be happy for her.

He was like a little boy slave, her father, sent out to toil for them that they might be well off and live life for him.

Lulu brought the sandwiches to the table, and they ate again, and again drank tea, the hot food and drink in the hot afternoon, with the sun beginning its amber stage above the roofs of the city.

'That light, it's like Arabia,' said Janey, using the ancient name since, that way, it did not evoke wars. And then, 'Oh go on, Hesta. Think how blue the sea will be. And Mum says this place is lovely. The sea, the sea – the edge of the earth.'

Hesta said again, 'No, Janey.' And turning her eyes away, saw the weird contraption on the work-top, pushed back well out of Lulu's way.

'What's *that*, Lulu?'

Lulu knew about changing subjects. Her aim was to abet this ploy, save where harm might be done. 'Of all things, it's a mousetrap.'

'What?'

Janey said, 'Old Smelly downstairs says there are rats in the building. I thought, yeah, and I know who it is, this rat. They're talking about demolishing these flats, you know? The state they're in.'

27

'Rats are beautiful animals,' said Lulu, as if the loss of her flat meant nothing.

'But they leap for your throat,' said Janey, with relish, not at this idea, but to prompt the coming reply.

'No. They leap for the space behind your head. It's mistaken for an attack. It's a bid for freedom.'

Janey said, 'Smelly put the mousetrap out for the rats and Mum picked it up in case a rat ran in it and got hurt.'

'Yes, I did. But I was coming upstairs so here it is. Frankly I don't know what to do with it. If I throw it out it's liable to hurt someone.'

Hesta said, 'I'll take it. I can wrap it in a lot of newspaper and dump it in our rubbish.'

'Thank you,' said Lulu. 'Actually, I'll wrap it up. We've got a ton of local newspapers. I don't know how they get up these stairs. Then they put six papers through one door, which is ideal, if you've got a cat.'

So it was with Manor House. Urine, dogs, rats. Paper deliveries in excess. And the bin men venturing near only one week in four.

But here too Janey had grown up, choosing her own first name on her fifth birthday. And Lulu let down her hair. And Venus shone in at the window.

A candelabra of twisted iron spikes burned with candles the shade of tomato soup, in the middle of the glass dining table.

Martin Peecey leaned back from the rather arid roast chicken and salad, and had another quaff of the red wine he had brought. It matched the dining room, if not the meal. Stephanie had seductively told him, you did not drink red with white meat. 'White wine gives me sinus,' said Martin Peecey, romantically.

Time now, however, to praise her. The unmoist meal – she couldn't cook to save her quim – her crimson strappy dress, and her expensive perfume, tindery as struck matches.

'Oh, thank you, Marty,' she said, lowering her eyes like a convent girl of fourteen. She was not, however. Unfortunately.

Hesta had gone off. With that friend of hers. Peecey had said something about that to Stephanie, a few months back. And Stephanie had reportedly rounded on Hesta the next night, telling her to watch out, she might turn into a raving dyke. Hesta had slammed her bedroom door in Stephanie's face.

Hesta wasn't a les. No, she just needed someone experienced. Win her over. Take care of her.

Really, Hesta was the main reason he kept on with Stephanie, because Stephanie was getting to be a bit of a drag. Always on about her stretch marks. Wanting to go out to the wine bar late at night, when Kev kept it going for paying 'friends' behind shut doors. Christ, in four years, Steph would be forty and he was only twenty-nine.

On the other hand, Hesta . . .

'And Hesta's off, is she?'

'Yes. The little bitch. Oh, Marty, she was so rude to me. I get frightened she'll get violent. I do. I *hit* her,' Stephanie added, unaware, it seemed, of a slight contradiction.

'Well. Two women cooped up together. It's a recipe for mayhem.'

'Marty, I just wish – I wish I could leave Iain. I do, Marty. He's never with me. He never was anything to me. I was so young. I got snowballed. And then I was pregnant. That horrible little flat we were in. And the hospital—'

'Yes. Poor Stephie.'

'Sometimes I feel so *old*—'

And you look it, baby.

'No, baby. You look just fourteen tonight.'

'Do I, Marty? Do I?'

She would not leave Iain, no fear of that. Though Martin Peecey earned a good deal from his co-ownership of the bar, Iain raked it in. Martin Peecey had seen Iain once. Iain was thirty-seven. Poor old bugger. At the back of Peecey's mind something scratched like the skull memento mori – *One day you shall be as me*. In a thousand years, Martin Peecey would be thirty-seven himself.

'You know, Stephie . . . I've got an idea.'

She stared at him. She had wanted to go on a while longer with her make-believe of deserting Iain.

'What is it?'

'Well, Hesta – you say she never gets back till after eleven thirty.'

'She doesn't. Or later. So *late* – I've got no control over—'

'It's just that . . . You see, baby, you look so young tonight. So very young. I mean, I feel I'm cradle-snatching. And, well – it's only nine fifteen.'

Stephanie listened. Her lips parted. If she felt any outrage it was not obvious.

About forty minutes after midnight, Lulu, who had switched on the portable radio, picked it up. She, Janey and Hesta, walked quietly into Lulu's bedroom.

'Ah, look at her,' said Lulu.

Janey went forward, and bending over a sleeping plushy tortoiseshell cat, implanted a soft deep kiss on her chocolaty-scented flank.

The cat raised her head, vocalized a purring call, and stretched, catching Lulu's emerald bedspread in wicked permitted vandalistic claws.

They had been to visit the cat earlier. Old now, she slept most of the day and night, on the beds of Lulu or Janey, or in moveable patches of sunlight on the sitting room floor. She was seventeen – a year the senior of Hesta and Janey, but, in cat terms, seemingly either eighty-five or one hundred and nineteen.

The announcer on Radio Four courteously bade the attending world a good-night. Lulu, her daughter and friend, stood to attention. The National Anthem was played. They solemnly sang:

> *'God save our gracious Cat*
> *Long live our noble Cat*
> *God save the Cat.*
> *Send her victorious*
> *Happy and clawrious*
> *Long to reign over us*
> *God save our Cat.*

The cat watched judgementally, smiled with her cheeks and eyes, and curled up again to sleep, emitting as she did so a minuscule fart.

'What scares me,' said Janey, as they went out again, 'is in a couple of years there won't be a Royal Family, and they won't play it.'

Lulu handed Hesta a plastic bag with the mousetrap wrapped in vast amounts of local news, half a cherry and pecan cake from Sainsbury's, and three bananas. It was Lulu also who supplied Hesta's schoolday lunches. Given over by Janey at the bus-stop in the High Street, on descending, in the mornings.

They hugged in a ring, three graces. Hesta held tensely, but did not cling. There was nothing to cling to. They were here.

The taxi driver, Mac, whom Lulu had known for ten years, waited by the door and escorted Hesta down. 'They should get that lift fixed, they should.' He looked elderly to Hesta, but he was brown and kind, Irish, with a lilting voice and wonderful eyes. He talked in platitudes to conceal a poetic soul.

When they presently came upon a drunken fifteen-year-old boy being sick copiously over a landing, Mac said, nostalgically, 'Ah, lad. Those were the days.'

Below, he helped Hesta into the back of his car, and drove off through the dark, as he must have done many hundreds of times, towards the better streets. And her mother's house.

That afternoon, about a year before, Hesta had walked into the Asian shop in the High Street. It had been September then, a grey hot day full of unspent thunder, and three o'clock because Hesta had skipped a French class. As she was selecting an ice-cream from the glass-fronted freezer to the rear of the shop, a man came in and began to talk to the Indian woman in a low hoarse voice.

The Asian shop sold old-fashioned ice-cream 'bricks' – something Iain had once described to Hesta. As her hand closed on a brick, in its pale blue and white paper, she heard a few words rise clearly from the counter.

'I want it,' said the man. 'I *want* it.'

'No, no,' said the Indian woman in her melodious rhythmic tone, 'no, please – we work so hard—'

'Give it to me, you shitty wog, or you'll get this.'

Hesta straightened without sound. She saw the man at the counter, blocking most of the view. He was big and darker than the day. Yet the thunder too was held in him. Then he made a sort of swinging movement, and he swung, by it, the Indian woman in her coral sari, swung her by her neck, and her bun came loose and all her hair poured down. In his other hand, pressed to her breast, was a big, dirty, shiny knife.

'Give me the fucking money.'

'All right,' said the Indian, but she hung there still, paralysed, between two dreads.

Hesta went forward. She made almost no noise, but the man heard her. When she was about six feet away he half turned his head. His three-quarter profile was squashed and yellowish and demoniac, like the rubber masks sold in this very shop for Halloween. But the mask was his face.

'You stay back, you,' he said. Incongruously he added, 'Wait your turn.'

'OK,' said Hesta.

She tore the wrapper off the brick in two quick soft strokes, and lifting it in her hand she ran forward, and slammed its icy freezing whiteness into his sweating grey and yellow neck.

He screamed. It was the shock. The knife fell from his fingers and behind the counter, and he let the woman go. Turning, he stared blindly at Hesta, then rushed out on to the pavement and away.

The Indian stood in her fall of hair, her face creased with terror.

'Oh God,' she said. She spoke then, probably in Urdu. Next: 'Oh, you shouldn't have. He might have hurt you—'

Hesta said, 'Can I take another brick?'

'Yes, yes. I will get the wafers.'

With trembling hands the woman pressed the new ice-cream together, while Hesta telephoned the police for her in the back room. After that, and after the son had come in and the husband had been called from his other job, Hesta left the shop. She ate the ice, but would in future accept nothing else free, though she allowed the Indian woman to show her once the small beautiful Krishna in the shrine behind the back room. He was white and black and azure, and at his feet lay a light in a rosy glass. Of this she told Janey. But not about the mugger.

For Hesta had not astonished herself, was not proud of what she had done. It was like the tea strainer, and the cosy. What worked best.

As she entered the hall of Stephanie's house, the flat-faced clock in the sitting room showed almost ten past one. There were no lights on, but this had been apparent from the street, when Mac's taxi pulled up.

'Your mum's in bed,' he said, 'do you think?'

Hesta said, 'Yes, I suppose so.'

But if Stephanie was in bed, it would be with Martin Peecey, and the light would still be on. And his car would be parked on the drive. More likely they had gone on to the wine bar to sit drinking until three or four. Then Stephanie would come home in a cab of her own, slamming the car door, the front door, stamping up through the house, disillusioned, depressed, hung-over, washed up.

The young girl, with her fire-chrysanthemum of hair, her dancer's boyish body, ascended the stairs as a prologue, without pity.

She could smell Martin Peecey in the house.

On the lower floor, the sodium sheen from the street came in, but upstairs she switched on a light. Her mother's door was closed, but that meant nothing. There was silence.

Hesta went across the wide landing, opened her own door.

She was sixteen. Every sense in her was primed. Within her own body she was new. And in the world, like a cat from the veld or the forest. If there is anywhere else before life, probably, on some level of her consciousness, she remembered that better.

But she had been brought into captivity, and perforce had made her lair in one corner of the large cage. Here she placed her trophies and her psychic bones, scent-marked with deodorant and hair-spray. It was her own place.

Then, returning, the leopardess finds her primal corner has been tampered with.

Hesta stood on the threshold, under the harsh overhead white-shaded hundred watt bulb Stephanie insisted on, for doing homework. Her eyes were stretched wide and the light made them yellow. Her hair, from its cut and back-combing and lacquering, already partly stood on end.

Only the bed, really, had been disarranged.

Normally, on Fridays, Den changed the beds – changed Stephanie's, that was, for Hesta changed her own on Saturday or Sunday morning. As usual Stephanie had left the clean sheets, madly printed with enormous Picassoesque flowers, on the chair.

The bed, however, that Hesta had left as usual tightly closed, the Indian shawl stretched over it, had been undone, spread wide and left lying, indecently open, *exposed*. Along the undersheet, where last night Hesta had lain sleeping, which, this morning, she had pulled smooth, there was a ruffle, a ripple, a ruck. On the pillow was a small, dark, oily stain.

She did not need to go near to be sure. The whole house reeked of him, of her mother's lover, his hair-cream, his aftersun and aftershave, his thin brown English skin. His *maleness*.

Now the bed also reeked of Martin Peecey, fully of him, since he had lain there with her mother not two hours before. Into Hesta's sheets he had given off his sexual sweat, the pangs of his struggling anti-perspirant with a picturesque name; he had rubbed his sweaty Brylcreem into her pillow. He had come, filling Stephanie to her brim and so spilling through into the virgin mattress.

There was one other thing. On the carpet. A pair of Hesta's slim white cotton pants, and the slender white bra which she had been told to wear, and, young and small and firm and flawless, had never needed.

That was all, then. Not much. A ruined raped bed. The underclothes worn by her skinny mother to tantalize him. For him a titillation. For Stephanie, perhaps, the means of another delivered slap.

Hesta turned. She looked back into the bright-lit upper hall.

Not a sound. Besides, Peecey's car, the deep blue BMW

roadster, had not been on the drive.

Hesta put her plastic bag down on the chair over the new sheets. She opened the doors of her built-in wardrobe, and took out what Stephanie called a 'robe'. Hesta shed her school clothes and underthings. She let them fall by the discarded knickers.

In her 'robe', Hesta went next door to the large 'family' bathroom (shades of puce), and running the shower full-power and cool, rinsed herself, washed herself with her tablet of melon soap, rinsed herself again.

Doing this, she was automatically careful of the large dark blue bruise on her arm – the work of Stephanie earlier, striking at her as she left the kitchen. Apart from this automatic care, established over the years, Hesta took no notice of the injury.

She had become, of course, accustomed to her mother's blows, which had begun in earnest when she was about seven (the age of reason). It was as she left her little-girl stage, which Stephanie had dressed in heavy 'Victorian' frilly cotton, and moved into another psychological and physical area to which Stephanie tried, but could not manage to affix, a satisfactory label.

The less control Stephanie had felt herself to have over this new being – no longer a toy, but an autonomous creature – the more Stephanie lammed into her child. For the child was going all wrong. The toy had been perfect, equipped with every proper function – it laughed a little, it cried, but never excessively. It became able to walk and talk. But dolls should know their place. Dolls must not grow up.

There had been one night when Iain, home from his rig, had seen the healing mark on his nine-year-old daughter's leg, where her sock had rolled down. Stephanie, in her bright dress for going out, had tensed, as Iain asked, 'How the hell did she get this?'

'A boy at school,' said Hesta, 'hit me with a bat.'

'Little bastard,' said Iain. 'I'll go up there—'

'No, Mummy did,' said nine-year-old Hesta. She added thoughtfully, 'He cried.'

She was a good liar, a good story-teller, the facility had come early. Stephanie did not stir, and later the scene was not discussed between them. Hesta had, naturally, not been protecting her mother, but Iain.

Hesta dried herself quickly, scarcely touching the towel – Stephanie's choice, very thick and purple. Hesta used the melon deodorant stick. Then she picked up the stick, the melon soap, wrapped in a disposable plastic shower cap, and her toothbrush, and went back to the room which was her room no longer.

Not, of course, that it ever had been. As with the playroom in the attic, Stephanie was often likely to come in with one swift rap of her knuckles, to show how courteous she was and aware of her daughter's privacy.

But there would never have been time to hide anything, between rap and entry. And Hesta had never bothered. Her naked body, her ignored homework – she disguised neither. There had only been one deception. Now, as Hesta opened the central drawers of her wardrobe, her fingers brushed without attention the box of Tampax, from which, once a month, she removed between ten and fourteen tampons, throwing the applicators into the bin provided, flushing the disposable pencils down the puce loo.

In this way, she had kept Stephanie from learning that she, Hesta, did not menstruate. Otherwise, it would have meant a visit to the doctor, an apocalypse Hesta had been threatened with from her thirteenth bloodless birthday onwards. Until one evening of her fifteenth year, when, with a little help from a defrosted steak, she had commenced her lie.

Stephanie, who was a fool, was also not a complete fool. In the beginning, she had checked the drawer regularly to see if pads, then tampons, disappeared.

She still did this from time to time, but now her reasons were different. Hesta had been irritatingly physically backward. Now she might be moronically pregnant.

In the bottom of the wardrobe was a medium-sized holdall. Hesta, standing naked, put things into it – tights, pants, soap, deodorant, toothbrush, lacquer, brush, scissors, make-up . . . her Reeves art pad, ten by eight, which she used for notes and drawings, Biros and pencils from beside her bed. Something made her think of the fountain pen Iain had given her, and she took it from her school bag, dumped – Stephanie – by the chair. Then she opened the plastic carrier Lulu had packed with food. Inside she saw again the item which was not food. The huddle of newspaper, layer on layer, like the nest of something.

Lulu had found the dress for Hesta in the charity shop. She had found one for Janey, too. Lulu had simply said, there were some clothes in they might like to look at.

Now Hesta wore the dress, which her mother hated, loathed, had threatened to throw out.

Janey's was green, but this was the palest, most-weathered

black, a sort of silky material that Lulu had called *Kosma*. It clung, making of Hesta's body, almost to her ankles, a shimmering snake. The hem was slashed over and over, as if it had been torn by knives. Openings ran up three or four inches, or all the way to the thigh. Foot-long frayed red tassels fringed irregularly down to this wild hem. The sleeves could be rolled to the elbows, revealing a scarlet silken lining.

The dress in turn had been dressed with chains of brass and silver, and a girdle of bronze links, with a red enamel clasp, two red roses gripping the face of a bronze demon.

Hesta's tights were opaque, the colour of the blood she had never lost, and did not care about.

Her black shoes had each seven straps, and five silver buckles.

She had turned out the light after all, and yet the faint upward flare of the sodium lamps caught all the narrow rings on her hands.

Hesta was changed, or had changed back into Hesta.

Or, she had only thrown off her camouflage, which had been forced, like her school bra, on to her.

At nine years old she had begun to spell her name another way.

She could remember Iain's face, full of interest. 'That's good. Hey, like a girl in a band.'

Iain, who sometimes had drawn a spider in gold ink after 'Daddy' on the postcard. But the female 'Mummy' spider eats the male.

Without the light, in Stephanie's pristine bedroom, smelling of a tinder-and-arson-like perfume called by some imaginative title, smelling of a flesh that the sun was making fifty years old before it had needed to be, Hesta located the big chest of drawers.

Nothing was out of place in this room. No one had done much in here. And in the lingerie drawer lay all the bras full of wire, and the lacy stockings and the crotchless knickers that Martin Peecey had not, tonight, been interested in.

Tomorrow, however, or next day, or a week hence, Stephanie would have to put on something from this hoard.

The mousetrap was uncomplex, its little plane of wood and the open metal shape that lay over it, waiting, for the slightest inner pressure, to slam shut.

Hesta arranged it neatly under the flower-burst of bras, the serpent beneath the blossom.

And then, taking up the holdall, she went down.

A walk through the streets did not daunt her. It never had. She took the ride in Mac's taxi because Lulu summoned the taxi. It was five to three now, and probably she would get to Fulton Road by twenty to four. There was an all-night tea place there. By eight Lulu was always awake and up, though Janey would doubtless sleep until eleven.

As Hesta closed the front door of Stephanie's house, a great quietness hung for a moment in the road of Victorian buildings. And then, from the cooler depths of night, a light wind blew, and stirred the tops of the trees in every garden. A sighing rush, vast strength, stroked soft ancient pages turning over for ever.

And in this she heard the presage of her journey, her arrival at the edge of the earth, the sound of the *sea*.

High Tyde

Before the sun rose the men came down the beach of stones to launch their boats into the long, black sea.

Moving lights slit the dark. Breath, steaming with strong tea, coffee, pre-dawn beer, made ghosts. The morning was cold. The first cold morning, autumn days, the last day of the Season.

Above, in the one grand, serviceable hotel over the promenade, the final holiday-makers slept, knowing in their dreams that today they would go home. Back to other places, back to desk work or redundancy.

The fishermen, running their boats down into the water, knew also well enough lean times had come. For now someone in a suit, and sitting far away in an office of chrome and plastic, told you when you might fish, and how, and where. They joked about it sometimes, these men in oilskins and black jerseys.

Large and big-ribbed, painted red or black or yellow or blue, the boats shouldered over their slides, pushed by the little bulldozers, down into the surf. Like dogs pushing at a wayward bitch, like children playing, the bulldozers, yellow and red as the boats, thrust, rammed, butted. And, when the tide had come in on the land, filling the beach like a bowl, each boat glided suddenly free, taking the slight swell, riding like a duck.

Old as men and the sea, this game, in some form.

By the time the sun rose, ochre and powdery through a fine film, on the brink of the tumbling cliffs beyond the town, they were long gone.

With the sunrise, a photographer had appeared on the shore. Using his filters, he sought to change the image of the sea that had no meaning unless tampered with.

He therefore, and a solitary dog snouting in the waves, noticed how one fishing boat came slowly back, out of the opened morning.

The dog grunted, wagged its tail, and ran on. The photographer snapped the boat, turning in towards the beach, the bobbing prow. A good catch? Presumably, to bring them home so fast. And the gulls thought so too, wheeling in, white as angels, screeching like the damned.

As the boat grounded, the photographer, a Londoner in dirty expensive jeans and designer-label shirt and jacket, crunched leisurely forward. He watched the man come from the winch-shed and cast down before the boat some wooden pieces – the slides. He was late. He too had not been expecting them. A big man in yellow oilskin trousers plunged off into the shallow water. He attached the winch wire to the boat.

The photographer took quick angled shots: the wire, uncoiling, snake-like, pulled taut; the two fishermen laying the slides like offerings before the boat, and when she had run, the wire singing and sizzling, over them, taking them up and carrying them round for her again. The ascent of the boat was slow. Now and then she rocked. Ceaselessly they laid her carpet, took it up, laid it once more.

If they saw the photographer, angling, snapping, seizing bits of them for history, as they toiled to live, they did not show it. He might only have been another gull.

In the end, the boat had gained the upper beach.

The photographer lowered his camera. Walked right up to them.

'Good morning. Everything OK?'

The men glanced at him now. The big one said, very politely, 'Yes, sir.'

'You're in very early.'

'Bit of bother,' said the younger man. 'Nothing much.'

'Any chance of a couple of close-ups?'

'If you've got the price of a drink,' said the bigger, older man.

The boat hung dark and silent on the bloomed sky.

The photographer, who could probably sell a suitably ethnic shot for two hundred pounds, pulled a tenner from his jeans and handed it over. 'Cheers.'

They let him arrange them, standing solid as granite by their vessel, revealing her name, *Stella*. Seen this way, she looked as if she could never return into the water. She hid her limber swimmer's knack in the breadth of her beam, her hard sides. Beyond her, the sea in lines, coming and going.

There were no fish, apparently. The gulls veered off.

When the Londoner had gone whistling up the stones, they returned into the *Stella*, called not for some wife or girlfriend, but after a star, and looked again at what their net had captured.

A huge bottle – a Nebuchadnezzar – black-green vitreous, covered over by barnacles. But corked inside, a glimpse of burning red, like one fish after all, or a flower, or even the star of the boat's name.

They pulled a sack up over the catch, the Nebuchadnezzar that once had held champagne, and now held something other. Hid it, as the boat hid her true nature. The bigger man carried this bundle up the beach, towards the town, and Hassinger's house.

Three

On the train they ate sandwiches and drank Diet Coke, and sometimes had a swig of the vodka Lulu had put for them into a small Evian bottle.

Janey was excited. She burst into little bouts of applause, seeing woolly sheep in grass, and firm, rounded cows, and fields of sun-bleached green. The establishing lemon leaves were on the trees. She began a game of geographical couplets. *I once went to Minsk, But I haven't been back there sinsk. I once went to Istanbul, But everyone said Who's this dam' fool?*

Hesta offered, *I once went to Tomsk, But someone let off a bombsk.*

The carriage stayed mostly empty. Further down, a boy in a leather jacket, whom they ignored and who ignored them, poked audibly loud bad music into his ears from a Walkman.

'Do you remember Tony?' asked Janey, nostalgic for her fifteenth year. She had fancied Tony, at the Milton School, and having cleared the situation with Lulu (who had already got her on the Pill for painful periods), Janey sent him a note: *I can can, if you can can. But I can't can't if you won't won't.*

47

It seemed Tony had never heard of Offenbach, or of pretty girls kicking up their legs in black stockings. He had approached Janey and said, 'Don't understand your note.' Janey had blushed. Tony said, 'Are you saying you'll fuck me?' Janey stopped blushing and replied, 'Fuck off.'

That morning, having knocked on Lulu's door at eight thirty, Hesta had been let in without questions to mugs of tea at the kitchen table. Janey had decided too to get up early. Usually on Saturday afternoons, she and Hesta went to London, or round the local flea markets, but Janey claimed she had had a premonition. 'I dreamt you were walking down Fulton Road and it was still dark.'

'It was,' said Hesta.

They ate toast, while Lulu made a sandwich spread, with egg and cheese and tomatoes, in a blue enamel saucepan. Then she vanished, and came back just before they left, with a bunch of black seedless grapes, also for the journey.

Only once had Janey said, when she and Hesta were about twelve, 'I wish Mum'd adopt you. Then you could leave *her*.'

Hesta had not answered. With Hesta, silences conveyed meaning, and those who cared for her – so far so few – understood.

The seaside station was shabby, littered with cartons, wrappers, and spotted purely white with bird excrement. Seagulls flew overhead, making a querulous bleating noise.

No one wanted to see their tickets. 'I can smell the sea,' said Janey.

On the wall outside the station, another wit had been at

work. Graffiti a foot high read distinctly:

DON'T WALK ON THE ~~GRASS~~ WATER

Above, the seagulls burst into raucous insane laughter.

It was the last day of the Season, and for the very last trippers, the town swung on, making believe that it was high summer still, the mystical seaside summer which can never end. For like flies, where does the seaside go in wintertime? Surely it shuts like a door, folds up like a tent, all is empty, and only the grey, wild, winter sea remains, blasting at the lonely land.

Outside the station was a ramshackle road, with other roads rising away from it, to crests of Victorian houses.

They walked along the road, which was like a defile between mountains. Nothing seemed to be happening. The shops were unlit, closed or apparently vacant. They did not seem actually to be selling anything. No one was there, or anywhere.

As they turned a corner, a bombsite opened, running off to either side, limitless. Rubbish crowded between the struts and bricks of lost buildings. A board for adverts had been stripped to flags of flying paper.

'I thought they got rid of bombsites,' said Hesta. It was not a condemnation. She was puzzled.

'In the war, the town was badly hit, Mum said,' answered Janey. 'The Nazis dropped their last bombs all on the coast before they took off out to sea. And there's never been enough money to put things right.' It was a little speech. Pre-learned.

Coming in like this, they saw the town was not inviting.

Janey had said there was another station farther on, but they had not got off there.

The seagulls wheeled and, looking up, Hesta saw how the gulls in their turn looked down. She had not known gulls really did this. It was like the video of *The Birds*.

Janey led the way unerringly. Through the bombsite, through an alley beyond, where plastered walls and blank windows leaned.

And there it was, suddenly, after all.

The seaside.

The shops along this road, this steep slope, had out awnings of red, white and green, and everything *fell* downhill towards an architectural open V, ruled right across by the horizontal turquoise line of the ocean.

'Look, there it is,' cried Janey.

Set apparently at the road's end, in misleading perspective, the sea was higher than the bottom of the street. Under the upper bar of turquoise, which held it from the paler sky, the water did not look like water, more metallic, milky, greenish-blue.

Janey started off at a run, as if her brakes had failed, but Hesta walked more slowly. She glanced at what she passed, the greengrocery oranges and tomatoes out on their table, the man in the butcher's smiling in a boater, the furry toys and china bells and knick-knacks. And presently nine brown bodies in Day-glo came by, sucking at their obligatory ice-creams and lollies, the women squinting at Hesta disapprovingly. There were now plenty of people.

Janey stood waiting at the road's end, and here was the

T-junction of the promenade, cut from them by a roar of fast cars.

Fumes, white sunlight, the mirror reflection off the sea. Everything for a moment in a haze, bleached in a prolonged solar camera flash.

When the traffic stopped for the lights, Janey hurtled over, raced through the strollers and children with their balls, threw herself against the railing, leaning far out, like a figurehead of the land.

'Did you come here with Lulu?'

'No, she never brought me here. 'Cos, see, the beach isn't sand. You know what kids are like.'

They gazed down on the piebald stones, amber, white and black, the slaty blue of pigeons. In dips and drops and swirls, the pebbles went to the water's edge, where waves moved softly in transparent fans. Only a scatter of human beings sat there. It was, after all, October.

'Listen,' said Janey. 'The sea *breathes*.'

They listened.

Then two boys marching by, stripped to the waist, in unbecoming shorts, shouted and whistled, insulting ugly words that meant that Hesta and Janey had been noted.

Neither girl seemed to hear.

When the boys were gone, Janey said, 'Can you see the curve of the earth?'

'Yes, I can.'

'Anything could be out there. Mermaids. A dragon.'

'A god,' said Hesta, 'walking from the water with seaweed on his shoulder.'

'Lovely,' said Janey. 'Not like *them*, bloody garbage.'

About half a mile away, to their right, an arm of glittering white pier pierced into the ocean. A sound of varied musics wafted from it, while to their left, burst up the screams of a large funfair. In both directions ran the lamp-poles with their coloured lights attached, waiting for the night.

Over the promenade, the rise of old houses, and the pleated galleries of older cliffs. A church tower spanned space with its glinting golden cross. Janey studied the view, as if she meant to draw it later, or was looking for something.

'I like it,' Janey said. 'It's good.'

Along the front were peeling buildings, barricaded windows. Here and there new paint. One hotel was washed in pink, balconies spilling geraniums. But only one.

Janey said, 'We have to do everything. Paddle in the sea. Find a stone with a hole in it. Look at the fishing boats. Have fish and chips. Look at the clock tower. Go on the rides. Get a present for Mum. Watch the sun go down – over there, probably. Walk under the cliffs where it says don't.' She glanced at her watch. 'The last train back is ten to seven. We've got six hours and five minutes.'

Janey, who had never been there, was the guide. She took them into the town streets, crowded with ancient churches and curio shops, to see the clock tower, where the bomb had almost fallen, passing over like a deadly wasp to lodge in a sixteenth-century pub.

A memorial marked the spot where ninety-two persons, drinking out the raid, had died, as one, in one second of red annihilation.

The clock tower was very pretty, with a blue face, and

gold figures. At three, it played the first bars of 'I do like to be beside the seaside'. This innovation had been added in 1946, to mark its personal victory over Nazi Germany.

There were small crowds in the town, not multitudes. They moved lazily, soaking up the sun. There had been a forecast of downpours for tomorrow.

In the fish and chip shop business was slack. A statuesque black-eyed beauty brought them huss and fries, and rounds of satisfying white bread with butter.

It was a little cooler, when, holding tights and shoes in their hands, they paddled in the sea, which itself felt chill as a fridge.

'Oh, I could live here,' said Janey. 'I just could. Even in winter.'

The town smelled of fish, cooked, and alive, of hamburgers and ozone.

Farther along the beach, a party of beggars was quietly getting stoned. (By the clock tower a girl busker had sung a tuneless song, not pausing for the music box of the tower, discordant, sad.)

'People without homes, in B and Bs,' said Hesta. It was only a comment, but Janey answered, 'That may be Mum and me any way, if they pull the flats down.'

They did not find a stone with a hole, but Janey chose two, an orange one with a white face painted on it by weather, and a blue one, whorled and striped with zebra black.

Notices announced: *Rock, Ice-cream, Buckets and Spades, Umbrellas*. Or, *Palms read. Mind the Step*.

In a dark little shop a beaming lipsticked woman sold Janey a seahorse brooch she could not afford for Lulu, while

Hesta stood by, refusing blandishments to try these earrings, this scarf, this ring.

They went in a pub with a crab as its sign, and drank vodka and orange juice. A tall old inebriated man tried to take them elsewhere. 'Poor old sod,' said Janey, when they were outside. 'Just think, he was young and nice once.'

'Perhaps he wasn't.'

'Yes. He had great eyes.'

'And he was sixty years old.'

'Was he? One day we'll be sixty years old,' said Janey.

'Do you think so?'

They stood a moment, and glanced sidelong into the veiled future that is the veiled future for all living things. Who dares to know? Mind the step of palm reading. The world is full of wars and weapons, illnesses and accidents. But then they raised their heads, for they were sixteen, lions, and alive.

When they went into the funfair, Janey fired at the line of tin ducks and missed them all. They rode on the carousel, horse by horse. But Janey sought the fibreglass rush of the Rocket alone, and came staggering off like a drunk. 'Jesus, I feel sick. I need some more chips.'

The chips were eaten after they had got down the steps on to the beach again, and walked away under the cliffs. The town curved behind and was hidden. Green holes watched above, and rock faces carved like those in mediaeval paintings.

The light was changing, the sun going over, and eventually they saw it begin its descent, towards a distant corner of the water. Time had flowed out like the sea.

'You've been really quiet today,' said Janey. 'I mean, you always are. But are you OK?' Hesta smiled. She put her hand on the top of Janey's head, a sort of blessing. And Janey shivered. 'It's getting late. You know, it's six. We ought to start going back to the station.'

'Yes,' Hesta said.

Cars were pouring away from the town. The last shops were closing, doors slammed, awnings poled up. The little train for the children was rattling to its shed along its Lilliput track. The last train of summer.

The gulls called and clustered, standing sentinel in the westering yellow light on chimney pots, walls, or flying the high sky in long circles, round and round each other.

Most of the holiday-makers had vanished, it seemed. Dolls brought out for show, now packed up. On the sea terraces of the cafés, and of the pink hotel, a few last of these prototypical people drank beers and gins, worn out by sea and sun.

Golden smoke now on the town, like polluted pollen.

Slowly, Janey and Hesta wended along the promenade. Janey was reluctant, her eyes taking lingering snapshots of the sea, which now was darkly blue as sapphire wine.

'I'll make Lulu come, sometime.'

'That's a good idea.'

Hesta stopped, and so Janey stopped. Janey said, 'You don't want to go home.'

'No.'

'Come and stay tonight with me and Mum. You usually do weekends, any way.'

'It isn't that,' said Hesta. 'I don't want any of it.'

'Oh,' said Janey.

'I don't mean you and Lulu. But that's pretending. I'm supposed to live with Stephanie. I'm supposed to keep my father from feeling bad. I have to go to the Aspens, and take GCSE, and then A levels, and then go somewhere and study art. And then – then some other fucking useless thing.'

When Hesta swore it was like the swearing neither of Janey, nor Stephanie. Hesta's word was cold. The curse of an old cold woman with bones of chiselled ice.

'Well – what will you do?'

'You knew I'd say this.'

'Yes. When you put your hand on my head like they do in churches.'

'How do you mean?' asked Hesta.

'I don't know. Like a bishop. Any way. I knew. What'll you *do*?'

Hesta shrugged. 'My mind's a blank.'

'It could be – dead weird here. Drugs and stuff. Dangerous.'

'Yes.'

They stood staring out from the prow of the land towards the sea. There were gulls on the beach, walking to and fro. And, jet black, a single raven.

'If you – if Stephanie—'

'Tell her I came back with you and left you at the station in London.'

'She'll go mad.'

'So what?' said Hesta.

'Yes,' said Janey, 'so what.'

Then Janey put her right arm round Hesta, and laid her

head for one second on Hesta's shoulder, among the chains.

'Don't worry,' said Hesta.

'All right.'

'Take care on the train,' said Hesta. 'Get in a carriage with more than one person.'

'Oh, Hesta.'

'Thank Lulu for me.'

'OK.'

They were apart, looking at each other. They had met when they were eleven, had known each other at once, and so for five years after. And now, here in this place where neither had come before, at the edge of the earth, against the backdrop of sea and sunfall, would they for ever let go?

'You know – where we are,' said Janey.

'Yes. Take care, Janey.'

'*You* take care, Hesta.'

A tear ran down Janey's cheek. She shook her head. She said, 'Parting is such sweet sore ow,' turned and went away, almost running, as she had arrived, the black banner of her hair the colour of the grapes they had eaten, and soon she became small as a child. And then this child cannily crossed the road among the roaring cars, and went up a street between the buildings, and was gone. She never looked back. She had not been able to restrain her tears, but her manners were too good to let her wave good-bye.

Four

The lights came on at dusk.

Beneath the pallor of the street lamps, twists and curlicues of bulbs, some in the shapes of seahorses, like Lulu's brooch, fish, dolphin, boats. Their extraordinary colours rained on the pavement, and down into the darkening sea below. Ruby and chartreuse, icing sugar pink, pineapple yellow, electric blue.

Hesta observed them. Did she remember this? Seaside lights . . . Surely she must do.

She sat on a bench on the promenade and watched as the sea and sky went to darkness. And the other way, how everyone seemed to be leaving.

A couple kissed under a lamp, with neon red in their hair. She felt nothing for them, for their temporary or enduring love, both perhaps equally tragic.

After they had gone, a family went by, with a happy little skipping girl.

Eventually the streets seemed deserted, and inland she heard the musical clock strike for nine.

She must have fallen asleep. Of course, she had not slept the previous night, only sat in the café in Fulton Road, with the drunks and homeless. Yes, she had slept about two hours.

Hesta got up, and crossed over the road, which was almost without traffic now. Windows everywhere seemed black, but for a handful of lights in the pink hotel, a couple of cafés.

The sea *breathed*.

It was getting cold, and out of her bag Hesta took the long black jacket she had packed.

She walked through the town, by the clock tower, through the streets where everything was shut. And then there would be a little cave of light, a café, or a more sombre cave, some pub.

Then there was a chemist's, open late, with a tall blue glass jar in the window. Above the shop the lettering read ominously, *Dug Sore*.

Hesta went in. There were no customers. A woman in an overall was standing at the pharmacy, eating cough sweets, putting them one after another into her mouth.

'Can I buy a Coke?'

The woman looked at Hesta.

'Oh, have it. Just have it. Look, there they are.'

Hesta looked and saw the line of cans, beside the rack of shampoos. She felt for her wallet in the bag. She had about five pounds left.

But, 'No. Just take a couple of cans. I'm just shutting. Do you want some hair-wash for your lovely hair? Look, that's a nice one, with extract of rose.'

Hesta looked at her. The woman was calm and serious and had even stopped eating the lozenges.

Hesta glanced at the cans of Diet Coke, and the dark red shampoo. What would happen if she took them? A

60

homosexual advance, an outcry and threats of the police?
Somehow either seemed unlikely.

'Season's over,' said the woman. 'Are you going home?'

'No,' said Hesta.

'No,' said the woman, 'I thought not.'

Hesta took one can of Coke.

'I'll leave the money here.'

'If you like. You needn't.'

'All right. Thank you.'

'Don't mention it,' said the woman primly.

Outside, the darkness seemed to have grown deeper.

She was tired. If she had slept, and she must have done, it
had not been enough. But where to go with five pounds, for
a bed. To Hesta it did not truly matter. She would find
somewhere. For although she had lived her life in reasonable
material security, still it had all been a bivouac in her
mother's house. Threats, attacks, intrusions – these were
familiar fare. And owning nothing – for what did she own? –
what was in her bag. The dress and skin she stood up in.

She was in a street now where part of the cliff came down
to the road, like the limb of a dinosaur.

Hesta paused and looked up at this bastion of rock. The
street lights were few, but even so, she saw the neat white
graffiti cut into the cliffside.

WE KILLED ROY, HERE.

And under that, CHRISTMAS 1925

Hesta laughed softly.

Three seagulls soared over, screaming maniacally.

After the Coke she was hungry, but again, in Stephanie's
house, she had got used to that.

Hesta walked on, up and down. It did not mean very much, the town. Janey had been so excited about it and had not wanted to leave. But she, Hesta, had been the one who remained. The bag was heavy now, as if stones had been put into it. And where was this? Old houses and winding streets, and faces of the cliff with ivy matted on them, and clinging autumn flowers.

Where am I?

I once went to Tomsk, but someone let off a bombsk . . .

She sat on a wall and, looking over, saw back down into the town, the curl of streets, the occasional light. Half the street lamps were out, or else had been removed. From somewhere came a human sound, a song it seemed to be, very loud, but quickly diminishing.

Beyond the streets she could see the promenade following the curve of the shore. The coloured lights that now apparently shone on no one. And a part of the funfare, all wrapped up against the rain or the dew, in types of plastic sleeping-bag or curtains.

Far out on the invisible sea, the peculiar mooing began of some lost ship, archetypal, strange.

And overhead in the black sky, the jealous moon, three-quarters full, was rising.

'You said I must, but you don't ever say that, do you?'

'No. Not usually.'

'You trust me.'

'Completely,' said Lulu.

'So why did you say that to me – over and over—'

'I said it twice.'

'Make sure you catch the train at ten to seven. The last train.'

'Obviously I wanted you to catch the train.'

Janey sat on the grey sofa holding the cushion with the painting of giraffes on it. She had been crying, but stopped. She was in her dressing-gown, and her hair was tied in two bunches, as she had sometimes worn it when she was ten or eleven.

'But Mum – I shouldn't have left her—'

'I think you had to.'

Lulu, in a black velvet tent lasciviously trimmed with lace, handed Janey the hot chocolate from the tray. It was nearly midnight.

'But what'll she do?'

'I don't know.'

'But she's all alone.'

'She always is,' said Lulu, 'alone.'

'No – there was me – there was us.'

'But we weren't enough, love. No, we weren't. And any way, she doesn't want comforting. She wants to *be*.'

Janey drank the chocolate. She thought how now, probably, she would never see Hesta again, and the sweet drink became flavoured with a little salt.

Lulu ate a digestive biscuit slowly. She said, 'I know it's hard on you.'

'And *there* – I didn't know what to do.' Janey stared at Lulu. 'Do you think she'll be all right?'

'Yes.'

'Why? Just because – no one else would.'

'She's very different,' said Lulu. 'She's very strong. I wouldn't have wanted it to be you.'

Janey got up and sat down at Lulu's feet, and put her head in Lulu's lap. 'Did it have to be one of us? What do you mean?'

'Oh, you know,' said Lulu. 'Give us a cuddle.'

Janey hugged her mother tight. She said, 'You mean I couldn't have handled it.'

'I mean you don't have to. I mean you have other things you'll have to do.'

When Janey lay on the rim of sleep, with the tortoiseshell cat warm in her arms, it was as if all the night was empty of Hesta. All the world. I didn't leave her. No, she made me go. I'll never see her again.

I once went to Minsk, but I haven't been back there sinsk.

And, on the stroke of midnight, the lights went out.

She heard it chime from the clock, and a fraction of the mechanical tune – *Oh I do like to be* – and then silence. And in the silence they switched off the illuminations. All the fairy colours, the jewels, the rainbow rain.

Now the street lamps stood stark. And only the moon shone on the sea, making there a road to nowhere.

Hesta stood up. She was cramped and very cold.

Even the moan of the ship had ceased. There was not a single disturbance – except the faintest murmur from the ocean, which so pervaded everything, it had almost become inaudible, like her own breathing, or her heart.

There was a café still open down there. She could see its brilliance. Go and get some hot tea and a bun. Something like that, something cheap.

There were steps, and she followed them down. A gull

perched in a crevice of the cliff, a few feet above. It regarded her, wicked but quiescent. They never slept.

As she got into the narrow byway, below, Hesta heard a car coursing along the streets of the town. The note of it was quite wrong, too throaty, cranky – and then, as it had come, the sound was gone, but not dying away, simply arrested. It must be some trick of the cliff wall, shutting off the noise.

When she reached the café, it was shut, though lighted up garishly, a tease.

A cobbled lane rambled away, with bow-fronted shops on either side, a pub, and above these, tall windows framed in architectural pilasters, vine leaves, urns and stone faces. Like something Janey might have drawn . . . and had she been here earlier with Janey? Hesta was not sure.

One window burned in a box of dull green plaster, and now Hesta heard a baby crying, a demanding and primitive, strident howl.

A shadow passed inside the window, back and forth. A woman, rocking her vocal and unremitting child. No sleep either for her.

The window was open, too, as if the whole street must suffer as well.

Hesta hesitated. There was something curious about the shadow play, about the yellow reflected pane thrown on the cobbles, and the form going over it, over it.

Then the woman came directly into the window, the baby held to her shoulder, wailing.

Something made Hesta step back, into the doorway of a shop beside the café, out of sight.

The woman was leaning from the window. Perhaps she

wanted the cold night to slap the baby quiet. But the baby only squalled harder. Then the woman lifted the baby forward in both her arms. And dropped it straight out of the window, on to the cobbles below.

How does she view this, the leopardess, alone in her red hair and the night? Is she shocked? What does she feel?

Hesta stood stock still, and as she did, she saw the dark liquid run from under the object on the cobbles, glittering in the window's gleam. It was not crying any more. The window above was gently closed.

'You don't want that, do you?' someone said, softly, beside Hesta. 'You're not interested in that?'

Someone, thin, elongated, young, male, standing just clear of her doorway, outlined in the glare of the shut café.

'Be better with me,' he said, 'won't you?'

Hesta did not speak. Nor did she resist when he put on to her arm a long pale hand with hard, scarred fingers. The touch was impersonal but explicit, an usher or policeman at some public event to which she had, innocently enough, got too close.

She let him move her away along the lane, away from the dead bleeding of the baby flung down on the cobbles. As they left the lane, she saw the promenade of dead lights ahead and the moon on the sea.

'Don't want to do anything about it, do you?'

'No,' she said.

'No. She was as wise as she was beautiful.'

The accent was educated, the voice modulated oddly, low, light, expressionless.

'Not too good here,' said the bizarre young man. His hair

was in thick short black spikes. His black eyes and crooked nose were clear enough in the pallid bony face. 'You can see that.'

'Yes.'

'Hungry?' he asked. 'I'm always hungry. You'd better come with me.'

'Why?'

'It's the end of the Season. You don't know your way around. I don't want anything. I won't rape you. Doesn't interest me, rape.'

Hesta turned abruptly. She walked back into the lane. All the windows were unlighted. She walked on, and there on the cobbles was – nothing. Nothing at all.

He had followed her a little way. He called mildly, 'Come on.'

She went back to him. She raised her head but did not speak. He said, 'If you saw it, you saw it. That's the only reasonable way to think. Even if it wasn't there and you saw it. Then you saw it.'

End of Part One

PART TWO

One

In the night it rained. She woke, and wondered why her bed smelled of must. But then she slept again. The window, in the same place as in the house of Stephanie, had deceived her.

Next, waking, it was light, a grey clear morning, and a girl sat on the end of the mattress, balancing a mug.

'You haven't half got good hair,' said this girl. Her own was mouse-fine and limp. 'Want some tea?'

'Yes, thank you.'

Hesta sat up, holding the sheet across her breasts and under her arms. She had slept only in her pants. The tea was scalding hot, a reviving amalgam of tea leaves and bleach from two tea bags left floating, and a drop of thin milk.

'Usually only one bag,' said the girl, 'but Skilt said you might need it strong.' She stretched. She wore a short skirt and sleeveless T-shirt. She was thin, like her hair. 'Hot innit?' The room seemed cold and dank. 'You're Hesta, right?'

'Yes.'

'I'm Phaedra.' There against the ruinous wallpaper, which once had depicted birds of paradise, Phaedra, fragile as a weed. 'It's a Greek play,' she added.

'I know.'

'Yes. Thought you would.' Phaedra rose. 'There's a bathroom along the corridor. Cold water. I've left a towel. Got any soap?'

'Yes.'

' 'S all right then. See ya.'

She went out of the door, closing it decorously behind her.

Hesta gulped down the tea, and got up, wrapped in the sheet which once, long ago, might have been pink, or mauve. She looked from the window. The road ascended narrowly, with two shops that had their blinds down. Over a wall was a rubbish dump, or an area that had become one. The gulls, pristine clean, picked through black plastic bags. Two fought over a fish-skin.

At the top of the road was a swarthy pub, low in stature as some ancient Saxon dwelling preserved by National Heritage.

Everything had been glazed by rain.

But for the mattress and Hesta's bag, the room held nothing. Skilt had conducted her to it last night. 'You can have this.' There was a pillow ready on the bed in a dingy case, two sheets and a blanket with one cigarette burn in it, like a seal of ownership.

'Doesn't someone else sleep here?'

'Not now.'

Skilt had brought her to the hotel about one in the morning. It was, in the bled-out light of the lamps, like a building made of paper. Many of the windows on the ground floor were boarded up, others merely smashed. In the second and third storeys, and the attic rooms above, ghostly concealments hung, like webs.

72

He had asked her name. Pointing up at these rooms he said, 'A proper place for a spider.'

Never talk to strangers. Never go with strangers.

A memory of Stephanie, slapping Hesta's six-year-old legs because she had answered a woman on the street. The woman had been asking the way to the supermarket.

Strangers, however, may be guides.

Skilt had not touched her, after the first laying on of a hand. He explained, as they walked along the promenade, void as if after some catastrophe, that this hotel had become theirs, his and the others'. It sheltered them.

When he knocked on the criss-cross boards of the side door, where a notice read *Deliveries only*, a huge man in a vest and jeans had opened up.

'Hi, Susan. This is Hesta.'

Susan, six foot five, bulging with muscle, his head shaved and crawling with thought, nodded. 'OK, Skilt.'

Black letters ran along the face of the hotel, VICTORIA, the last thing Hesta saw of the outside before they went in.

As Susan shut the door and shot three powerful bolts, a great black dog came like Cerberus out of the gloom.

'That's Susan's Dog,' said Skilt. 'Let him sniff you. Then you're known.'

Susan's Dog came forward like a beast of moving basalt, tasted with his nose Hesta's fingers, snuffled at her groin. His forehead, like Susan's, wrinkled, thinking, then he was satisfied. A large sheathed penis, like something stuffed, hung between his equine legs.

Under a shelf an iron bar leaned on the wall. Two candles burned there on a saucer, and from these Skilt lit another. By this appropriately Victorian light, they climbed a back stair, and came out in a corridor, and so on to a landing. An amazing stairway, with ornate brass balustrade, descended to a wilderness of broken floor. Ripped floorboards and a sign for a powder room fleered in the candlelight.

They crossed into another corridor, and so arrived quickly at the room.

'You're tired,' said Skilt, like a courteous bridegroom willing to forego his first night. 'Decay can bring you something.'

'What?' said Hesta.

'Decay – that's the initials, D.K. – what was for dinner? Sausages. Cold sausages and some toast. Do you want tea or gin?'

Hesta said, 'It's very good service.'

'Hotel, wasn't it?'

Hesta went to the mattress and sat down.

'I'll pay you back.'

'For what? In a perfect world, everything would be free. Consider this a perfect world.'

She closed her eyes, and fell asleep sitting there in front of him, and woke up again because Decay or D.K., a fat girl in bursting corduroy trousers, came in with a blackly toasted bun with sliced cold sausage and mustard in it, and a quarter cup of gin.

Skilt had gone, Decay went, and Hesta, after a couple of bites, a couple of swallows, got out of her coat and dress and tights, crawled under the musty coverings, and slept. Who knows where we go, asleep.

But on the way to the morning bathroom, Hesta passed

three other doors, all standing wide open. Inside the rooms were mattresses, carrier bags, and in one, a portable radio.

The bathroom was functional, once meant to be shared by poorer guests, a slim white tub, a basin with cracks, a stained lavatory. But the flush worked, and the basin filled with the cold water to which they had somehow reconnected themselves. A towel had been put over the side of the bath, with a sticky label attached to it which read *Hestar's*, an approximation of her name. The towel had a picture of a red cat. Had it been chosen with care?

When she re-emerged, Decay was in the corridor at the end window, talking to a pigeon on the ledge outside.

'They say they're dirty, don't they,' said Decay. 'They ain't no more dirty than people.'

'No.'

'Less dirty. Do you know, there are one million pigeons and three million seagulls in the town? Yeah. And they shit on everything. You see it all the time, in Season. Women going Ooh, Ooh, and guys rubbing at their hair. But they ain't never shat on me. Wouldn't care if they did. Everyone shits on you, don't they. But you can wash bird shit off. Do you want breakfast? It's down the ballroom. Have you seen the ballroom?'

'Not yet.'

'Come on, then. Skilt said show you around.'

Hesta put her towel in the room. She had dressed in her alternative clothes, the long black skirt and loose white shirt.

'You've got a lovely figure,' said Decay judiciously. 'I never did. My dad kept on and on. Go on a diet. But I looked bloody horrible whatever I did. So I run off. You know sometimes I don't eat for two whole days. Never lose a pound. It's fate. Kismet.'

Decay peered through another opened door. Someone had upset some spaghetti on the floor. 'What a waste,' said Decay. 'I'll send up the dog. Yeah, kismet. Have you seen the musical? I like that. Everything comes out right. And *Seven Brides for Seven Brothers*?'

'No, I haven't.'

'Well, you might not like it. My dad said I was an ostrich, stuck my head in the sand. You got to, sometimes.' They had come to the grand staircase. In the daylight, clots of carpet were visible. Decay looked over. 'This was all lovely once. But then, I'd never have got in here. Don't lean on the railing, by the way. It's wonky.'

They took a side corridor and descended some cold stone stairs behind two glass doors off their hinges. At the bottom they went through a wide foyer with rose-coloured doors marked *Ladies* and *lemen*. A telephone lay in cream pieces like bits of meringue. On the thick emerald wallpaper, lime-green fungus grew.

'Now, this is impressive,' said Decay. She pushed at a pair of white door panels ornamented by gilt wreaths, and scratched all over by words and names . . . *Tyler*, *Johnny*, *Kiss me Dick*, *Pete loves Deb*.

The ballroom was enormous.

Marble pillars supported a gallery of wrought iron and fake gold, and the ceiling was like the inside of an iced wedding cake, if wedding cakes did not contain cake.

In the middle of all this, a hearth had been built on the floor, of cement, walled in by bricks. Here a fire burned, reflected on the marble, the gold, the cracked and holed panes of the long windows and the cracked and holed mirrors between them.

Outside was a terrace, where rusty garden furniture clustered. A sunken garden had nothing in it but weedy summer grass, flattened by rain, and a stone bird-bath where a gull was inspecting its feathers.

'There was a palm tree once,' said Decay. 'But it died. So we cut it down and burnt it. The wood didn't half smell triffic. But it was a shame.'

Three men sat by the fire, toasting bread. Phaedra was buttering it with margarine. A vast canteen teapot stood by, and three kettles gibbered quietly on the edge of the flames.

'Domestic, ain't it?' said Decay. 'People think, if you live in a squat like, you got to live like pigs. Mind you, pigs ain't dirty, not if they're looked after proper.'

The men were introduced. Bod, Brillo, Catsmeat. Only Catsmeat had truly long hair, blond, and shining with attention.

There was a packet of cornflakes and a can of condensed milk. The thin milk in the carton was saved for the tea.

Presently, the doors shouldered open, and Susan's Dog walked in.

'Hello, mate,' called Catsmeat.

The black dog came over and sat down, and Brillo filled a plastic bowl with cornflakes and a generous amount of the condensed milk. The dog ate with involvement.

'Susan gets money off the social for the dog,' said Bod, admiringly.

'I really like a bit of the dog food,' said Brillo, 'but then, he likes the cornflakes. Give and take, you see.'

Phaedra gave Hesta toast and margarine and another mug of tea.

'Well,' said Brillo, 'Season's over. Get some stores in today. Want to come, Hes?'

'Call her Hesta,' said Decay.

'Sorry,' said Brillo. 'Forgot. Most of us, like, change our names.'

'I already did,' said Hesta.

Brillo nodded. 'Right.'

They ate after this in silence. Outside, the gull patrolled the terrace. It sprang up on an old iron table and effortlessly released its bowels. Then flew off.

No one asked questions.

There was a sense of blind intimacy and knowing, as if of warriors before some battle. But life was the battle, that must be it. No one needed to ask. Respect a name, respect a secret, all in it together, sink or swim. You are thrust here, abandoned here, and finally driven forth into nothingness. So, about the brief camp fire of the world. And Hesta was used to a bivouac.

The small group left the hotel about eleven fifteen. It was the time, Catsmeat explained, when people begin to want their dinner, and so, hypoglycaemic, lose concentration.

Decay carried a shopping bag, the young men, Catsmeat, Brillo, meandered behind. Everyone but Hesta wore long coats.

The road was dry, and although the sun had not come from the clouds, it was beginning to be hot. As they turned on to the front, Hesta looked towards the sea. Still and grey, it was

78

a different element from yesterday, and from the night before. No one else moved on the Sunday promenade.

They crossed a number of streets, and Catsmeat said, 'You don't use the little shops. Not fair, 'cept in an emergency.'

Hesta, wandering along with them, seemed to have assumed she owed them this. For they had fed her, and now were going shoplifting. Stephanie would have been appalled, censorious and frightened.

'Don't worry,' said Brillo, to Hesta. 'It's easy.'

She glanced at him. 'I'm not worried.'

It was all a dream of course. Really she had gone home on the train, was with Janey and Lulu, and tomorrow she would be returning to the Aspens.

The big shop was attached to a garage.

Decay went straight in and began to put into a wire basket a paper, a carton of milk, a tin of beans and a can of dog food. She drew Hesta over to the eggs and started examining them carefully. 'Get a lot broke, then you've paid for nothing, they leak out.'

Hesta sensed rather than saw Catsmeat and Brillo idling between the shelves. No one else seemed to be in the shop but for the girl painting her nails at the check-out. There were two security cameras. These showed the same views of the shop over and over, and Hesta suddenly noted that they also showed, now and then, the spot where she stood with Decay and they were not there, even the eggs were not. It was some sort of pre-recording on a loop.

Catsmeat and Brillo idled back. Both looked bored, almost petulant, but Brillo muttered, 'Bread, chocolate, bacon, and a *Home and Garden*.'

Decay snorted.

Catsmeat went up to the counter. He shook his moonlight hair at the girl and said, 'Hallo, luv.'

Decay reached over and took, without fuss or subterfuge, four cans of lager. Then she turned and stowed them, one by one, in her flapping pockets.

'Bar codes,' said Hesta.

'Not here. Not out of Season.'

On impulse Hesta went around the shelves, and standing out of sight of the dud cameras, the check-out, and Decay, took a slab of cheese in sweaty Cellophane and dropped it into her skirt pocket.

The check-out girl was deep in converse with Catsmeat, ignoring Decay, who arriving there, abruptly barked, 'Oh come on. I ain't got all day.'

Nothing happened until they were at the door.

Then the overweight manager, in his tie and neat trousers and stomach-bulge, emerged from nowhere.

'Wait. Just a minute. *Wait.*'

They froze. And Decay turned protectively, her own bulk dividing them all from him, her face red with animosity.

'My God,' said the manager. 'You silly sods.'

'What's up?' said Brillo. He was pale.

'Open your coats.'

'Oh fuck,' said Catsmeat. 'Oh come on, mate.'

'Do as I tell you.' The manager stepped forward and pulled Catsmeat's coat open wide, and there it was, the lining stacked with tins and packets. A bag of Wotsits fell to the floor.

'Can't trust you. Bloody idiots.' The manager turned to the

nails-girl on the counter. 'Get some more beans for them. And that macaroni's on special offer. What's this –' he felt into Brillo's pockets. 'Get him another couple of packs of the smoked back. Useless, the lot of you.'

He swivelled then to Hesta. 'I don't mean you. Take this. It's quite nice, herbal. My wife uses it.' He handed her a green bottle of bubble bath. 'Look, there's some fresh flowers there. Maybe the roses. If you want.'

He watched them loaded, shoved some French bread into Decay's carrier with two slabs of butter and a jumbo pack of tea bags, then stood aside to let them go.

When they were outside again, they hovered on the pavement. Hot globules of rain dropped, with yards between them.

'He never done that before,' said Brillo.

Decay removed a Mars Bar from Brillo's pocket. She bit off its head.

Evo, a boy of fifteen, was on a kitchen chair, guarding the door, and let them in as he had let them out. His long, unwashed hair crept on his shoulders, and his greenish face, alive with blackheads and scabs, threatened an awful beauty to come.

'You was quick.'

'We was lucky,' said Brillo. High with wild success, he handed Evo a can of beer, and Decay removed page three carefully from the paper and slid it on Evo's knee.

'Cor, en't she big,' said Evo. He sat back happily, the picture of the bare-breasted model held up reverently to a trace of light.

As they climbed the stair, Evo called, 'Skilt wants *her*.'

'He means you,' explained Decay to Hesta.

On the grand landing above the ruined floor, Susan, avoiding the 'wonky' balustrade, was throwing darts into a cork-board fixed to the wall. The dog sat meditating at his feet.

'Skilt,' said Susan. 'I'll take her.'

Hesta handed the cheese and the bubble bath to Decay. Escorted by Susan and Susan's Dog, she was drawn away again into the warren of hotel corridors.

They climbed another stair.

'Magpie had a nest in there,' said Susan, pointing into a chaos of room where two ceilings had fallen straight down and a fretted gap showed rubble and, ultimately, the rainy sky.

'Why does Skilt want me?' Hesta said.

'Ask him. 'Spect he'll tell you.'

They climbed on.

Susan was massive. Even his jeans appeared to have muscles. And the dog was the same. Neither seemed actually unhelpful – enigma might well be indigenous here, with some.

It would be impossible to run away. It had been from the first. Whoever guarded the door to keep others – authority, the law – out, also kept in those desired to stay. By stealing she had given them a hold on her, because of which they might permit her some freedom. It had sometimes worked that way with Stephanie.

They came to the attics.

A broken window showed how dark the sky had become, like dusk, and as they arrived in front of it, thunder tumbled, low as a drum in the hills. And next the rush and rustle of thick rain.

'Needs it,' said Susan. 'Down there.'

Hesta went alone to the door, which hung ajar. Beyond was a space. A great doorless storeroom gaped to one side, full of strange rickety chairs and settees. A doorway was ahead, also without a door. Skilt's private room?

What was Skilt any way – their leader, their founder? Had he captured them all, wandering aimless on the shore or in the streets, runaways, misfits (that is, those who did not fit the system), the impecunious and afraid and angry?

It was dark, and in the room were only the usual things, mattress, a few bags, one table perhaps salvaged from the store, with twisted butterscotch legs. On the table lay a book, open and face down, a bottle of Abbey Well water half full, a Biro, a gull's feather, some stones from the beach. And a disposable syringe.

Skilt stood at a window, over which drooped a green shrimp net, tangled like mohair. He turned.

'It's not heroin.'

'You're diabetic,' said Hesta.

'Oh no.'

She had been meant to see the syringe. But perhaps not, perhaps it was part of the decor, like the feather and stones. Or he had overlooked it. Or genuinely did not care.

'Sit, why don't you,' said Skilt.

'Where?'

'Anywhere.'

There were no chairs.

Hesta went to the wall, and sat facing him, her back against the bare plaster.

Skilt walked to the table, picked up his book. He read out,

'And the moon and the sun, and the stars, and all the seas.'

Then he moved to his mattress, and himself sat there, crossing his legs. He was very, very thin. He wore a white shirt shoved into black trousers, a costume rather like her own. His feet were in black plimsoles.

On all his fingers there were scars, long diagonal scars, as if he had warded off the blows of knives, but too, scars that circled his fingers like rings.

His teeth were good, solid and white, but the two front left upper incisors were visibly chipped.

'How do you like it?' asked Skilt.

'What?'

'Here.'

'Fine,' said Hesta.

'And do you think you'll stay?'

'I've nowhere else.'

'Your home.'

'No.'

Skilt gazed down at the floor. He said, 'What you saw last night. Going to tell me?'

'If I must.'

'Don't have to. Just wondered. They call that Old Street.' When Hesta did not reply, Skilt said, 'I walk around that part of the town, sometimes. The others don't like to, much. Not out of Season.'

'So it's out of Season.'

'When they turn the illuminations off and everyone else goes home.'

Hesta again did not speak.

Skilt said, 'Mix with the others. They'll put you wise.'

'All right.'

'You're willing to do anything,' said Skilt.

'No.'

'Then what won't you do?'

'I don't know,' said Hesta.

'If someone broke in here,' said Skilt. Hesta said nothing. 'Don't want to say or not sure?'

Hesta said, 'If I'm no use, you can always tell me to go.'

'That's fair,' said Skilt. 'We'll leave it like that.'

Hesta got up. Skilt watched as she did so. Hesta said, 'I'd like to make a phone call. Is that allowed?'

'Of course. If you've got some money.'

'I've got a card.'

'The local box is probably vandalized again. Happens in the summer. Go up to the pub. Someone will take you.'

'Thanks.'

'Don't mention it.'

'You don't want to know who I'm calling?'

'Don't give a toss, Hesta.'

Susan and Susan's Dog were waiting by the rainy window and took her down again, but it was Bod who went with her to the squat Saxon pub, on whose grimy board hung a picture of a fat rabbit sharing a pint with two dogs. The name of the pub was the Hare and Hounds.

'Picture used to be these beagles coursing this hare,' said Bod. 'Got a lot of complaints from the animal rights. So they changed it. I like it,' said Bod. 'Don't eat meat. I had a rabbit when I was a kid,' said Bod in the bar, over a half of some murky ale. 'Used to take it to bed. It lived for years, y'know. I still miss him.' Bod had another drink. 'Sometimes Skilt goes up the Cancer in Old Street. Not keen meself. Other end of town.'

Hesta drank Perrier and drew in her sketch book. It began as a doodle, and ended as a drawing, quite detailed, of the tall old man who had tried to pick up Janey, and possibly Hesta, yesterday. He had had a shock of greying hair scraped back in a pigtail, and a rich man's suit, of washed-out fawn. There had seemed to be a sort of amusement in him all the time. Even when, after he had bought them two drinks apiece, they left him there.

His hands, and his throat – seen inside the open-necked shirt – were very strong. She realized this as she drew them. Was he younger than he seemed? Acting up, playing some game?

'Phone's free,' said Bod.

The barman, squat and swarthy as his pub, waved her card and her fiver away.

She had not seemed to see Bod pay for their drinks. His any way looked like the rinsings from last night. Perhaps her Perrier, which had had, abnormally, a flat salty taste, had only been tap water with a spoonful of Andrews.

Lulu answered after five rings. Her voice was very seductive because, sometimes, on Fridays and weekends, an obscene caller rang the flat. He had been doing so for years. Lulu gave him vivid descriptions of her invented twenty-five-year-old body, its underwear and lusts, until he came with gasps and groans. She had asked him never to call before eight or after four p.m. He always thanked her respectfully.

'It's Hesta.'

'Hallo, Hesta.'

'I'm OK. Can you tell Janey?'

'Of course I will.'

Lulu did not, as Hesta knew she would not, demand Hesta's whereabouts, her condition, why she had not come back, how she dared.

'Is Janey all right?'

'Yes, fine. A bit tired. She's asleep.'

'I thought she would be. Give her my love, please.'

'Definitely.'

'And the cat.'

'I will.'

Hesta paused. She said, 'This place – I mean, down here – it's weird, isn't it?'

'Yes, Hesta. Yes it is.'

'I'll go now.'

'Take care.'

'And you.'

Hesta put down the phone. As she did so a curious pang seemed to pass through air and space. It was the note of severance, surely. The conclusion of a sequence.

Looking back across the bar, everything seemed unreal. It was as if she had entered a film, and the film had now ended, and yet, inside the film, she and it went on, unseen, together.

Her Face

The main room was L-shaped, three bedrooms knocked through. The window that shone into the long stroke of the L reached from ceiling to floor and was glazed in two hundred small round panes.

This light – this dark light – fell now on the unrolled portion of canvas that had been laid flat on a table made of ebony, with enormous legs ornately carved. Five objects held the painting open, at the four uneven corners, and at the torn-away part on the left side.

No one was in the house.

It had the secretive silence of any building devoid of animate presence.

Below the upper rooms, where shafts of iron held the second floor intact, and the first floor, neglected, crumbled, sometimes things scurried, shifted. A little drip of rain had run down, as it always did.

The faint transparent sun had at three o'clock appeared above the sea. Two pencils of gilt respondingly swelled in through two holes, but above, the window of two hundred eyes refracted the light in two hundred tiny golden bubbles.

The painting felt the sun, and showed a pale blur of a face, throat and bosom of a woman in uncertain clothing. For she had no features. They had been ground away by time, or a seepage of water, slight as the rain on the lower floor.

Yet her hair, both fantastically bound up and riotously loose, was red as a blood-orange, its heart and skin.

By one of the legs of the table stood the base of the barnacled and green-black Nebuchadnezzar from which, once its neck had been smashed, the painting was extracted.

The style of the painting, the ghost of its brushwork, something in the bizarre design of the dress, seemed indicative of the seventeenth or early eighteenth centuries.

You might be inclined to stare at the face, which had vanished, or which, conceivably, had never been described. After a while vision might play tricks with vacancy and fill the face in. A certain pair of eyes, a nose, lips, chin. This forehead. That angle to the cheeks, tilt to the jaw.

But it was guesswork.

Even the ravenous colour of the hair, that had flamed straight through the closed glass like fish or fire or star, might have been corrupted and altered by its years under the sea, or the sea's entry into some slight crack or lesion.

Could she, in fact, have been painted as blonde, or black-haired?

Truthfully the bosom had lost any expression of curves.

The portrait after all could have been a child, or a young man, wearing a fantastic wig.

And so under the wig a child's face, a boy's face. Even the unclad face of a skull.

Two

Stephanie Web, a half-drowned swimmer, sank and surfaced in and on her sea of drugged sleep.

Her dreams were horrible, of humiliations and failures, a disco where no one would ask her to dance and she was not allowed to dance unless asked, a street where, incredibly overweight, she tried to find a lavatory, but all of them were open to the gaze of passers-by.

She was so hot in the dreams, and nauseous, and all of her ached, just the way she had been when she was carrying Hester.

Then she would wake up, or almost wake, but the fever followed her, the ache, the pain, and a feeling of ghastly dread. Until the drugs dragged her back under.

Up and down, rising and sinking.

Wanting to urinate, but not able to come to sufficiently to seek the bathroom. And besides, now it was so difficult, something that had been so simple, something that had been *Just going for a pee*, a major undertaking.

Trying to cry in her sleep. Crying in the dream. Why would no one help her? It was because she was so ugly and so fat. And the awful sickness, not pregnancy but over-indulgence.

'What have you eaten?' cried the thin unknown woman with highlights in her hair. 'Come on, spit it out.'

'Chocolate. I ate chocolate.'

'Yes I can see it. Under your skin.'

'And I made a sandwich.'

'Bread? You ate *bread*?'

'And mayonnaise. And cheese.'

'Go to the toilet and sick it up.'

'Not toilet, loo –' but Stephanie retched in her sleep.

Somewhere, at the end of the leafy Victorian road, church bells rang dimly. It was Sunday. But for Stephanie Sunday did not matter much. As Saturday had not mattered much after eleven seventeen in the morning.

She had not got in until four thirty a.m. Martin, as normally, had not bothered to bring her home, she had had to take a cab, and it had cost fifteen pounds of Iain's money.

By the time she had let herself into the house she was leaden, full of acid wine, overtired. She did not think about Hesta, not really. Of what she, Stephanie, and Martin Peecey, had done in Hesta's bed.

High on alcohol, much earlier, it had seemed funny, clever, serve the little bitch right. But it was degrading for Stephanie, squeezing her thin dieted hips into those sixteen-year-old's panties, made for other hips never spread by the carriage of a baby.

Yes, he fancied Hesta all right. They were like that. Men. She could remember, when *she* was fifteen, sixteen, all the dirty old men looking at her. But Martin was not old, of course. Simply immature.

After the sex, Stephanie, feeling herself begin to come down the sharp spiral from wine and action, wanted to go on, rev up the evening.

In the wine bar, she could sense his boredom. She tried to please him. It did not work. At last, about ten to four, she was angry. She left.

In the bedroom, she threw off her clothes, the expensive dress dropped on the carpet, and rolled into bed. She was asleep in five seconds.

But on Saturdays, as on Wednesdays, Den came in to clean, using the keys she always remembered to leave for him, under the sculptured stone, on Tuesday and Friday afternoons. And when Den started the hoover downstairs, at ten thirty, Stephanie woke up.

She was not hung over. She could 'hold her drink'. But she felt dry-mouthed, depressed, and nervous.

It was useless to try to resume her rest. So she got up.

As she scrubbed her teeth and showered, Stephanie looked at herself in the large bathroom mirrors Den would presently scrupulously clean with Sparkle.

She was slim. She looked – about – twenty-nine. And just put on some eye make-up, and lip gloss, brush her hair, smile – she smiled.

Her eyes looked very heavy. She could see lines under them. Some trick of the hot overcast morning light. Well, it was sexy. Heavy eyes . . . a hard night.

But she had not done her exercises for three days. She'd really have to stop being lazy. It was vital. Not today, though.

After the shower and the scented sprays, she stopped to

listen for Hesta. Sometimes music, or the little radio, would sound from Hesta's room. Silence.

But then. Hesta had been a bloody beast again and flounced out. Probably she had not come home at all, stayed with that stupid little Janey and the awful fat fool of a mother. If she didn't look out, Hesta was going to end up the same size. And then what would Martin think of her?

The hoover stopped.

Den would be in the kitchen now, cleaning the stove, and, no doubt, he would be making coffee in the cafetière.

Stephanie looked at her body again, now in its silky robe pulled tight at the waist by a cord to twenty-seven inches, the lowest she had been able to attain after Hesta's birth.

What would Den say if she went down in her robe? Not just the robe, perhaps, that was a bit much. Robe over bra and pants. She wasn't a slut. And . . . the bra gave her a good line, better – well, a decent bra always helped anyone. (As she had endlessly told Hesta.)

Den was rather dishy, wasn't he? About nineteen, wasn't he? Making a bit on the side while he waited for a job in computers. Stephanie had picked him out herself. Easy on the eye, Den, with his short-at-the-back, long-at-the-front black hair, and brown eyes, and tight buttocks and nice teeth.

She didn't mean anything. God no. Much too young. But just a little flirting, perhaps. Like the time she gave him a piece of her apple, and he left half and she finished it. It would be fun. And he'd love it, wouldn't he. Of course, it might be special, that young body on top of hers, that silky head . . .

Stephanie took off her robe and opened her lingerie

94

drawer to pull out the white lacy pants and white lacy wired see-through bra.

As the clock in the clash-blue sitting room put its minute hand on to eleven seventeen, Den heard Stephanie scream in the most astonishing, unbelievable manner. The kind of cry he had listened to on the late news often, coming out of Bosnia or Rwanda. Not what you expected in a posh street of outer London on Saturday morning, as you were pouring hot water on to dark-roast, full-aroma coffee.

For a moment or so Den hesitated. Getting involved was not always a wonderful idea.

But then he thought probably Stephanie, who could be a bit hysterical, like the time she saw the squirrel tearing up the small bed of flowers, had spilt something on the floor, or stubbed her toe. And he had to go on pretending he was caring, since she paid him fifty pounds a week, which even his mother had never credited.

Den ran up the stairs, calling, 'What's wrong, Steph?'

And banged on the bedroom door.

When he stopped banging, he heard Stephanie being violently, frighteningly sick. And after that, he heard her fall right over, and the floor shook, although she only weighed, she said, nine stone.

So Den, careful, brave Den, opened the door, and there Stephanie lay naked on the carpet by a pool of vomit, making peculiar sounds, and something unrecognizable had happened to her hand, which was actually the mousetrap.

Some of the night shift were still on at the hospital, and their eyes made the hollows that had been under Stephanie's into nothing. Now, however, Stephanie was rather a mess.

A nurse came and assessed the situation.

'My God,' she said. 'A mousetrap? No, you were sensible not to try to get it off. Yes this is a priority. Just bring your mum straight through.'

'She isn't my mum,' said Den, faintly affronted. His mother was younger than Stephanie, having given birth about fifteen. Any way, he had always assumed Stephanie was in her forties.

In a little cubicle Den helped Stephanie to lie on the high narrow pallet. She seemed to be delirious.

Christ it had been awful. He had known he had to get an ambulance, but then he had another thought, and phoned a taxi. He needed to get Stephanie dressed.

Her body looked quite alien to him. It would never have aroused him in any event, because Den was gay. But poor cow, she'd wet herself. And so he brought a towel and wiped her, and some tissues to wipe her mouth. He had realized the contraption that had got hold of her right hand was beyond him.

He was required practically to lie on top of her, pulling on her pants and her jeans. He could not clothe her upper torso, so wrapped her dressing gown all around her, and being excruciatingly careful of her hand, tied her up in a bundle with the cord.

The taxi driver, looking upset, helped Den help Stephanie into the car, but she was sick again on the way.

'It's all right, mate. She can't help it. Fucking hell, I've never seen the like.'

Stephanie could not talk, her mouth worked only like a

drunk's. Den gave her name and particulars – Stephanie Web, forty-five, etc – to the hospital reception area, as Stephanie was wheeled off sedated to have the mousetrap removed and her two broken fingers set.

'I need to get back, you see,' said Den. 'I have to help my mother with the shopping.' It was one o'clock, and at two Den was meeting his lover. He felt vaguely guilty, leaving her there, but it was life that had left her there, and someone else, who must have it in for her pretty badly. Den was afraid of hospitals, just the smell made him giddy. He had been brave, in the end, to stand it as long as he had.

So, when Stephanie was brought out to be conducted home, she was found to be alone.

'Who can I contact, Mrs Web?' asked an efficient, exhausted nurse. 'Your husband?'

'Hiss on a rah,' Stephanie drunkenly mouthed. Then she viciously laughed. 'Thas all use hiss.'

Her awareness was coming back, through the haze of sedative and hurt. She looked out through wool and smoke, inside which she was shut with her core of hideous pain, but her brain functioned. She felt bitter.

'He's where, Mrs Web?'

'A dull rah,' said Stephanie.

The nurse deduced, from the sound of it, that this might be unhelpful.

'Is there anyone else?'

'Marhn.'

'Marni. Good. Do you have her number?'

'Hiss – *hiss* nummer.'

Somehow, across the gap of years, a peculiar memory

assailed Stephanie as she floated there in agony, wool and smoke. It was of Hester, three years old, and herself bending angrily forward: 'What are you saying, child? I don't understand. Speak clearly.'

Hester had done it, of course.

Hester had done it.

Hester had.

Hesta.

The nurse put Stephanie on a padded bench, and after several tries, reinvented a number which took her to the wine bar and Martin Peecey.

'I'm afraid your friend, Mrs Web, has had an accident. She's all right now, she'll be fine. But she needs someone to fetch her from casualty.'

'Haven't you got an ambulance?' asked Martin Peecey, nonplussed and non-pleased.

'One or two,' replied the nurse, 'they're rather tied up. Things like bringing in a cardiac arrest and a child the fire brigade just cut out of a car wreck.'

'All right. OK. All right,' said Martin Peecey.

Had Martin tried to be kind? He got to the hospital an hour and a half later, drove Stephanie to the house, assisted her inside, made her a cup of tea that was too strong, examined the two extra tablets she had been given and opined he could sell them in the bar for twenty quid.

He then guided her upstairs and she got with difficulty into bed.

Martin did not clear up the dried vomit on the carpet. He put newspaper over it.

When she said would he stay, Martin told her he could not,

it was impossible, this was Saturday. He would call her this evening.

Would he come round, then?

'I want to, baby. But you've forgotten. Some guy's having a party in the bar. Can't not be there.'

He did not ask about Hesta. And Stephanie did not say anything about Hesta. But after Martin had gone, Stephanie, creeping like an ill woman of ninety, went down again and locked and bolted the front door. This was not revenge. It was from fear.

Then began the horrible sinking and surfacing, the prolonged sleep that could only cover her in stages, that must always let her go. She kept it up as best she could, all through the night, with another of the pills, and on into Sunday. Sometimes she switched on the bedroom TV, but then she switched it off again. She drank the two bottles of Evian Martin had put at her bedside. If he called she did not hear.

In the midst of Sunday she woke mostly for an hour, got up, went down, tried to spread, one-handed, a crispbread with low-fat spread, and watched as everything slid off the counter on to the floor. She left it there.

She was a cripple and no one cared for her. No one loved her. She wept. And could only employ her left hand to blow her nose.

As she desperately swallowed the third pill, about five p.m., she did have the fleeting vision of the weight she would lose by not eating all Saturday and Sunday.

But her hand, which hurt through her entire body, her fingers which now might never be whole in their casing of gauze and splint and sling and purple swollen flesh, these made her desolate. It should not have happened. Everything could have been otherwise. In a parallel world, where she had not touched the mousetrap, or where a loving daughter had not laid the mousetrap for her, Stephanie was laughing in the wine bar. Stephanie, unmaimed, was her old golden self.

But Stephanie was here, and as she went down again into imperfect oblivion, it was as if, injured out of the proper image of herself, mutilated (ruined?), she did not know any more who she was.

Three

Now the sky over the ocean was pink, but the far water was silver ice. It was about ten to six, something like that. Yesterday she had watched the sun go down with Janey. Sky and sea had not looked as they did this evening. Things change.

Hesta had put Skilt's tribe to the test. Whether they would let her out alone.

A young man she did not know, about eighteen, nineteen, whom she had passed on a stair earlier, was by the door. All his head was shaved, like Susan's, but for a mandarin pigtail of black-brown hair. He had a scar under his left eye and a tattoo of a heart cut by a dagger on his left hand.

'I'm going out, all right?'

'Sure,' he said.

That was all.

There was no one outside. No one.

Hesta looked towards the Hare and Hounds and neither was anyone there. Along the promenade a lost soft drink tin rattled up and down in the gusts of cooling wind.

She walked out, over the empty road, and on to the promenade.

Reaching the railing, Hesta stopped.

101

You had to stop here, after all, or below, on the beach. Unless you walked on, into the sea, which some had done.

What would that be like?

Her thought was not remotely the suicide's. It was curiosity. How did the sea seem, closing over your head?

The pier was a little away on her left now. No more music lifted from it. It had lean domes and a shut gate, but below, its legs went down into the stones, legs barbaric and scabrous, revealed by the receding tide.

You could believe you were alone in the world. Some epidemic had wiped out the town. All the buildings empty.

A rusty squeaking noise overtook the withdrawing rattle of the can, the *hush* of the sea.

Hesta turned, to the right now, and saw a shapeless small figure coming along the promenade, pushing ahead of itself an old-fashioned maroon pram.

Above the figure with the pram, the white gulls wheeled on the pink sky.

Hesta moved back against the balustrade rail.

As the apparition got nearer, she saw a little woman in a brown coat and a squashed velvet hat. She pushed the pram rapidly, leaning into it rather, and in the quiet Hesta heard her say, 'Baby, baby, baby,' in the tones of a mother. But she must be a grandmother, she was elderly, more than that. She was like a caricature. Something in her gait, her demeanour. And the pram had been stylish in the 1950s probably.

Hesta saw in a glance, before she averted her eyes and head, how the woman's face was puckered, like her hat, but in firm pearly layers. She had the skin of a country girl grown old from an ancient photograph.

'My baby,' said the woman.

The pram went squeaking by, perhaps six feet behind Hesta's back.

Baby . . . like the baby dropped from the window to the cobbles?

A lioness does not wonder if she has hallucinated. Hesta knew she had seen it happen. As Skilt had said, whether or not she had, she *had*.

The pram and woman were by, going up the promenade towards the end of the town Skilt and remarked the others did not care for out of Season.

There *was* something in the pram, the baby, on a white pillow – Hesta saw it move, under the shawl, but not anything else.

And now a new thing had occurred with the sea. It had gone far enough out that a second beach was revealed, this one of smooth sand beyond the pebbles. And the fading pinkness of the sky made the second beach, wet and reflecting, also into a pink mirror.

A man was standing under the pier.

She could see him now.

Tall and bulky, in a leather coat, a flag of fair hair. The unidentifiable mask of his face seemed turned up to her.

Hesta ignored him. She looked out to sea.

'Full fathom five,' she said, 'my father lies. Of his bones are coral made.'

Behind her, from an upper window of the Victoria, Decay's voice shouted down:

'Supper's up, Hesta!'

Called in from play.

103

* * *

It was like the Great Hall in Greek or Celtic myth.

The central hearth where burned the life-giving fire. Marble pillars glinting on the edges.

Skilt sat on a sofa to one side. The rest were on the floor balanced upon mildewed cushions and rugs.

Supper, cooked on or at the fire, had been fried bacon and eggs, tinned peas and mushrooms, French bread and marg, and slabs of cheese. They drank tea, but after the meal, cans of beer and lager were passed around.

A kind of iron stand protruding over the lower end of the fire, where the bacon and eggs and tea had been prepared, now received a large saucepan with something watery in it. This simmered slowly.

There were about twenty people gathered in the room, and Susan's Dog. One of the boys had gone out after his food, and then the young man with the ponytail and skewered heart had entered, presumably relieved from duty at the door.

Skilt said to Hesta across the fire, 'Despite appearances, none of us has AIDS. You can share the beer if you want.'

'I don't like it,' said Hesta.

'Decay,' said Skilt, 'break out the gin.'

When Decay brought the gin, she offered it to Hesta. Hesta took the bottle and drank a mouthful. Then Decay drank. Skilt said, 'Decay makes speeches, don't you, dear.'

'I do,' said Decay, 'sometimes.'

'It's her way of showing us the rules. What she can tolerate. For example, don't kill a spider or fly in front of Decay.'

Decay said, 'They're not – ' and stopped.

Skilt said, 'Go on.'

'They ain't dirty,' said Decay. 'My dad used to kill flies. They carries disease. That's what he said. I said, People carry disease.'

Skilt murmured, 'Now your speech on AIDS.'

Decay did not seem embarrassed or offended. Instead she got off her knees by the mysterious saucepan, rose to her feet, and addressed them.

'My dad said AIDS was the judgement of God on homos. Like, he was always saying to me, Go on a diet, then you'll be able to get married. What I think about AIDS is this. If you believe in God then He's got to be pretty great. And if He's great, He ain't going to make a lot of filthy rotten illnesses to hurt people. Just like He ain't gonna cause earthquakes and train crashes. I think, like, God is so far from us, He just don't see it, how it could hurt, but He don't *make* it happen. He wants us to be happy. He does His best.'

Bod said, 'God's all right. It's them others.'

'Any way,' said Decay, looking around, a speaker from a platform, 'AIDS is either some horrible mistake, something that just happened. Or it's some stinking experiment. Probably the Americans. Or even that lot in London. Well, they experimented on pregnant women didn't they, with radiation. And let some virus out a bleeding tube to see who caught it.'

Bod nodded loudly. '*Yeah.*'

'And people say in the Bible it says,' said Decay, 'if you're a queer God hates you. But the Old Bible was wrote by a lot of old geezers what probably had to wank if they saw a little kid scratching his head. And Jesus *never* said nothing about it,' announced Decay, freshly arrived with the hot news from just-AD Palestine. '*He* said, Love one another.'

She nodded, and knelt down again by her cauldron. Perhaps her vehemence had caused an odour now to rise from this with the steam. It was the smell of ancient swamps.

Firelight on faces. Shadows. The glitter as the gin bottle passed.

Before Brillo passed it back to Hesta, he wiped its top.

Hesta drank a sip, to be polite, and passed it on.

Skilt, the mediator, said, 'Decay came here after running away from this bigot she so beautifully conjures.'

'I told her,' said Decay.

'Bet you did. So, Hesta has been introduced. Anyone want to be next?'

Bod said, 'I can, if you like.' He looked at Hesta, and then down. 'I couldn't get a job and I went on the streets. That's me. Never liked it. And I got beat up. Later I got sent to a B and B down here. But they said I had to go on a course to learn how to read and write.' His face fell with remembered terror. 'Never could learn. Like they tried to teach me to swim. Nearly shit meself every time, I thought they'd stop me money, so I come here.'

'And I taught him to read,' said Decay, bossy and proud, 'in six weeks.'

'She did too. Look,' Bod held up the *Home and Garden* Brillo had apparently stolen for him. ' "The Michaels have renovated this lovely sixteenth-century cottage." ' Bod showed them the cottage to prove he had not lied. 'Smashing, ain't it?' He had no jealousy. The Michaels were fairytale people, into whose unreal world the written word could effortlessly take him.

Catsmeat said, 'I'm about the same. Not prostituting with men. No one'd have me. But I got down here. Funny thing, I was going bald. Look at it now –' and he shook out his Rapunzel hair.

Skilt said, 'Is the stuff ready yet, Decay?'

'Think so. Have to cool a bit.'

She took her swamp saucepan off the iron and set it by a tray of used batteries, laid near the rejuvenating fire to warm.

Beyond the long windows it had grown black with tepid night. There were no sounds above the crackle of the flames, their own intermittent noises, Bod turning pages, Phaedra hugging herself into her jumper. Once seagulls screamed overhead, a crazy battalion setting out across the town.

'One more,' said Skilt, 'before the dreaming starts.'

Hesta did not know what he meant, but the man with the heart tattooed on his left hand said, 'I'd tell it, Skilt, but you know. Can't find the – can't speak it through.'

'Phaedra,' said Skilt, 'tell his story.'

Phaedra uncoiled. She said, 'Cold, innit? Winter's coming. He's called Bish-Op. He was brilliant, weren't you, love? Could do it all.'

Bish-Op said, quietly, 'First in maths. First in English. Paint. Athletics. Do it all.'

'When he was seventeen,' said Phaedra, 'he got appendix. Routine. No problem. When he comes round, he can't do anything. I mean, he can eat and go to the bog and all that. But he can't do painting. He can't play football or jump. He can read, but it doesn't make sense, see?'

'My brain,' said Bish-Op, 'changed. My mother kept on. Just try, darling. Just work at it.'

'Tried to throw himself off a carpark,' said Phaedra. She reached out and punched Bish-Op lightly. 'But he didn't. Came here. Yeah.'

'It was my name,' said Bish-Op. 'Raymond Bishop. But – changed it. Like the oper— like the op. Fucked op.' He looked straight at Hesta and smiled. 'You're beautiful, aren't you?'

Hesta sat in silence. Then she said, 'Thank you.'

'I – never had the chance – paint someone like you.'

'I'm sorry.'

'It's – I don't mind. You see, I can't – get round it enough to mind.'

He turned, and shivery Phaedra put her arms about him. '*You're* nice and warm.'

' 'S ready,' said Decay.

She dipped a mug into the saucepan and brought it out. Then she glanced uncertainly at Hesta. Then at Skilt. 'Do I—?'

'No. Hesta won't have it.'

'What is it,' said Hesta, 'drugs?'

'Yes. No.' Skilt stretched out his legs. 'Sea water. Seaweed. I get it down under the pier, or from the shore along by Old Street.'

Hesta said nothing. Decay supplied, 'She's thinking it's all polluted and poisonous.'

'Are you?'

'Yes.'

'Not here, Hesta. An example. Brillo.'

Brillo said, 'I cut me finger on me blade. Blood everywhere. Put it in the sea. Two minutes, perfect. No scar.'

Decay brought the mug of simmered sea to her lips, and

took a mouthful. She held it in her mouth a moment, then swallowed it down. And passed the mug to the unidentified girl on her right. Who did exactly the same.

Hesta watched the mug circulate. She had seen the taking of drugs before, three girls hiding in the trees at the Aspens with a joint; Stephanie and Martin and a couple of friends, once, in the kitchen with a little mirror, snorting repulsively.

Perhaps there was that ambience to this. Or was it only the element of sharing, that basic instinctive human thing that binds all addicts to anything together, be it cocaine, alcohol, or a pot of coffee.

A boy across the fire, the mug having passed, spoke up suddenly.

'I found this antique. Amazing it was. Black turd in glass, seventeenth-century shit in a bottle.'

Laughter went over the group. Ritual laughter.

Excluded, as seemed her right, Hesta sat silently, the fire making her hair into a copy of itself.

The sea sounded. Had it been audible before? The tide, coming in . . .

Round their hearth, the fire in the camp of warriors, night before the never-ending battle, bivouac in space.

Evo spoke. He spoke in a new voice, over-educated, almost a distortion. Older than he seemed.

'My friends, the Honourable Hugo Briggs, and Lady Jocasta. My father thought I'd probably marry Jocasta. Even though she was five years my senior. That day in Harrods. She bought everything. We thought she'd never stop.'

The sea sighed.

Evo said, in his too-excellent voice, 'We drove out into the country and ate pâté and strawberries, and drank Dom Perignon. She liked Dom Perignon the best. Hugo said it looked like a good place for foxes. He hunted, you understand. Very oddly, he seemed to admire foxes. He once said he used to fantasize that they were chasing a fox and one sprang out of a hedge with a gun and shot his father.'

Not even Decay responded.

Evo sighed with the sea.

'When we'd finished, Jocasta emptied three carrier bags. All the costume jewelry she'd charged on her American Express, and some ties Hugo had bought, and some stupid things. A stole with metal fringes. A thing to peel cucumbers.'

There was a long pause.

Evo said, 'She offered me a bag. I said I didn't want to after all. Jocasta said, Oh come on. Don't be a bore. You know you're not going anywhere. You know it's finished. But I wouldn't. I cried. Then she threw the cork of one of the bottles at me. I got up and walked away, and as I did that, I could hear them putting the glue into their bags.'

The pause now went on and on.

Someone said, very soft, 'What sort of glue?'

'Oh, out of a big tin. She spooned it out like syrup.'

A wait now.

Evo said, 'I thought I heard her singing, she had a marvellous natural soprano – something from Mozart, was it? But when I came back, they were both dead. The bags were stuck to their faces. The whole place stank of the glue. I used to love that smell when I was a child. It meant making things – model planes, playing. Now when I do it with the

110

bag, I'm always careful. I like the hallucinations.

'Once I seen,' said Evo, altering totally, becoming the first Evo again, 'a horse wot was flying. But she wanted to top herself. And Hugo, he was screwing her. And so he went too. She said we'd all be dead in five years, any way. Crucial. When I remember, I see them sat under the trees, with these bags on their heads. Can't remember the faces. And two little coronets with real strawberry leaves on the top.'

Evo's voice changed yet again. He said slowly, as if he sailed upon the words: 'You see the fishing boats go out. Once a boat went out. Four men. It never came back. They were all married. The women cried. Then they got married again. They got older. When they were in their seventies, one morning the four men walk back into the town.'

'Were they still young, like the day they left?' asked someone.

'No,' said Evo softly. 'No, they was quite old. About the age their wife-widows were now. But each man had a big puffed-up stomach. They lay down in a row, where the houses were, and stopped moving.'

Someone said – Hesta thought it was Phaedra – 'They were dead.'

'Yes. But their bellies. Something moved in those. So the doctor cut them open.'

'Fish,' said Brillo clearly. 'They was full of fishes.'

'No,' said Evo. 'Four babies. Alive. The town looked after them and they grew up, four big blokes, looked just like their fathers. They'd come back full of their own sons.'

The mug had arrived again and Hesta passed it on untouched to Decay.

Susan said, across the fire, 'I'll tell Hesta. Listen, Hesta. When I was twenty, I fell in love with a little girl of ten. I never touched her, mind. I held her hand, that was all. If I'd been thirty-five and she'd been twenty-five, I could've told her, told anyone. But I was twenty and she was ten. It wasn't she was a kid, you see. It was because she was her. She liked me. I used to take her on the swings. I thought, keep your job, save up. I thought, in six years, I could maybe make something of it. They'd say, cradle-snatcher. That was all.'

Was it the sea, or the sounds of their breathing?

'Then her mum got the idea I hung round 'cos it was her I fancied, and she makes a pass at me. And when I don't want to know, she tells me to get out. She said I was a pervert, she seen me looking at her – at her Susan. That was her name, you see, my little girl. The old whore mother said she'd get the Bill on me. So. I never went back. And a year later they moved away.'

Catsmeat said, gently, 'How old are you, Susan?'

'Thirty-two,' said Susan. 'She'd be twenty-two. She's married now. I heard. Married and got a kid of her own. She lives over Leeds way.'

Bod said (he must have said it before), sullenly, 'Couldn't you go and see her?'

'I called her,' said Susan. 'She said, Oh, it's you. She was surprised, scared. Her mother had spoken to her. She said, My husband is just in the garden. He don't let me see no one. He's possessive. I've got to ring off now.'

Hesta saw, across the fire, the golden points of the dog's eyes burning. Susan laid a hand flat on the dog's head, and the eyes half closed.

'Bottles wash up here,' said Susan. 'And they got messages in 'em. There was one from a Roman galley. She was called the *Goddess Livia*. It was in Latin. It said, *I miss my wife*. That was all. He wanted someone to know.'

'There was a champagne wreck,' said Brillo. 'They brought the bottles up. All sealed tight. The wine was ace. Knocked you out for a week.'

Over the fire, a girl said, 'Do you know about Moses, Hesta?'

Someone laughed. Several of them made a sudden noise: *Brum-brumm*, the motor of a car.

Bish-Op said, carefully, 'Moses parted – the Red Sea.'

Skilt said, 'And now he drives a car around the town.'

'Some nights, you see him.'

A lull fell over them, like a long wave. Hesta perceived it, sensed it, apart from them, for she had not drunk their communal drink that might only be a rite, or might be a cause of 'dreams' only because of the wastes and chemicals in it.

Another girl said, 'It's a long black car. A collector's item. All burnt out, and it smokes. But he's all smart, like 1920s, or 1914. Blazer and boater.'

Skilt lay back on the sofa now. He said, in his odd, actor's voice, 'All those dead thrown over from the ships wrapped in the flags of nations, and with a stitch through their noses to keep them still. On the Day of Resurrection, the sea gives up its dead.'

A young black boy sang out, 'I see them come up from the water wrapped in them flags.'

Bod cried, 'One after another. Red, white and blue. Union Jack, French flag, US flag.'

113

'And the women too,' said Decay in a low sweet tone, 'the dead women with their dead babies stillborn.'

'On the funfair,' said Catsmeat, 'the old pictures of the fat lady and the clown and the baby, where you stick your head through to be photoed. And severed heads were stuck in there. Yeah, I saw them there. Till they rotted and the gulls had out their eyes.'

Phaedra said, 'Once a man dressed up as a mermaid, and sat on the rocks under the caves, where the sea comes right in and goes right out. And they shot him, 'cos he wasn't real. Then a real mermaid comes up. And no one goes to see.'

Another man said, 'Jehovah's Witness comes into the town. Knocks on a door. Real heavy stuff. Asks this old guy, Are you prepared to die for Jesus? The old man shouts, Mother, fetch the axe. The Witness laughs and then the old woman comes and cuts the old man in bits. She says to the Witness, who's all smothered in blood, Y'see, mister?'

Silence now. A deeper wave spread and covered them, and it seemed to Hesta they might be asleep with their eyes wide open. All but the eyes of Susan's Dog, which had shut.

In her head Hesta heard the song, 'Full fathom five thy father lies'. She had not taken the potion, but she was in its proximity. She did not say the song aloud although it was on her tongue, tapping at the inside of her lips.

Driftwood and old boards settled in the fire.

And then, across the partitions of the night, there began a swift rushing, rather like rain, but not the rain. And the end of it was a dull resonant crash.

Hesta got to her feet.

The others only turned their faces a little.

114

Skilt said, 'Another wall's come down. The hotel, Hesta, it's going to rack and ruin. Microcosm of the world.'

Then Skilt got up, and he and Hesta were facing each other across the fire.

Skilt said, 'The name *Hester* comes, like *Esther*, from the Babylonian goddess Ishtar.'

The dog, too, had risen, and went padding round the fire, licking up remnants from the plates and spilled cans.

Decay said, 'In my dreams I'm slim, and I have wings. I'm like that now, a bit.'

Skilt walked towards the doors, half turned, and beckoned to Hesta.

'What?' she said.

'I want you to come with me.'

Would she say no? In his stronghold, surrounded by his people? Hesta walked after Skilt without hesitation or denial, but her footfalls were canny as those of a tiger.

Outside the ballroom, Skilt said, 'Not worried, are you? I won't hurt you. Feel you haven't got much choice?'

'Have I?'

Skilt continued to the back stairs and began to climb. She still followed him.

'Maybe. Maybe not. Am I a nasty vengeful cretin like Susan's little girl's mother? Or am I a weak, easy-going, fair-minded stoic? Any way, what do I want you for? Rape you? No. Molest you? No. Guesswork. You'll do what I say until I say something you won't do.'

'Yes,' said Hesta.

'And we still haven't decided *what* you won't do.'

At a higher window he stopped and pointed out.

There was blackness, with only one street lamp showing for about a hundred feet. The illuminations, turned off for the winter, hung like dead insects under this light. No moon.

Otherwise, the street, the empty road, the promenade, the railing.

'Can you see it?' Skilt asked.

'What?'

'The water.'

'No.'

'Can you *feel* it?'

'No.'

'Anything?'

'Yes.'

'What?'

Hesta considered. 'Openness.'

'Think of it. The boat, the ship. Floating alone in miles of *that*. And after all, that's what the land does too.'

'Seven-tenths of the earth is water,' said Hesta.

'And most of us is water.'

'I know.'

'Been to school. What a good girl. Why did you leave?'

Hesta said, 'I don't tell stories, like the others.'

'Didn't think you would. Neither do I, much.'

When they reached Skilt's room, beyond the furniture store, Skilt again went first, and lit a candle that had migrated on to the table with the feather and stones and book. The syringe was gone.

Skilt sat on his mattress.

Hesta stood in the doorway.

'Feel you've learned anything?' Skilt asked.

116

'Perhaps.'

'Out of Season,' said Skilt, 'it's strange here.'

'Yes.'

'The fee for the lesson,' said Skilt. 'Take off your clothes. I'd like to look at you. That's all. No touching. Now, is that one of the things you'll do, or not?'

Hesta came into the room. She pulled her white shirt up over her head, undid her skirt and let it fall, stepped out of her pants. As she bent, flexible as a cat, to undo her sandals, Skilt said, calmly, 'No. Keep those on. There are splinters in the floor.'

She straightened, and waited in front of him. Only her head was a little turned, her eyes looking right away through a wall. She was not pale or flushed, and just visible now, her heart beat quite slowly.

Hers was almost a boy's figure, the waist very small, but the hips also narrow, and her breasts, young and high and not large. But she had the smoothness of a girl, the creamy overlay of the feminine thing. The hip bones, although they showed, were like two half-sheathed pearls. In her long legs the knees were rounded. At the joints of thighs and inside arms, a hint of lushness, after all. There were no marks on her. Not a freckle. Only the outrageous heat of hair at her groin as on her head.

'Raise your arms,' said Skilt.

She raised them, her fingers pointing straight at the ceiling.

'Now turn your back to me.'

She did not move, and Skilt said, 'You'll hear if I do anything. And look, I'll be reflected in the window.'

Hesta turned her back.

After about a minute Skilt said, flat and dry, 'You're like a narrow white vase with red flowers spilling out of the top.' Then, 'That was pleasant. Dress now,' in the manner of – a doctor.

She did so.

When she looked up, Skilt was lying back on the bed, gazing into the air above him.

'Didn't hurt,' Skilt said, 'no?'

'No.'

'You'd do it again.'

'If I had to.'

'Don't have to,' said Skilt. 'My memory's very, *very* good.'

Four

Ringing. Bells.

Answer the bells.

You don't answer bells. Yes. Not bells. Telephone.

Wake up and sit up and answer –

'Mar – tin – Marty—'

In the dark of a morning that was probably Monday, and the luminous bedside clock unticking and unwound, orphaned of light and time, Stephanie listened.

'I'd like to speak to Mrs Web.'

Stephanie was Mrs Web.

'Yes – speaking – what time is it?'

'Very early, Mrs Web. I'm sorry.' The voice was a woman's, cool, professional, not sleepy, or hurt or sick. 'Mrs Web, is your husband there?'

In a sort of slow-motion horror Stephanie glanced about. But Iain was not coming home yet. Next week – the week after next—

'No. Of course he isn't.' Stephanie marshalled herself. She sounded like a well-drilled child. The child Hesta should have been. Talking on the phone properly in an adult way. At six years old. And then Stephanie felt her head begin to clear, as if the layers of wool were wafting off, leaving only the pain and a deep hard rage. 'Who the hell is this in the middle of the night?'

The woman replied courteously and frigidly. She was speaking on behalf of the Company.

Into the cup of Stephanie's clearing skull, the image came, the rig standing flame-puffed and garish, up to its heart in the sea.

'The rig,' said Stephanie.

'That's correct, Mrs Web.'

'For God's sake what's happened?'

What had happened was that – though no helicopter had visited the rig for two days, no emergency means of escape had gone missing or been tampered with, and in his personal space, the clothes lay folded, the socks in their compartment, the bunk neat, the notebooks stacked, the pen capped, the coffee mug half full – from that yellow stage in its vast arena of wild water, between midnight and six a.m., Iain Jason Web had vanished.

End of Part Two

PART THREE

Last Rights

Her two-roomed flat was above the toyshop. For years she had found the stairs difficult, but now she would never have difficulty with them again. When she had to descend, for the last time, there would be assistance.

Although she had been plump in her youth, Miss Lawrence, at ninety-seven, was thin all through, her taut skin, her hollow bones, the cobwebs of her hair. Today she had dispensed with her wig, but put in her teeth. As she lay back on the pillows, her eyes were bright.

Outside, noises rose sometimes from the street. But not many. The Season was over and it had been raining.

The room smelled of lavender essence and Olbas oil.

As Hassinger entered, the bare thin arthritic hands of Miss Lawrence lifted from her counterpane like startled birds.

'Oh, Mr Hassinger. How kind. How kind of you.'

Hassinger came to the bed and asked her permission to sit on the side of it.

Miss Lawrence consented, smiling.

'We've never met before,' he said. 'Miss Lawrence.'

'No indeed. I've seen you, of course. I remember when you first came here. It's wonderful, Mr Hassinger,

123

wonderful that you've come to see me.'

'But of course I would, Miss Lawrence.'

She looked up at him, taking in all of his face, hungrily. It might have been a mother with a son. A most respectful, admiring mother, a most famous, talented son.

'Do call me Catherine. You'll have to excuse me, Mr Hassinger. You know how it is. I haven't got long. Has everything—'

'Everything's been arranged as you wanted, Catherine. And the budgerigar has gone to the pub, to Mrs Joy, as you wished.'

'Is she pleased?' asked Miss Lawrence eagerly.

'Delighted. The bird is right now sitting on her shoulder, singing.'

'Ah yes, yes, he does that. He's happy then. And I knew she liked his colours. I didn't want him to be in the room when I go. They sense it, don't they?'

'They do.'

Catherine Lawrence lowered her eyes. 'The other thing. I feel rather shy about it.'

'If you want to change your mind, Catherine.'

'Oh – no – no. I *don't*. I truly don't.'

'But you understand that it will probably be the end.'

'Anything could do it, the doctor said,' answered Miss Lawrence firmly. 'Even – excuse me – visiting the lavatory. The doctor told me I'm hanging by a thread. Isn't that poetic. It sounds so delicate. It will be very easy. My sister had a terrible lingering time, but of course, she was in London. And she was only seventy.'

'That was a shame.'

124

'She was cruel,' said Catherine sadly. 'She had a very bad marriage, but she used to say to me I wasn't *Miss* Lawrence, but *missed* Lawrence. I'd missed my chances with a man.'

Hassinger reached out and took her hand. She glanced up at him, and flushed a little, somehow, the palest rose hint behind her skin. 'You should have moved down here earlier, Catherine.'

'Yes, I should. But then, you know, I never troubled. Once I was over fifty. I've never even done anything for myself. They used to tell you it was wrong. In the end, you don't know how. Then, when I started to fail – well. You've read my letter.'

'I have. And I've arranged it, Catherine. If you're still willing.'

Again she lowered her eyes. She said, 'He won't mind?'

'He says it's an honour. And it is.'

She blinked. 'I'm nervous,' she said. 'I suppose every woman is.'

'Also every man,' said Hassinger. And when she looked up again he smiled. 'But Mr Aims is experienced and most gentle. His hands have been praised.'

Miss Catherine Lawrence gave a little low laugh. 'I mustn't keep you then, Mr Hassinger. I can't tell you what it's meant, meeting you properly. I wonder if there is anything after death? I'm not afraid. Only a bit curious. If there is, shall I send you a postcard?'

Hassinger laughed to himself. 'Yes, Catherine. I'd like that.'

Outside the door, sitting placidly on the sofa, Mr Aims was waiting.

He wore an elegant old-fashioned suit, a silk tie; there was a red rose in his buttonhole, and a white rose in his hand. He was about sixty-eight or nine, aristocratic, with thick grey hair and a tanned corrugated skin.

'You can go in now.'

'Thank you, Mr Hassinger.'

'Thank you, Mr Aims.'

Mr Aims rose and crossed to the door, and knocked. At the feather of her reply, he opened it, entered, and shut the door behind him.

There was the softest murmur of two voices.

Hassinger did not need to see. How Mr Aims spoke to Miss Lawrence, handing her the white rose with a little bow. He would woo her for a minute or two, and then he would bend and kiss, with the softest, closed-mouth kisses, the dry petals of her lips.

With his beautiful praised hands, manicured and clean as laundered linen, Mr Aims would caress the fragile body, light as a moth. At last, Mr Aims would reach the sexual centre of Miss Lawrence, the secret country that no man or woman, not even she, had discovered, and here, his smooth fingertips traced with oil, he would begin the faint sweet caress that might, after ninety-seven years, bring Miss Lawrence one of the wonders of the physical world she was leaving, the orgasm she had never known.

Four minutes later, by the clock on the mantelpiece above the gas fire, Hassinger heard her utter one long, animal, heartless, abandoned cry. How passionate after all had been Miss Lawrence.

Five minutes more, and Mr Aims came from the room.

'She's gone. She went out with it, as it were, on the tide.'
Hassinger nodded.

He looked once into the bedroom. She lay there, eyes and mouth closed, perhaps by Mr Aims, the white rose between her hands, a lovely ancient virgin, launched upon the sea now, bound for that other undiscovered country.

One

October became cold and still, and the sea crept on the shore. Rain fell outside and, here and there, inside the Victoria Hotel. November began. Frost formed on the windows. Tea and breakfast at the fire. Blankets airing. Torn quilts on the beds. Time allotted to spend alone in your room with the single Calor gas heater. Going out to one of the supermarkets to lift provisions. (Hesta was not asked to participate.)

It was not that they spoke to her – *with* her. They told her things. Used to the knack of solitariness in assembly they went about their own business by the fire and left her to hers.

She had not heard a news item for perhaps four weeks. But then, to Hesta, the unstoppable terrors of the world had nothing to do with her, until they came near.

One morning Skilt took her down to the beach, at first light, and she saw five fishing boats set off, free of the pebbles, into the high, barely moving sea. Phaedra, who had come with them, rubbed her fingers through her hair. She looked into the clear pale sky still touched with yellow, and at the flatness of the sea.

'Innit windy,' said Phaedra.

Hesta said, 'It's calm.'

'No, it's blowing up really bad.'

Skilt said, 'It will be windy later, you see.'

Phaedra blushed.

They went behind the beach, where the sheds were with a first catch of gleaming fish all laid out, boned and clean, in the icy morning. Fish that was white and fish that had a pewter skin, coralline lobsters and blue crab.

On the stones had lain a tiny shark, dead, with its sad face turned to the sky. A gull tore at it, and nearby sat one of the dogs that had walked up and down the beach as the boats escaped from their wires.

Among the sheds, however, three white dogs ran barking at them. Phaedra said, 'It's all right. Their tails are wagging.'

'Thinking how good we'll taste,' said Skilt.

He walked into a shed and began to order fish extravagantly from the big woman in her apron. She did not hesitate, but brought the fillets, and put them into bags.

'Decay does smashing chips,' said Phaedra hungrily.

Then, as the white dogs and Hesta watched, Skilt took out of his big black coat a cheque book, and wrote a cheque for the fish, and the woman accepted this, again without demur.

The name Skilt signed was S. MacQuenna.

They walked back along the beach, trudging and sliding on the stones, towards the pier. The white dogs trotted after them, then lost interest. Barking, they began to play with the edge of the sea.

'Out there, once,' said Skilt, 'a fossil forest, with dead ships caught in its branches.'

'There's an old town sunk there,' said Phaedra, 'like Atlantis.'

Under the pier they paused. A skeletal black cathedral, wrapped with weeds and rags and broken nets. Above, the ruin of a ghost train that no longer ran.

Skilt and Phaedra gathered muck from the poles of the pier, and put it into brown plastic medicine bottles.

It was here Hesta had seen the man, the blond man, looking up at her on the promenade above.

She thought she had seen him since, three or four times, once walking down the road from the Saxon pub, the Hare and Hounds, in the early dusk.

'Do you like to read?' Skilt asked Hesta.

'Yes. Sometimes.'

Phaedra said, 'Bod said you're writing a book in your notepad.'

'No,' said Hesta.

They came up from the beach, up the wooden steps from the stones, and stood by the shut gates of the pier. On the wall there had once been a notice that warned, WET PAINT. But both Ts had been crossed out.

'You see,' said Skilt, but he was pointing to a black weathervane inland. As they glanced at it, it rapidly turned, and a gust of icy cold lashed down the street.

There were never any cars on the road now. There must be, obviously. Somehow Hesta never saw them.

At a noise of gulls, she looked back along the beach. A cloud of the birds was hovering there, shrieking, and underneath three figures in tight white clothing ran to and fro, shouting, calling.

Phaedra said, 'We're going to the library this afternoon.'

But Hesta was distracted a moment. She had realized the

people on the beach were naked. Leaping and running, they offered some kind of food to the gulls.

'We all like fresh fish,' said Skilt MacQuenna.

The wind was blowing violently as Decay, Phaedra, Bish-Op and Bod set out for the library. Hesta walked with them. When they asked her to do these things, she simply did them. She had not been asked to take any particular drug, to steal, or even to accompany them when they stole, to have sex, or attempt the chores. When she had offered to wash dishes in the powder room, Decay and the other two girls already there had said, friendly enough, that was fine, she need not.

Of course, there was a camaraderie amongst them she could not share, did not need to share, felt no urge to infiltrate.

Skilt had not called her again into his room for any purpose.

She wrote fragments in her notebook, and she wrote a sort of on-going letter to Janey that probably would not be sent.

It seemed the winter, like an obstacle, a vehicle, would have to pass.

The winter was a presence.

The library was shut. A board announced that it would not re-open until 1 May.

In the streets a few people had scurried by, heads down against the wind. Like the library, a multitude of shops were shut. But outside the supermarket, two old men were throwing a red apple to each other, back and forth. A woman at a check-out stroked a cat sitting on the till.

They went around the side of the library, under its high

gothic windows, into an alley. A narrow blistered door slit the brick, and here Decay banged with her woollen fist.

A panel was opened in the top of the door, and through a grill reminiscent of monasteries, a pair of eyes gazed down.

'Decay,' Decay called. 'Bod. Bish-Op. Phaedra. Hesta.'

The eyes swivelled, vanished, then the door was opened.

A thin man was standing there inside, scanning them.

'Parky today,' said the man.

They went up a wooden stair and came out by some inner doors.

Within, the central heating roared through its tubes. At the tables men and women sat reading. In spots, a bottle, vodka, meths, stood on a folded newspaper.

No one was in charge. You chose what you wanted, read it, replaced it.

The elderly tramp drinking the meths was very careful to spill nothing on the pages of an Edwardian travelogue. Though he stank, his hands were pared clean as peeled potatoes.

Presently Bish-Op had a book of paintings from the Renaissance. He stared at each one, sometimes running his fingers over the peach-like forms, the blue dresses, and camels painted gold. Decay, Phaedra and Bod seemed to be reading novels.

Hesta moved along the aisles. She came across a little girl, about seven years old, filthy, sitting on the floor with a King James Bible open on her lap.

There was jam in the child's hair. Her face was serious, scholarly, and as Hesta went by, the child said, 'Mind Poppy.' Hesta beheld a tortoise poised about a foot along the aisle. It was not reading a book.

The library was a club. Slightly salacious, clandestine.

The wind raged and the windows shook. In here it was warm and humid from the heating and the human breath.

A seagull pecked at a window ledge.

Hesta took books at random, read a couple of lines, put them back. The words and phrases joined together, as in a game she had played with Janey years before, making absurd or arresting sentences: 'He left the car and found an apple tree grew where he had last seen his wife in Cairo.' Or, 'After all there is nothing to fear in the sounds of a lion rushing towards one in the corridor of the train providing I know there is no God.'

Hesta, leaning on a book stack, took her notepad from her jacket pocket. She wrote instead what she had seen that morning: WET PAINT — WE PAIN

Below in the street, a squeaking pram bumped by, maroon, with an elderly woman in a velvet hat pushing it. (Baby, baby.) The gull flew from the ledge.

Instinctively, Hesta looked along the street for the blond man. He was not there. She had never seen him close, and yet he was familiar.

Hesta thought of her father, but did not know why. The gilt spider and the word *Daddy*. Perhaps she should call Iain Web. But he would surely say *Go home, Hesta, please, please, you must.* Pleading. Anxious.

This place is very strange.

She could take a train tomorrow. Would there be a lion in the corridor?

Baby, baby. Dropped, dropped.

It was getting dark when they left, a smear of painterly

crimson madder in the west over the curve of the sea. They half ran, as if now to evade the area, for the library was beyond the pier, nearer to the end of the town they were not, apparently, too keen on.

The people on the beach had been naked, but on the street only a man in a tabby raincoat exposed himself to them as they passed, and then bowed low. 'Lovely cock,' called Bod.

'Thank you, kind sir.'

Hesta saw his face, so pure and sane that it was, or must be, deviant and mad.

She said abruptly to Decay, as they raced along, 'I saw a woman drop a baby out of a window.'

'Yeah,' said Decay, 'you ain't the only one seen things like that.'

'I heard,' said Hesta, 'Moses' car.'

'Least you ain't seen *that*.'

As they passed the supermarket, a girl in a pink overall ran out and threw packets of crumpets to them, one, two, three. Bod and Phaedra caught them balletically.

'Skilt?'

'Yes.'

'This place.'

'Make a pun, shall I? Plaice with chips. Place with ships.'

'What if I just go and catch the train?'

'You don't have enough money.'

'I could get hold of it. Or you could lend it to me. Cash a cheque.'

'The money isn't for you to go. It's for the ones that want to stay.'

Hesta stood in the doorway and Skilt sat on his mattress.

'Something,' said Hesta, 'is happening.'

'Something always does.'

Hesta said, 'You won't explain it.'

'Can't, possibly.'

Hesta left Skilt, and went down through the hotel. In the ballroom they were toasting crumpets. Firelight within, night outside. Hesta went into the night and up to the Hare and Hounds. It was busy. No one looked at her. When she asked to use the phone, a girl with long earrings waved her to it.

Lulu's number rang and rang. Hesta counted methodically. After the twentieth ring, she put the receiver down.

From the pub, Hesta walked up the sloping streets. Everywhere shut. Everywhere a secret. The loom of lightless buildings, churches with steeples, silent. One or two windows, high up, cosily lit behind coloured curtains. Lit like the window in Old Street with the crying baby.

She reached finally the bombsite, a tall shattered wall with ivy clustering, blown in the harsh, fitful wind that Phaedra had predicted, as Phaedra predicted every aspect of the weather unfailingly. Swells of buildings with gaping rooms revealed, bleached wallpapers, fireplaces, chimneys. Windows black. Seagulls flying over, five or six of them, screeking to each other, shrieking, phantoms on night sky.

The bombsite went on and on, away on either side, circling the lower town, the paths to the sea.

And over a piece of raw masonry, black on white, just visible, again those words, *We Pain*, the Ts crossed through.

Down among the smashed bricks and weeds, the dead

winter bushes that had sprung from eroded drains, did anything wait to hold her back?

Not afraid. Yet hackles rising.

No door to keep her in, no guard. Nothing tangible.

Before the bombsite, had something else been here, circling this part of the town, a moat about a fortress . . .

Half the street lamps were not working.

She returned downhill towards the sea, as if it was her fate, as if she were drawn there, as once other things had been drawn out of it to the land.

When he drove back down late in November, reaching the road that ran parallel to the promenade and the ocean, he cruised beneath the Victoria Hotel. Though he gave the boarded edifice not a glance, from their windows Bod, Catsmeat, Susan and Susan's Dog, stared at the car.

Sometimes, out of Season, traffic passed, not much. And on this rainy afternoon, the sea draped in greenish fog, the vehicle was slick with cold moisture, shining and incongruous.

Moses, the town ghost, drove a Bugatti. That had been established.

This was an American car, a 1958 Pontiac Chieftain, white, with two bronze streaks running flank-long into its fins.

The photographer was very proud of the car. He had given it a stylishly unfeminine, funny-domestic US name: Chuck. Chuck was carefully revamped inside. Chuck could do a hundred. Girls liked Chuck. And there was lots of room for the cameras, the Nikon and the Olympus, the ancient Ensign, and their myriad accessories and gadgets. Lots of room for the physical soul of the photographer, normally called an ego.

His shots of this shore, certain buildings, the fishermen, had done well – at least, when he described them to his publishers. However, when the films were printed, something had gone wrong. Blotches, scratches, blurs. A mess. And a lot of hassle after, arguments with technicians, invective through darkroom doors.

The only thing was to come back.

Neil Bolton didn't give up – no way.

Driving down into the town and around to where the huge cliffs stepped amid the streets like giants, Neil was high with tenacious optimism and a little blow of something. He noted possibilities in the misty wastes of November sea, and in the dying peculiar winter light. He knew that no one saw quite as he did. He had always had a good opinion of his gifts, and in the pushy, superficial, easily titillated world he inhabited, so did others.

Eventually he drove round into the carpark of the pink hotel on the front, where a nasal receptionist had told him over the phone, twenty rooms were still available for guests.

The rain made the car gleam on the lot. It was heavily armoured with locking devices and alarms. Nothing else was parked there, not even a tawdry bike or ridiculous Mini.

He carried all his cameras and bags into the hotel, and located the desolate foyer.

The carpet had been taken up, presumably for an out-of-Season repair. A plastic plant in a tub appeared to have died. No one was on the desk.

He rang the bell loudly.

And no one came.

Impatient, tolerant, Neil began to devise some amusing comments, text to go with these photographs that might form a book. People made him laugh with their lack of insight, let-go figures, pathetic ideals, sad lives.

But he never allowed them to see. He had, he would have said, what they had once called the 'common touch'. He could get on with anyone. Talk them round. Persuade. And after all, if they didn't agree, you could use a telephoto lens.

The first picture that had made his name had been a secret London shot of a middle-aged woman dressed like twenty, but her skirt caught up by a freak gust of wind, and so revealing the varicose veins bubbling on her legs above the four-inch high heels. These marks, to him, were not inspirations of pity for what forty-eight years of neglect and standing had done, but of the disgusting contrast, the parody of Monroe, the clownishness of those who were too thick to *know*.

And she had never known. If she had known – her broad bottom focused in French knickers and her life-blown legs, and the pigeon on the pavement staring at it all apparently in amazement – no hint of *her* at all, of the illusion she had tried so hard to create – if she had *known*—

A thin bowed female was coming in answer to the third *tring* of the bell. She glided out from all the quiet and grey glimmers of the unlit hotel and, insinuating herself behind the desk, switched on merely a small shaded lamp.

It was an island now, the reception desk, in the midst of that great half-formless dimness. But the photographer, with his canny eyes, did not see the relevance of this potential scene. The strangeness of it, symbolic of the many tiny fortress spaces of real life. He did not know about fortresses.

He was busy getting his room with bath at the knocked-down price of winter, like the cheap rate of a whore with only basics to offer, the one who can only ask a fiver, for her unknowledgeable fallen breasts and hilarious varicose thighs.

Two

'Skilt's taking us up the Cancer.'

'Where?'

'Cancer.'

Bod said, 'It's called the Kissing Crab pub. Old Street.'

Cobbles. Baby. Blood.

'I'm going,' said Phaedra, 'so's Bish-Op. And Skilt said you.'

'No,' said Hesta.

'It's OK,' said Phaedra, 'if we're with Skilt.'

'Ale's good,' said Catsmeat. 'But wasn't asked, was I?'

'You go,' said Hesta. 'I shan't.'

Bod said, 'The guy what runs it is called Mr Joy. It's got figureheads. It's a great pub.'

'You go, then,' said Hesta.

They had almost cornered her, there on the landing. On the gilded balustrade a candle burned in a saucer.

In Hesta's brain, the vision of the pub was emerging. The timbered front and small windows, through one of which had flushed the modern migrainous lights of a fruit machine. She and Janey had gone in there, under the sign of a rose-red crab, and drunk vodkas and orange, which, twice, had been bought for them by an elderly man in a suit.

The Kissing Crab.

Old Street.

She had not realized, finding the street again, or not properly, that she had been there before. It had been altered at night, after midnight, after they had switched off the illuminations. And the one lighted window. And the baby crying, and dropping.

Hesta turned to go away, and Skilt was there. Skilt wore a white shirt with a high Russian collar, white trousers, a black coat, black boots.

'At last. Something she won't do.'

'That's right,' said Hesta.

'Scared?'

Hesta waited. He blocked her way.

Phaedra said, 'I'm scared, up there. But I like the Cancer.'

'Cancer is a disease,' said Hesta.

'It just means a crab.'

Bish-Op appeared behind Skilt. He had undone his pigtail of hair, which made a fringe of long fine black silk around his shaven skull and face. He said, very slowly, 'I got so – I couldn't go anywhere. Not into a shop. I was – sick – if I had to go to the – the Boots shop – the chemist – or into the vegetable shop. Anywhere.'

Phaedra said, 'That's *really* scared.'

'Sure. I was – scared when I woke up,' said Bish-Op. 'When I opened my eyes. Like – I'd gone somewhere then. Didn't know where. Scared. I thought, I'm here. But where is it?'

Phaedra said to Hesta, 'My dad killed my brother. He beat him to death. It was my fault.'

Hesta looked at her.

In the glares of the flickering candle, Phaedra's face was tragic and feral.

Bod said, 'They mean you oughta go.'

'Why?' said Hesta.

Skilt leaned on the balustrade which was wonky. 'A meteor could hit the earth,' said Skilt coolly. 'They wouldn't tell anyone. Panic – useless. We'd all be gone in five seconds.'

'You sound like Evo's Lady Jocasta,' said Hesta.

'She had a point. It's that precarious. But what do you do? You run away. Or you stay with it and see. If you run, you don't stand a chance any way.'

'It's just a pub,' said Hesta.

'Right,' said Catsmeat, 'so why not go?'

Hesta shrugged.

Phaedra said, 'Put on your dress. That black dress with the red. That's great.'

Hesta said, 'This jumper is warmer.'

'Close innit?' said Phaedra.

'It's November.'

Phaedra giggled like a nine-year-old. 'Lied, didn't I?'

Out of Season, they had switched off the TV and moved the flashing fruit machine, and put in the battered black piano made in London in 1901. The way from one bar to the other was easy. You walked through a low corridor whose beams brushed the crown of anyone over five foot four.

It was called the Kissing Crab because, as not many visitors had seen, the red crab on the sign was embracing a full white moon. Yet Hesta saw this, when now she walked in under it. Oil lanterns fluttered light like wings in the windows. The electric light was low, and also fluttered fitfully, reminiscent of turn-of-the-century gas.

Real logs in a tiled fireplace burning. Figureheads put up, a mermaid, a soldier.

Behind the bar stood a large woman in a crab-red dress. On her shoulder was a green budgerigar, to which, now and then, she talked. Then the budgerigar sang. Its song was unusual, resembling that of a robin.

Bish-Op and Phaedra sat down side by side, and Skilt, going to the bar, called Hesta.

Across the counter, in the other bar, crowded with locals, a movement. For a second, it seemed they had all shifted, looking at her, but it must have been an illusion.

'What'll you have?'

'Perrier, thank you.'

'Anything in it?'

'No.'

The large woman came. She had a square face. She put her finger out to the budgerigar, which hopped on. She held the bird, singing green, between herself and Hesta. The budgie opened its wings but did not fly. It was a display, as if Hesta might have been in doubt as to the nature of a bird.

'Have a drop of ice, dear,' said Mrs Joy, whose first name was also Joy. 'I'll tell you what we do. We get an old white brandy here. The smugglers, them as used the caves down from the promenade, used to bring it in. And we put it in the ice tray. Do you good, raw night like this.'

Hesta looked at Skilt, to see what reaction he had to this.

(Seen sidelong, Skilt's face was very chiselled, and had a carious embattled delicacy.)

Hesta said, 'All right.'

'I can see you can hold your liquor,' said Joy Joy, 'or I wouldn't have suggested it.'

For the rest of them, Skilt bought ale on tap from a barrel bound with black iron.

A man had come through to the piano and was playing 'Apple-Blossom Time', which Hesta did not know. He was rough, in an enormous black jersey, and had sausage fingers. There was not one wrong note.

The budgie flew over to the piano and sat there, watching the pianist closely.

'Look at the copper pans over the fire,' said Phaedra.

The brandy in the Perrier had a crystal tang. It went to Hesta's head, but gin and vodka did that.

'We'll have another,' said Skilt.

'No, thank you,' said Hesta.

'Not for you, then.'

Both the bars were quite small, but, save for the four of them, the pianist, the budgerigar, their side of the counter was empty. The other bar, presumably the locals' side, though not noisy, was crammed full.

There had been a couple of times, last year, when Martin Peecey had cajoled (demanded) Hesta go with him and her mother to his wine bar. A kind of greasy boredom had therefore come to be associated for her with drinking places, a threatening tedium.

The time had always come when Martin would find her leg under the table, or, if she did not go with Stephanie to the loo, swiftly move over and sit by her, squeezing her shoulders, saying, 'Stolen moments, eh?'

What would happen here?

The warm mellowness, the glow of copper and hearth and lamps, the clink of glasses, the smell of alcohol and smoke – did they lead the blind night, like creatures in disguise, towards some confrontation?

It was the third round now, and Hesta had been given another Perrier, but with no brandy in it. Could she trust Skilt? It was herself she trusted, keen eyes and the unhampered senses of taste and smell.

Then the door opened from the street. A cloud of darkness and thin fog entered the room, theatrical, as in some production of Ibsen or Chekhov, Janey might have said.

Skilt glanced up, sidelong. His eyes were like a lizard's, black, unblinking. Then he looked down into his beer.

The man wore a leather coat. He was large and tall and his hair, taking the lamps, was like a sheet of coarse fluid silver over his head and neck and collar.

Joy Joy bustled to the counter.

'Good evening, Mr Hassinger. Usual?'

'Yes, Joy. Thank you.'

A foreign voice – from where? European. Strong hands with long fingers. A fisherman's boots, and a fisherman's jersey.

Hesta had seen him before. He had watched *her* from a distance. But also he had been here. The old man of sixty in the noble suit, in this pub, trying to pick up Janey. Had he sounded foreign then? Had he been sixty then?

With the flood of hair, the leathers, the way he moved,

turning, going by, not seeing them, or not concerned by them, he looked younger. In a tall greenish glass a long transparent drink. The smell of it – spicy, laser-white – floated after him with his own scent of leather and fog.

Were the group intimidated now, this new stranger in the bar with them? Phaedra had certainly drawn closer to Bish-Op.

The pianist stopped playing. 'What'll you have, Mr Hassinger?'

The old man who was not so old, Hassinger, turned to the piano. (No look for Hesta now. Not one.) He smiled. He had the long teeth of a wolf, very white.

'Something from Wagner,' said Hassinger.

The pianist drank from his mug. 'He was a terrible old anti-Semite, was Wagner. Used to put on gloves to play Jewish music. Then threw the gloves away, like he'd have liked to throw the Jews.'

'Then we must hope he is in Hell. But his music may enter Heaven by itself.'

The pianist laughed, his teeth also long, but brown. He slammed some monumental chords into the piano.

'*Flying Dutchman*,' said Skilt. He leaned across to Bish-Op, spoke under the music. 'Why don't you show Hesta your trick?'

'Shall I?'

'Yes.'

The piano recital fell to a softer passage, and in his corner the blond man seemed sunk into thought, absorbing his drink. Across the bar counter, the locals murmured and rumbled, their tankards clattering quietly.

Joy Joy was talking to the budgie.

'Bish-Op's trick. It's good,' brightly, Phaedra. 'It's really clever.'

Bish-Op swallowed his third pint, and put the empty glass, scummed with froth, in the middle of the table. Then he sat back, and his sad dark eyes settled on it. After about three seconds, the glass began slowly to move, rotating gradually on one spot.

Hesta noted that all their hands were to be seen, including the hands of Bish-Op, which he had clasped together where the red rent heart trembled.

Still spinning, the glass rose in the air. It went up about four feet over the table, and revolved there, shining like the Holy Grail.

Hesta saw: the glass, Skilt and Phaedra, Bish-Op, at the counter Joy Joy looking interested, and a couple of the regulars over the counter, leaning on the surface, nodding, and Hassinger, his gaze that was like the blue of mapless winter sea—

Then the door opened again and the glass turned over and smashed on the floor.

'Whoops,' said Joy Joy. 'Don't worry, my love. My hubby's a champion with the dustpan.'

While through the door came the old woman with the maroon pram, beaming with pleasure at her own arrival.

And, 'Hallo, Duchess,' called Joy Joy, while from its shawl and the blankets, the woman lifted out her baby, a black and white gull with razorous topaz beak and glittering eyes.

Dinner had been so foul that Neil Bolton believed they had

done it purposely. He preferred more exciting food, any way, everyone knew the English and Americans couldn't cook – Thai or Chinese, Japanese raw fish – not this pathetic muddy thing served, stewed, in its skin, with wilted overdone potatoes and apparently tinned peas. The cheese was supermarket cheddar. The wine was lousy and the tonic flat. Even the ice was wrong, *fishy*. Christ, what a hole.

After the dinner, for which the last serving had been an insulting seven thirty (these people were mediaeval), Neil got his authentic RAF flying jacket, and his camera bag, and swung out into the doleful seaside winter night.

He paused at the rail above the beach. The fog lay almost white on the water, faint drifts ebbing up into the town. What was needed now was a doomed three-masted ship, drifting aground out of the whiteness . . . Neil liked his little fancy, and took a quick shot of the shore using the night apparatus and twenty minutes, because after all, a ship could be faked.

He passed no one as he walked on, although, overhead, unseen, a bevy of gulls screamed.

About one street light in ten was working. What a place. Divinely derelict, you could say. It was worth the rotten food.

As he turned into Old Street, heading for the pub the fishermen had mentioned to him, Neil Bolton had one of his premonitions of success. He was going to get something tonight. Something that had never come his way before.

The first thing he saw, as he pushed open the street door of the bar (and the raucous noise hit him), was an incredible-looking girl, not in keeping with the town at all.

She had dyed her hair a crazy red that probably would need toning down, and she had on a sort of statement-making

dress, when she'd have looked better in something severe – a
uniform, perhaps. But her body was slim as a snake's and her
face was real class. About nineteen, although she could be a
bit younger. Old enough to be had, he was sure.

He stood a moment in the doorway, so she could be aware
of the effect he made, his expensive appropriately modern
image, everything perfect. A shame he hadn't driven round
in Chuck.

The girl did look, for about half a second.

They sometimes pretended, but they didn't miss a thing.

The two boys at the table were nothings. And the other girl
should have been put down at birth, poor bitch.

The rest of the room was full of the local men, hustling
and jostling, and overhead a TV was announcing the Ten
o'clock News.

Neil pushed, smiling, and patting in a firm masculine way
that would be correct here, to the bar counter.

An obese woman in red came over from something odd on
the far end of the counter.

'Good evening, sir.'

'You've got real ale here, I understand.'

'Indeed we do.'

'Let me have a pint, please.'

A short bent man straightened like a gnome from under
the counter.

'Gentleman wants the ale, Ted.'

Ted put down a dustpan full of broken glass and hopped
across to a line of barrels.

On the far counter, there, a seagull was washing itself in
what appeared to be an ashtray filled with milk. A green

150

budgerigar ran up and down the counter, sucking up the spilled drops.

'Quite a pet you've got,' said Neil.

'One of our regulars,' said Joy Joy.

Neil Bolton's small clear eyes ran off and over and over the humans in the two bars. Craggy faces, hands like rock. Only a handful of women.

It surprised him slightly, a television being on. They had a piano. Somehow, he would have thought, home-made music not TV.

The screen flashed to a change of mood.

It seemed the Queen Mother had had another operation and was doing excellently, and a young woman with a round animated face, who looked as though she had never been kissed, was telling the camera how wonderful the Queen Mother was, and how well, a miracle, such a privilege to see her.

Across the counter an old bag in a soiled bursting coat was drinking gin. She shouted loudly above all the noise, 'Lovely and well. There you are.' Unexpectedly, she had an Oxford accent.

Joy Joy said, 'It's a real pity all the old people couldn't have lived like the Queen Mum. If they'd had her life, and her money, and were looked after the way she is, I expect they'd all look lovely and well, too.'

'Yes,' said the old woman in the coat. 'But if you were to offer it to me, all that, and I had to go and shoot birds for it, I wouldn't. Not I.' And she bent foward and kissed the milky seagull on the head.

Anti-monarchists amused Neil, as did monarchists. He took care not to grin.

He glanced round, and saw the red-haired girl, sat there drinking water, was not looking at him.

After he had studied her for a moment, Neil decided to take a chance on her. He went to the table.

'Good evening.'

All of them looked up. What a weird crowd they were. Drop-outs, but for the girl. Mad eyes. Her eyes, on the other hand, were a hazel colour, or it might have been the lights. Besides, she had looked away again. All women had one of two gambits. Stare at you and pant, or act cold. This was a chilly one. Fun to warm her up.

'Let me introduce myself. My name's Neil.'

The ugly bit who was nearly bald, said, 'I knew a Neil. Neil Down.'

The boy in white and black, who looked most like a hideous woman, gave a crack of laughter. The other guy was obviously stoned or nuts; out of it.

'I'll be frank,' said Neil.

'I thought you said you were called Neil,' said the bald girl.

Neil smiled at her charmingly. 'So you're a comedienne.'

'No,' she said, 'just rude.'

'Oh good. Then I can be rude too. It's not you I want to talk to, I bet that's a surprise. I wanted to ask your friend with the red-hot hair if she'd like me to take some photographs of her. Here's my card,' he added, slipping the black and white item on to the table before the redhead. 'Can I join you?'

Skilt sat back. 'Why not.'

'My round,' said Neil. 'What'll you have?'

'A triple Pernod,' said Phaedra.

'That might make you more rude,' said Neil.

Skilt said, 'She'd like a triple Pernod, and we'll have beer.'

'OK. Fine. And what about you . . . Scarlet?'

Hesta said, 'Nothing, thank you.'

'Go on,' said Phaedra, 'he wants to get in your knickers. Ask him for a proper drink.'

Neil Bolton laughed a little and appealed to unseen beings who floated in the air. Then he went to get the Pernod for the cunt, and a vodka-tonic for the redhead.

Bish-Op said, 'Skilt, how – do we handle this?'

'Don't worry about it,' said Skilt.

Phaedra shook herself. She was flushed from drink and from the prospect of drink. She said, ' 'S all right, darling.'

Bish-Op said, 'He's a bas-tard.'

'Yeah.'

The bastard returned with the drinks. As he set the vodka before Hesta, he pulled an unused chair over and sat beside her. The TV news was coming to an end.

'And what do you think of the Royal Family?' said Neil to Hesta.

'Nothing.'

'Republican?'

Phaedra had started on her Pernod. She said, 'A king and a queen had a place. In the old kingdoms, like in ancient Greece. The royalty were the high priests. They represented the people and they had to be without flaw. In time of need, they were the sacrifice. They'd die for the land, or the kingdom. That was why they got the best of everything, and no one minded. 'Cos they gave the best of themselves and they were prepared to die to appease the gods.'

'Does she always go on like this?' asked Neil. 'It'll be a cancan on the bar next. What an awful thought.'

Bish-Op stood up. His eyes were as focused suddenly as if rectified by the skills of Neil Bolton's cameras, and his heart-and-blade hand was raised.

Skilt pushed Bish-Op down.

'Don't matter,' said Phaedra. She hiccupped. She looked at Neil. 'You enjoy yourself while you can, I say.'

Neil got up. He said to Hesta, 'I'm at the hotel. The one that's open. You've got my card. I'd like to see you.'

As he moved off through the small space, he brushed by a man in a leather coat. That was an interesting face, like some 1950s film star gone to drink – wild eyes—

But the TV was off now, and they were gathering at the piano. The corridor between the bars had been revealed, the doors at either end propped open.

There in the crowd, an accordion, and a man with a whistle . . . The budgerigar, animated, was fighting with the old gull, and the Duchess had poured the last of the gull-tinctured milk in her gin.

'You're going to play? That's great. Would you mind if I took a few snaps?'

They beamed on him, the rough youths and rugged men, characters from some book, doing what should be done, flattered. Was it to be a sea shanty?

Someone hammering a tune out of the piano and the roller of the accordion, the twang of a Jew's harp.

In their midst, a massive sailor with a face made of rope and pale eyes like salt, opening his mouth of broken dentures.

The rich voice pealing, an organ note.

'*She comes in wearing blue,*
No fish today, me boys, me jollys.
When she comes in wearing blue.'
And then the roar, most of the male voices in the pub,
'*We'll go hungry, we'll go poor*
When she comes in wearing blue.'
The light had changed. (The barwoman had turned the electricity off?) Neil quickly adjusted the camera.

As the leader in the song began again, Neil took him, this way, that. They loved these shots, his patrons. These old men they would never have to be.
'*She comes in wearing green.*
Fish in plenty, fill nets, me jollys,
When she comes in wearing green.'
'It's the sea,' whispered Phaedra. Her huge bright eyes were soft with thought. 'Sea colours – weather—'
'*We'll have plenty, we'll go fat*
When she comes in wearing green.'
The penny whistle soared, as the budgie soared up from the bar.

Neil caught the flight of the bird on film.
'*When she comes in wearing grey.*
Stormy morning, me boys, me jollys.'
Hesta had moved her body round. She watched the huge man singing. She caught the intimation of the power of his life inside him.

The air was hot as midsummer, flavoured with kipper and ale, with fire and smoke, with rum and brandy and oil.

The lamplight dashed against the figureheads like moths. The mermaid with her yellow curls, the soldier in his hat, the woman holding a fish to her breast—

> '*Break the nets, cave the timbers*
> *When she comes in wearing grey.*'

Phaedra was whispering the words now as they sang.

> '*She comes in wearing red.*
> *The land's abed, me boys, me jollys,*
> *Make new sailor boys, me boys,*
> *When she comes in wearing red.*'

Hesta felt the song rise up her backbone. She felt hard and spare. She wanted to stand up. Found she had.

She visualized her father abruptly, his red hair against red sunset sea.

'*She comes in wearing black*,' sang the man, like a sea bear. He closed his eyes for sorrow.

> '*Remember the dead, me boys, me jollys,*
> *When she comes in wearing black.*
> *We'll sleep that sleep, and our women'll weep*
> *When they come in wearing black.*'

In the long silence, Neil said boldly, 'My God, that was terrific. Bravo. Really.'

He had sloughed his priceless coat, which still had one tiny uncleaned Battle of Britain bloodstain in its sheepskin lining, uncaring on a chair. There were lots of chairs, for everyone was standing. He had used a whole reel.

The green bird perched on the figurehead of a mermaid. The old woman had the seagull in her arms, was feeding it gin, which it seemed to like.

He had some bloody brilliant shots.

Fuck the redhead. She didn't matter. She'd come round any way, they always did.

The sea bear walked through the crowd. He towered over Neil.

Neil said, 'You've got a fine voice.'

'You shoulda heard me grandpa,' said the man.

They were leading Neil to the bar counter. All at once he had their friendship and their trust. Inside himself he congratulated himself. But he was also overwhelmed. Jesus, he could live here. Buy something amazing, a conversation piece, prices were so cheap. Do the book. Really do it. The sea. These men.

Now look . . . they'd rolled back the carpet. A dance next?

The cameras were on the counter, the men were careful not to touch them.

Joy Joy handed Neil a pint. 'On the house.'

Neil laughed with pleasure. He drank, and was, despite himself, half turning to see what the redhead thought of it all, when the piano struck up again. And as it did so, the notes went right through him.

Hesta beheld a spray of crimson that jetted up and hit the ceiling, and she thought someone had thrown a mug of drink.

Then the burst came again, and again.

So many men were pressed at the bar. She saw arms rising and falling, as if someone were being thumped on the back. And – cries, she heard cries, but the piano played so loudly.

And Joy Joy's voice cut between the tumults, 'Another pint for you, Joe?'

'If you will, missus.'

'Ted, that's the new barrel.'

'Right you are.'

And then through them all Hesta saw Neil Bolton plummet, face astonished, one arm off, torso sliced from neck to groin, and covering the world with his crimson blood.

It was out there. Down beneath her. It flowed against the shore. The sea.

It was all change, and changes, all colours. It moved and yet seemed still. It was unthinkably deep. All things came from it and might be in it yet, in other forms, or the same. Women who were mermaids, animals that were fish. Cities of coral, towers of pearl, heaps of gold, dragons. Treasures and bones. Plants unknown and unnamed.

And the seas shall rise and cover up the land.

How could you stay sane, so close to it – to *that*? It was not the going out upon it but the dwelling by its side. The lullaby that rocked you. The voice always in your ears, so familiar as to be unheard. What subliminally did the sea say, sea say, soaking silking in and out upon the shifting sand?

The alteration had come after the glass fell on the carpet and smashed.

Short Ted Joy had emerged with the dustpan, said, 'Shall we take the carpet up now, Joy?' And Mrs Joy Joy had said, 'Better wait. Just in case.'

Then Ted Joy swept up the glass. And as he did so the pianist stopped playing, and Joy reached up her big sunny arm and turned on the TV.

Men started to filter through into the bar where Skilt's group sat. It began to be noisy, like a normal pub. Except for the seagull drinking milk and washing itself in the clean ashtray.

Then the man with the camera entered.

To Hesta, he was a manifestation of Martin Peecey, only a

little more up-market, worse.

She thought nothing else of him, and yet she knew. For with his entrance she saw how the pub had camouflaged itself, and, disturbingly, how also it was revealed.

The sea song had come to her as sometimes music, or a piece of writing, might do. The aura of it was entirely real, but in fact in some manner that had nothing to do with words or melody, but with *sounds*, the sound of the piano, the whistle, the accordion, the Jew's harp, the singer's baritone voice.

She had thought Skilt would get between her and the photographer, but he had not bothered. She had felt slight contempt for Skilt at that moment, but nothing more. She could easily elude Neil Bolton of the trendy black and white card.

Then Neil Bolton was hacked to death in front of her by unseen or barely seen knives, his blood hitting the ceiling, splashing the walls.

She was not conscious that Skilt had guided them all back from the table to the hearth, and that the blood did not reach them, except once, when Skilt put his arm across her face, and the blood hit the sleeve of his white shirt, missing her.

Hesta walked quickly to the door and went out.

She did not attempt to bring any of the others with her. Outside, the fog had cleared, and above she saw November stars, frozen and blue, lidding the town. She walked up the cobbles, passing below the unlighted window from which the woman had dropped her baby.

Hesta did not run.

She felt nothing.

She could hear the sea.

Behind a church with a Norman tower, a flight of steps went up among the ridges of the cliffs. Hesta climbed, slowly now. This was not getting away from the town, but somehow farther into it.

A gull shrieked from the cliff-top, one hundred and twenty feet aloft.

There was a level, and a railing. She looked over, and saw how the wandering bombsite that ringed the town began its ending here, against the flanks of the cliffs.

Nearby stood a brick wall, on which, a couth, carefully formed line of graffiti had been traced.

A garden rose inside the wall, a precarious garden with vast ancient trees that leaned away to one side, and a house above the garden, also seeming to lean. Everything overhanging the bombsite below, only the pillars of granite and limestone circling, assisting, beneath and above. The masonry of the house crowded at one end into the cliff. A light burned there, very dull, dismembered by a curious long pane split into atoms.

Hesta looked back at the graffiti on the wall. She could see it, in the gleaming, starry darkness.

OH I DO LIKE TO BE POSEIDON SEASIDE

Like one of Janey's puns.

Janey . . . I saw a man slashed to bits tonight in the quaint local pub. He was a prick. They played the piano. I can hear it still – I think . . . or is that only the piano nocturne of the sea?

Debussy, *La Mer*. Were they playing Debussy in the Kissing Crab?

Hesta looked back and saw a thin frail figure climbing up the steps after her. Phaedra raised her fey waif's face.

'Blimey what a slog.'

'Yes,' said Hesta.

'Won't be a tic,' said Phaedra.

'I'm all right,' said Hesta.

Phaedra came on, and presently reached her.

They stood together, and Phaedra lifted her arms and stretched.

Hesta said, 'Will it be cold tomorrow?'

'Yeah. Bloody freezing. Look, I've got two jumpers on. But don't worry. You'll be OK.'

'Will I?'

'He's got everything.'

'Skilt.'

Phaedra smiled. She pointed. 'See that house.'

Hesta said nothing.

Phaedra sat down on a jut of cliff.

'You see,' she said, 'my dad used to have sex with me. I thought it was what everyone's dad did. Mum died when I was four. Everyone said what a terrific father we had, me and Brian. Thing is, Dad used to get nasty and then he'd lam into Bry. So I used to run up to Dad, to distract him, snuggle up to him. And in the end, when I was about – oh, six or seven, I guess – he'd say, Look how you've upset your sister. And then he'd carry me into the other room. It stopped him going for Bry.'

'You killed him,' said Hesta.

Phaedra glanced up, startled.

'Me? You're kidding. I couldn't kill anyone. I'm useless

like that. No, I put up with it. And I lied to Bry, as he got all worried. Bry was older'n me, and . . . he was lovely. And really good-looking. He looked,' said Phaedra proudly, shining, 'like Daniel Day-Lewis in *The Last of the Mohicans*. Once when I was out with Bry one Saturday, shopping, when I was about fourteen, some of the girls from my school saw us. And after, they said who was *that*? And I said, that's my best boyfriend. Didn't know I went out with *him*, did ya? They were *green*.'

Hesta leaned on the railing, looking at Phaedra.

Phaedra said, 'Well, you see, I sort of fell in love with Brian. Pitiful, innit. I mean, my dad doing me, and I fall for me own brother. But he was – he was so beautiful. And he was so *kind*. And he made a real fuss of me. He used to say I was pretty. Though I never was. And, silly thing is, I know he really meant it. To him I was pretty. And he went out with some nice-looking girls.'

Hesta said, 'And you told him.'

'Yes, I did. I told him I loved him and I wanted him to come to bed with me. Oh, the performance I'd made. All this frothy bath and perfume, and done my hair in curls, and put on mascara – all the things they say do in magazines. And he was horrified. He went red. He walked out of the room. I ran after him. I said Dad did it to me, so it didn't matter. Then Bry – he burst out crying. He was twenty-three and he cried like he was a kid. I was just fifteen.'

Hesta stared out across the town. The line of the fogless sea was just visible, fluorescent, essential. You come so far, go as far as you can, what else could be there at the world's end, but this eternal otherness.

162

'I didn't have the sense to leave him alone,' said Phaedra. 'I kept on and on. I tried to put my arms round him and he threw me off. He said I was sick and mad and dirty. He said he never wanted to see me again.'

Hesta could no longer hear the piano, if, up here she ever had.

'Why are you telling me this?' she said to Phaedra.

'The others did.'

'So what?'

'People want to, Hesta,' said Phaedra. 'You make them do that. Didn't you know? Tell you things. Do things when you're there, things they wouldn't do otherwise. Or *you* do things like most of us can't.'

Hesta said nothing. In the starlight her hair was darkly grey, or some unknown colour close to grey. So foxes look, under certain stars.

'What I did,' said Phaedra, 'when Bry didn't come back, was I told Dad Bry had had a go at me. Tried to screw me. And I'd said no. And Dad shouted and swore, and he said I'd done the right thing. He said – can you reckon it – he said I should save meself now for me husband.' Phaedra threw back her head and laughed melodramatically, the way some people have truly done since the dawn of mankind, at colossal and idiotic hurt.

'Poor Phaedra,' said Hesta. Her tone was remote.

Phaedra said, 'Yeah. My name wasn't Phaedra. Course not. It was Shirley. Shirley Cork.'

'Phaedra's better.'

'Phaedra's my punishment. You know the Greek play? Phaedra's the king's wife but she wants the king's son to sleep

163

with her, and when he won't she says he raped her and the king goes and kills his own son.'

'You told me your father killed your brother.'

'It was on the tow path. There'd been some muggings. Bry was going to the caff. He liked the river. Dark by then and no one about. Dad took his golf club – he played golf, right. Yeah, he played golf.'

Hesta waited.

Phaedra said, slowly, 'The police came and Dad went to identify the body. They never found the mugger. There was one copper kept coming back. He kept looking at Dad. They couldn't prove a thing.'

Phaedra began to cry, but very simply, without volume or struggle. High up, the seagull called the scream of unvoiced human agony, on her behalf, to the ears of a God too far away to realize she had suffered.

At last Phaedra dried her eyes and nose in sections, on the sleeves of her two jumpers.

She sounded now as if she had a cold, but was cheerful.

'Bish-Op's like Bry,' said Phaedra. 'I mean he's cleverer than Bry. But he's sweet like that. And he sees me, I mean who I am, under me stupid yukky body. If you go down that path, you'll get into his garden.'

'Whose garden?'

'Mr Hassinger. That's his house. The dishy old guy in the pub. With the *eyes*.'

'Why would I?'

'There's a side door – I think. Just knock.'

'Then what?'

'Don't know.'

164

'I don't think so.'

'Oh, Hesta,' said Shirley Phaedra Cork, 'you know you will. Skilt's the beginning.'

'What about the photographer?' said Hesta.

'They kill people,' said Phaedra. 'They can do that. I can't. I don't need to.'

'Why did they kill him?'

'Out of Season,' said Phaedra.

She stood up and came over to Hesta, and held out her little left hand politely.

Hesta shook Phaedra's hand.

'Skilt'll send your stuff,' said Phaedra.

Phaedra went down the steps.

Hesta watched her. Then she looked back at the house above the wall.

She had no intention of going anywhere near it, or no nearer than she was. For some reason, Skilt had cast her out, or given her over, to the blond man – Hassinger? – by some bizarre law of this place of dire wonders.

Perhaps the 'adventure' was over now. It would be sensible to find a call-box that worked and get in touch, even so late, with Iain Web, her father.

If she told him the truth at last, he would not expect her to go back to Stephanie.

But perhaps, as she had always thought, she could not do this.

As with Phaedra, the telling of sexual disloyalties to fathers, was ill omened. Although Iain was not a monster, he was a man. He might do anything. Probably, she should risk that.

In the house above the bombsite, against the cliff, the light burned on. There were hundreds of tiny panes in that window. And timbers clasped the plaster, and a gigantic chimney ascended, phallic, decorative, with a chase of smoke now issuing from its cup.

A car gunned its engine in the streets below. Hesta recalled cars did not often negotiate the town in winter. She looked down again, and found, between the buildings, the twist of Old Street that had cobbles, and no road for any car. But there the car was, running with a huffing noise, long and low and black, with the curved hips of nine decades ago. Smoke drifted, or seemed to drift, up from the car, as it did from the chimney of Hassinger's house. This smoke was black. And a black being drove the car. Not a man who was black. A man who had become black. Over the cobbles, down the street to the sea. Vanishing at a bend, if there was a bend there . . . any way, vanishing. And the noise instantly gone, leaving only the voice of waters.

The night was cold beneath the stars.

For the first time in her life, sitting now where Phaedra had sat, on the cruel stone, Hesta saw the end of time, her own, the earth's. Like the hag or wise-woman, she gazed to the horizon, the ashes and the grave, the sun burned out, the oceans covering all. It made her very calm. Yet it was only a moment: she was sixteen.

End of Part Three

PART FOUR

One

A stupid rhyme was going round and round in her head. She could not get rid of it. Her mother had said it to her, when she was about six. 'Listen, Stephanie. Here's a riddle.' *Adam and Eve and Pinch Me*, said the rhyme and Stephanie's blowsy mother, paddling her fingers, with chipped nail-varnish from the housework, in Stephanie's bath. Stephanie listened, carefully. *Adam and Eve and Pinch Me went down to the river to bathe. Adam and Eve were drownded, who do you think was saved?* 'Pinch me,' said Stephanie, logically.

And her mother, with her chipped nails, pinched her hard on the thigh. How unfair it was. What a trick to play. But then, Stephanie had soon found out, most quickly by listening to her father, that her mother was a bloody fool.

'Would you like some tea?' Stephanie asked.

She hoped they would. She could go to the kitchen then, and have a quick nip out of the opened wine bottle. What alcoholics did, of course. Not that she was. But her nerves were bad, and no surprise.

'How kind of you. Yes, that would be nice.'

The woman was about twenty-seven, called Ann, apparently, tall and slim in a slick blue suit with a short skirt, and low-heeled but pristine shoes that probably cost a hundred and fifty pounds. The suit would be much more. The man was in a smart suit, too, his grey, with matching briefcase, and with a blue tie – perhaps to match Ann. He was called Roger Cover, a peculiar name, but not so peculiar as Pinch Me.

Adam and Eve and—

'Shall I come and help?' said Ann. 'I'd like to see your kitchen. I'm keen on kitchens. I just let the rest of my flat go to rack and ruin.'

The man had sat on the long couch. His tie, the suit of Ann, clashed with the other blue clashings of the room.

'There's no need.'

'But with your hand. It must be difficult.'

'Thank you,' said Stephanie resentfully.

She led the way into her kitchen.

'Oh, white. Yes, that's so clean-looking.'

The kitchen was not actually as clean as it had been.

Once she had got hold of the private doctor she had not seen since two years before, for a dose of 'flu, Stephanie had let herself go and burst into tears. As she cried, she had the most outlandish sensation, as if her grief and outrage were not real, but as if she should act them now, because someone was here who must commiserate.

The doctor, having checked the cast on her fingers, not bothering to ask – as Martin Peecey had not – how this had happened – gave her a number she could left-handedly ring in order to hire a help. He also gave her a prescription for some tranquillizers. He then charged her forty-five pounds, and left. He had, it seemed, beheld tears before, and often.

Stephanie had already rung Den.

At first Den had been out, all day, all evening, for two days and nights. (Stephanie had thought she heard his voice somewhere in the background. Maybe she imagined this. From the drugs the hospital had given her, she still tended to hear occasional noises, especially at night, that were not there.)

In the end, the third day, Den came to the phone. 'I'm really sorry, Steph. You see, a friend's got me an ace job in a photographic studio.' This was a lie. It sounded like one.

'But, Den, you saw, didn't you. I'm stuck. My hand – I can't – we can make it seventy, if you like.'

'Steph – I'm really sorry.'

'OK. Eighty pounds. Why not. I'm desperate.'

'I'm really sorry.'

'Oh,' said Stephanie, 'I thought I'd been quite good to you.'

Silence.

'You little fucker,' said Stephanie, and slammed down the phone.

Perhaps it did not occur to her Den, even if he had been older and heterosexual, might not wish to stay involved with a household where mousetraps were left waiting in drawers.

The 'help', when she manifested, was a plump and comely woman, about forty. When Stephanie began on her list of needs, the help, who was named Alex, told her what duties were her province. She would shop, and prepare light meals. She would tidy Stephanie's bed, and attend to Stephanie's hand. She would arrive at nine and be gone by three.

'I thought you'd clean, too,' said Stephanie. 'I'm used to a clean house.'

'Get a cleaner,' said Alex. 'I live in a pig-sty.'

There was trouble, too, over the shopping and the food. Alex would insist on giving Stephanie what was 'good' for her. This included omelettes, soup, fried fish, stewed apples, yoghurt, toast, bananas.

'I'm used to watching my weight,' said Stephanie.

'Don't watch it now. You're too thin for your height. Put your hand first. That needs nourishment to heal.'

Stephanie bit back a retort about Alex's large bosom and curvaceous rump. She simply left most of what Alex gave her and meanwhile observed the dust gathering in the rooms, the bits on the carpets, the cobwebs, the olive oil splotches on the badly wiped cooker.

She did interview two applicants to replace Den, both female. One chewed gum and had mad lost eyes. The other, a very fat, elderly woman, confessed her husband would not allow her to do heavy housework, which was represented by bathrooms and hoovering.

All this while, Stephanie was moving in a sort of dream. The horror-trance that had followed her injury, was gone. To herself she seemed normal – almost normal. Although sometimes, in the quiet and dark of night, she thought she heard the furniture being moved downstairs, or the church bells at the street's end ringing at three in the morning. Although, now and then, a gust of vertigo would make her grab the back of a chair, a wall.

The seamless, always-potential rage in her guts seemed to her utterly legitimate. Martin, for example, had not been near her, not since he brought her home. And that evil bitch Hesta had obviously decamped to live with common little Janey

and her obese mother. Den had deserted her. While Iain—
Iain.

As the days passed and she arose from the shock, and the
pain lessened in her fingers, Stephanie puzzled, in what
seemed to her a reasonable way, over the disappearance of
her husband. But this was superficial. What she thought was
not what she felt.

After the phone call, in the midst of the blackness, the
cold voice of the woman – *Is your husband there?* – trying to
catch her out. And then the news – the red-haired man,
leaving all his belongings, vanished away, vanished by no
known means. And all around, the hungry sea. After this, a
wave of tremulous relief had come on Stephanie.

In the state that had her, then, she had been able to
acknowledge that Iain, dead, was of great benefit. She would
have everything. The house, the insurance, the compensation
that the Company would give her. And no more would he
come, sadly, self-deprecatingly smiling, to put himself,
without ardour or skill, into her body. Nor would he try to
anchor her to her unwanted and terrifying child. She could
be free.

But through this lightness gradually stole the shadow.

Until then the mousetrap had been so appalling that, like
the chance of cancer or nuclear war, she had never analysed
it. Now the dim question rose, nebulous and poisonous, who
had really left it there for her? Hesta – yes, she had decided
it was Hesta, who was insane. But *was* it Hesta?

If Iain had vanished from one place, might he not be in
another. And if he was, why not here. Those hours of her
absence with Martin . . . Iain letting himself in (somehow

Iain wet, as if after heavy rain, or risen straight from the sea). Iain setting his trap, in revenge at her infidelity.

Under the compilation of fury and fright, and rejection by and of Hesta, this new thing, stealing up on Stephanie. Insidious and horrible. For Hesta had gone. She had run off, and Stephanie had been glad of it. But Iain – where had Iain run to? What did Iain yet mean to do? Was he spying somewhere from the obscure edges of things, down under the trees in the street, from some other window, from some loophole in life itself.

Though Stephanie did not frame such words, their concepts slithered through her.

Suddenly, when the disliked Alex arrived in the morning, Stephanie was pleased. When, at half past two, Alex left, Stephanie went down and bolted her doors. Turned on the lights early.

It was a week after that dramatic Saturday, when bones and properly coherent existence broke, that Stephanie played back the messages on the downstairs answerphone, hoping for something from Martin Peecey she had missed.

She had not been sure the telephonic twitters she had heard had not been further drug-bells in her ears. But some it seemed were not, for the three messages were all from the Aspens, Hesta's school, each asking her what had become of Hesta.

Stephanie had called the school that afternoon, holding the first glass of her second bottle of white wine. She explained she had been in an accident, and kept Hesta at home to help her. She apologized for not contacting them. When the woman on the other end entered a lecturing mode, Stephanie put down the phone.

Then, turning to her hallway, where a bright yellow vase supported once bright yellow chrysanthemums, now dead-and-Alex-unremoved, Stephanie felt a deep flood of panic rising from the very earth, engulfing her, like the wicked in the days of Noah.

However much of an oaf Janey's mother was, she would not keep Hesta away from school. It was, after all, against the law.

Iain. Hesta. Vanished. Not – *there*. Then – *where?*

And even as she thought these thoughts, in the strange dislocated condition that to herself was rational, another call rang through on the upstairs phone, the second line. Distractedly she hastened to it, and answered. And found that a Mr Cover from the Company would be coming to talk to her. Mr Cover and his assistant. Would that be all right?

'I'm not –' said Stephanie, 'I have to—'

'Please don't worry, Mrs Web. This evening then. About five?'

'No, that won't—'

'Thank you, Mrs Web.'

'Sit down,' said Alex five minutes later downstairs, stalking from the kitchen with a tray: cream soup, a sandwich, a banana. 'You're drinking too much, do you know that? You know what the doctor said.'

Stephanie downed her glass and continued to the fridge for more. 'Leave me alone!'

'I can, if you want. But the agency may not replace me. You're rather difficult, aren't you?'

'Don't talk to me like that.'

Alex shrugged, put the lunch tray on the dining room

table, and went to make the bed. By two o'clock she was gone, leaving – not a salad, but a *potato* salad and quiche – *pastry* – for dinner.

Stephanie downed another glass and flung it on the floor where the thick carpet did not permit it to shatter.

Outside the thickness of November was gathering.

And from this grey clarity that was a fog, at five precisely, Roger Cover and his Ann stepped down from a large black car, and rang the doorbell.

'You use tea bags,' said Ann. 'That's sensible. So do I. My mother won't hear of it.'

As the kettle slowly boiled, and the wine stood, shouting at Stephanie from the fridge, Ann had come out with lots of small snippets like this. It was light social chat, meant to make you relax. Because people who made confidences wanted to be friends. Had nothing to hide. Could be trusted.

Stephanie seemed to know a lot about Ann. Her neglected flat with the designer kitchen, her mother in Cambridge with the spaniels and the teapot. The allergy to new paint. Her plans for a holiday in Cyprus. About her assistant rôle, Ann said nothing. And nothing as to why she and Roger Cover were there.

Ann put the china tea mugs on the tray Alex always used, and they went back into the sitting room.

Roger Cover sat exactly as they had left him. As if he had switched himself off after they were out of the room. Now he invisibly let current back through his batteries and smiled, rising to his feet.

'How are you, Mrs Web?' asked Roger Cover, when they had all been served by Ann with the tea-bag tea, and sat down again.

'All right, I suppose.'

'The worry over your husband must be severe.'

'Yes, of course.'

'And you haven't heard anything from him?'

Stephanie stared at Roger Cover, who was still robotically, encouragingly smiling.

Inside the tight skin of her nerves and fluctuating fear, Stephanie felt this indigestible lump of her anger, swelling.

'Obviously not.'

'Do forgive me, Mrs Web. You see, sometimes in these cases, a wife may hear something. But her husband may say, don't tell anyone, not yet.'

'You think Iain and I have concocted some sort of insurance scam?'

'Did I say that, Mrs Web?' Stephanie sat stonily. Roger Cover smilingly glanced at Ann. 'Did I say that, Ann?'

'Certainly you didn't,' Ann laughed. 'But Mrs Web is under such a strain. I'd be frantic.'

Stephanie wanted to slap Ann viciously. But then, Ann looked the type, under her vivid make-up and gossipy gambits, who would slap right back, threefold.

'There's no means for Iain to have got off the rig,' said Stephanie, 'no helicopters. I was told that. No life-rafts or whatever they are.'

'That's so,' said Roger Cover.

'And no one could find him *on* the rig,' said Stephanie, keeping her voice, with difficulty, from rising high. 'But there's a limit to the places he could be on a rig, for God's sake, surely.'

'Yes, exactly, Mrs Web.'

'Then,' said Stephanie. Her voice cracked like an aging soprano's, hitting a high note after all, 'there's only the sea, isn't there?'

'Well, apparently.'

'Or a bloody flying saucer,' nearly screamed Stephanie. 'Is that what it's supposed to be? Close Encounters—'

The two of them sat in silence. They did not look upset, or embarrassed. Not contrite.

Ann said, 'It must be very hard for you, Mrs Web. We know that.'

Stephanie said, she believed quite levelly now, 'He must be dead. Tell me he's dead.'

'We don't know that, Mrs Web.'

'He jumped into the sea.'

Adam and Eve—

Roger Cover said, gravely, 'It *is* a possibility.'

'What about the police,' said Stephanie.

'Naturally, the police are involved.'

'I'd go mad,' said Stephanie, noisily. She put her tea on the floor. Her hands shook. She noted randomly that the tranquillizers seemed to make her worse, but maybe that was because she drank with them as she had been told not to. 'On a rig like that, in the middle of nowhere. *Mad.*'

'Did your husband ever say that he felt like this, Mrs Web?'

'Iain? Iain say that? No – Iain never said – he couldn't express—'

'He was uncommunicative?' prompted Roger Cover.

'Yes, totally uncommunicative,' said Stephanie, words flowing before she could stop them, 'one of his many problems. Married – my *God* – for sixteen years. And conversation really isn't a talent of his. Does he have any talents? Sixteen years of yes and no. When he was here. He went on a rig when he was twenty-five – Hesta was only, what? – four, five – left it to me, you see. Bringing up a child. Everything. Well.' She broke off, picked up her tea, sipped, put it down. 'Excuse me.'

When she came back from the kitchen, the gulped wine still hitting the floor of her stomach like paint stripper, she toted the biscuits Alex had bought. Challengingly, she offered these, her reason for going back to the kitchen.

Ann declined. Roger Cover took two. He said, 'I can't resist chocolate.'

Another little harmless confidence.

Stephanie sat down again.

She saw Roger Cover, in her absence, had got some papers out of his briefcase.

'We mustn't take up too much of your time, Mrs Web. I expect your daughter will be in soon.'

'Hesta . . . She's staying with a friend.'

Ann said, 'That's probably a good idea. Take her mind off all this.'

'You know,' said Roger Cover, shifting the papers on his knee, the tea and the biscuits concealed now within him, becoming a part of him, 'these things do sometimes happen. A man can go missing – and then turn up. It's for this reason, Mrs Web, we can't make arrangements yet on the go-ahead

179

for the insurance. Please don't be concerned that if – well, if it comes to it, you won't receive all the benefits to which you're entitled.'

Stephanie hiccupped. It startled her, but not either of them. They paid it no attention. Just as when she had screamed.

'Meanwhile, your husband's salary will continue to be paid into your joint account in full. So, no problems there. Was there anything you needed to ask, Mrs Web?'

Stephanie said, 'But he's in the sea.'

Adam and Eve were drownded.

'Let's hope not, Mrs Web. There's absolutely no evidence to support that. Nothing has been found. I gather your husband is a strong swimmer?'

'Yes.' Stephanie glimpsed Iain, as intensely as if that scene had momentarily psychically overlaid this one, Iain twenty-one, swimming up and down the public swimming baths, his hair darkened red as Martin's claret.

'Don't give up hope,' said Ann, sincerely.

Roger Cover brought the papers to Stephanie, with some sort of stiff light board beneath them. He put a fountain pen into her hand. 'If you'd just sign here, and here.'

'What am I signing?'

'A formality, Mrs Web. Just to show we've had our little talk.'

Stephanie did not care. Through the image of the swimming Iain, to the strain of Adam and Eve and Pinch Me, she signed.

The other doctor, the one she called out in the middle of the night, when she came to the conclusion she might go mad, mad like Iain before he jumped into the sea and swam away, was named Townsend. He was a locum.

When she unbolted the door to him, it was as if the night had taken form and walked into her house, for Dr Townsend was black – as Stephanie's father would have said – as the ace of spades.

Stephanie shrank in terror.

But Dr Townsend took her into the blue room and got her to sit down.

He examined her broken fingers through their casing very gently. 'I think I'd like you to see a specialist, Mrs Web.'

'More money,' said Stephanie. 'It's my husband's money. He's been lost at sea.'

'So I understand. I'm extremely sorry. Please don't start to worry about your fingers, but I do think they need a little more attention.' He asked her a great many questions, during which he told her to stop taking the tranquillizers, that wine was much better for her than the tablets, although she should cut it down, and preferably switch to red, at which, thinking of Iain's hair, she shrieked with laughter.

He gave her the name of a specialist at the private clinic. He asked her if there was anyone who could come in to be with her.

'No one,' said Stephanie, bitterly. 'No one bloody cares.'

'I believed you had a daughter.'

'She was the one who broke my hand.'

'How?' asked Dr Townsend. He had – again as Stephanie's father, a great classifier, would have said – a 'cut-glass accent'.

Stephanie told Dr Townsend all about Hesta and the mousetrap, about Iain – and perhaps the mousetrap – about Martin. She fell asleep in the middle of it all.

Dr Townsend gently woke her to take his leave. He had calmed her, but being once gone, ceased to exist.

Having bolted the door, she went back to bed.

She realized in the morning that Dr Townsend, prince of night, had not charged her any money. Then she had an impulse to look to see if he had stolen anything from the house as a form of barter.

Stephanie had met Iain when she was nineteen. It was in a pretty pub whose garden sloped to the river, on a ripened evening in late summer.

She had gone with girls from her temporary job, a Friday night fling, some drinks, giggles, a Chinese to end up with.

Stephanie was aware that she was a notch higher than her girlfriends. She had been to grammar school and was due to start her training, in the autumn, as a beautician. But she tried not to flaunt herself, to keep her improved accent soft. She thought her companions quite admired her, never knowing they called her clandestinely *Toffee-Stephie* for her toffee nose. After all, the florist's where they all worked belonged to Stephanie's father.

'Bit of pocket money,' he had said, putting her into the work. He was proud of her and she was accustomed to winning his praise. He himself had wed her mother for her cuteness (she was then a cockney naive seventeen-year-old), the 'bloody fool' of his later parlance – and then tired of her as she lost her looks. But Stephanie he appreciated. She did

182

all he said, growing up diet-slim and well groomed, 'clever', 'improving herself', due for a good – but 'feminine' – career.

'My girl,' he called her. But he had named her for an actress or character from some play.

All three flower girls were on their second gin and tonic, when out into the pub garden came an apparition from a dream.

Young men of this era grew their hair, and the hair of this young man was below his shoulders, thick and shining, the red of fires, and those atomically induced sunsets of the late 1950s, that the girls might have noted from their prams.

'Look – look at *him*.'

'Isn't he *beautiful*.'

He was, and although Stephanie did not verbally augment this effusion, she – as her father might have said – set her cap at him. After all, she was the princess, the other girls just slaves in her father's shop.

Most of the women in the pub, in fact, in some way looked – squinted, peeped, gaped – at Iain Web.

One or two went so far as to speak to him. But he sat on at his table with his pint. Alone.

He brooded. Yes, he seemed to have deep, perhaps painful, thoughts. He had broken up with a lover? But no girl surely would have cast him aside. Some obstacle then. She did not, this girl, understand him. Was not good enough. He left her, though it hurt him deeply, there in his heart behind that wide-shouldered yet slender chest.

Stephanie had had sexual experience. She was on the Pill. (This one thing her father did not know. Fondly, she grasped that she protected him by not telling him. Things were different now.)

The flower slaves sighed and mooned. They would fantasize all night and do nothing.

After all, some five attractive girls had spoken to him, on one pretext or another. And he had smiled indifferently, spoken politely, evidently with no interest. But those girls were not so wonderful. Frills and too fat.

Finally Stephanie got up.

'You're not going to, *are* you?'

'I'm just going to the ladies,' said Stephanie.

She was nineteen and she knew she looked stunning. Slim as a wand, tight white jeans and white silk shirt, fair hair the same length as his, all scented with non-cheap perfume, and with priceless youth.

She walked over and drew out a chair and sat down facing him. When he looked up, astonished, she said, 'Hallo, Mike. It's been *ages*. How are you? How was Australia?'

'Greece,' said the young man. And then, 'I'm not Mike.'

'Oh come on,' said Stephanie. Then she did a double-take. She clapped her exquisitely manicured hand to her perfectly painted lips, and blinked her cool eyes in their blossom of mascara. 'Oh no – no – you're *not*, are you. Oh God. I'm so *sorry*. But – you *look* like Mike. No, not that much. It's the hair. And – well. Well, you *do* look like Mike. But you're not Mike. I do feel an idiot.'

'That's all right,' said the young man.

She could see that, jolted, he was noticing her properly.

'I'm a *twit*,' said Stephanie. 'Can I buy you a drink? It's so rude, isn't it, to mistake someone for someone else. You see, Mike – well, I haven't seen him for a year.'

Iain Web thanked Stephanie, but said he would buy *her* a drink.

He was a 'gentleman' it seemed. Even her father would have approved.

The flower slaves went off without Stephanie to their feast. They shot her leers of envy and congratulation and pure spite. But, passing the table, did no more than say farewell.

Iain and Stephanie sat on, drinking a little, until the time came for them to be thrown out with all the other non-existent people.

In later years she could never recall what they had spoken of. She thought perhaps his two-month trip to Greece, islands, light, beaches. His training at engineering college. And her own neatly arranged suddenly unreal pursuits. She had scarcely heeded what he said, what she herself said. For when she spoke she was busy projecting her own image. And when he spoke, she was adrift in him, all at sea.

He had golden eyes – so she would presently write in her diary, the last diary she ever kept. And his lovely hair, like that of a Renaissance lord in Shakespeare.

They walked from the pub and down unseen streets beneath lunar lamps, and all was magical. They came upon a common, set there by God – or the god of Love. Or of something.

Stephanie's liaisons had been conducted decorously on mattresses, indoors. Now, under the great wild trees of a city parkscape that seemed like a jungle, or Eden, she coaxed and leaned to him, until he kissed her, and so, dissolving, drew him down. 'But Stephanie –' 'It's all right. I'm on – you know – the Pill.'

The sex was useless. Clumsy, hurried. It stuck out of the divine night like – oh daddy – a 'sore thumb'.

When Iain pulled away from her and apologized, he also said, 'I've been trying – to be celibate. And now I just couldn't – wait. God, I'm sorry.' And turning to her, he added, 'You're very beautiful. Too beautiful.'

She had been too beautiful – he could not, after his abstinence, control his passion. Irresistible Stephanie.

'Darling – it's all right—'

'No. But you've forgiven me. That's very sweet.'

'Perhaps,' she said, 'next time—'

'Yes, but not now.' And once more the piercing accolade. 'Right now, you're too much for me.'

So, the salve upon the sore.

They wandered back into the city, and he left her at her house, the semi-detached house in Mimosa Grove, and went away, he with her telephone number, and she, insufficient spent wetness in her loins, her climax ungained, masturbating over memory under the rainbow sheets. *Next time*.

Next time was almost two months later.

She had given up on him.

Into the rainbow pillows of her lust, wept, Iain – Iain—

Again, apologies. Family disturbances – over now. Come and celebrate. There was a really great Indian restaurant just opened.

She tried to be stand-offish ('play hard to get'). Not too much. She gave in.

The restaurant was sumptuous. There were chandeliers and plush, and, after nine o'clock, they doused the lights and left only burning candles.

Iain was flush, and generous. They had cocktails, starters, a main course (table subsumed by dishes; hers a prawn curry), dessert, a bottle of champagne, coffee and liqueurs.

He spoke throughout, softly, compulsively. She had reasoned that perhaps he had needed the extra time to slough utterly the ghost of the preceding girl. He did not talk of this. Not quite.

'When I was in Greece . . .'

Stephanie was rapt. He was more marvellous even than she had remembered, and garbed all in black, and scarlet hair. The scent of him made her tremble.

He had been given the holiday by an uncle. A reward. Something like that. And in Greece – he could not properly describe. She did not properly hear him, any way. There had been, amid the crystal light, the reflections of the blue crystal sea, some house, villa. And a man. An employer who, it seemed, had bullied Iain.

'Why did you put up with it?' she asked. It was one of her interpolations, proving that she attended. She had not needed to make many.

'He was crazy. Dynamic. Not Greek, but he'd lived there a while. Spoke it well.'

'What did he want?'

'Oh,' Iain was vague, 'just passing time. He was very rich. He had a yacht. I think he sailed there, this island, in it. She, I mean. Ships, yachts, he said, you call them *she*.'

'What did you do?'

'Lazed about. Swam. I'm a really strong swimmer. He was impressed by that. He wanted to practise talking English. That's how we met. I was trying to earn a bit extra.'

187

Iain looked melancholy. He must be thinking of the other girl. Had she been in Greece, too?

'What happened?'

'Nothing,' said Iain. He looked straight at her. 'Nothing.'

'Something,' said Stephanie, coyly, like the star in a film.

'Well, we had a fight,' said Iain. She watched him – it was all she wanted to do for the moment. His golden eyes met hers in a sort of defiant collision. 'It was over a girl.'

Stephanie experienced the expected pang.

'And,' she said.

'We were in the sea. We'd been swimming, he and I. I – I can't remember it all. But that was the end. I came home. And after that – after – after that girl – I didn't – I haven't had sex for six months.'

'Poor love.'

'Stephanie – when you and I – I didn't come.'

Another pang. This time not anticipated. She, wet enough for both, had thought that he had.

Instead of losing control, he had lost his hard-on. An insult after all. She tried to be magnanimous.

'Never mind.'

'Stephanie, you do believe I want you.'

'Do you?' (Of course he did.)

'So much, Stephanie.'

He told her he had booked a room in a small hotel, not at all seedy, it was nice. Would she come with him tonight?

Play hard to get. Men wanted that. Hadn't she heard her father with her poor common mother: 'You acted like a slut from the first, making eyes at me. You're just a bloody fool.'

'I don't think I should.'

'Please, Stephanie.'

They were both rather drunk, and the spices in the food, used by centuries of rajas to inflame desire, also worked on them.

By eleven o'clock she had called home to say there had been rough men on the last bus, and she was staying over with Carolyn. Carolyn was a school friend, no longer ever seen, but ever useful for excuses.

By twelve, with a half bottle of vodka on the bedside table and the lights out, Iain and Stephanie were violently making something, not perhaps love, in the hotel bed, while a cold rain fell on the world outside.

The coupling was again very swift. But by now she was so hungry for him that, once penetrated, she came in a matter of twenty-three seconds. And at her cries, he came too, there was no mistaking, the spasms running through him under her hands, his moans, the tide of him that burst into her and, a little while after, trickled out.

It should have been a long, special night, following this initial tumult. Slower and more exploratory joinings. Tenderness, and a little luxurious sleep.

But instead, after they had fallen apart, Stephanie was visited by a boiling urge to seek the bathroom down the hall.

Here it was she spent most of the night, fortunately not throwing up, but otherwise copiously and continuously voiding herself.

Her stomach, used mostly to cottage cheese, crispbread and lettuce, had rebelled at the unaccustomed food. Prawns, however faultlessly prepared, fresh from the coast as the waiter had assured her, demonstrably had not been the best choice.

In the morning, pallid and drained, ashamed of her looks, she let Iain take her to the end of her street in a taxi. He kissed her over and over. 'Poor baby. My poor Stephanie. My beautiful pale girl.'

'You will phone me?' almost tearfully she asked.

'I will. Tonight. I promise.'

And he did. By which time she was quite recovered. It seemed her illness had only made him more caring. They talked for an hour. They created plans for future nights, for excursions, they told each other, along the wires, that they loved.

The awful thing, perhaps the worst, was that she had been so happy. Never before so happy, surely. And not for very much longer.

When she went to see the doctor then, it was at her mother's insistence. 'You've got one of them bugs.'

'*Those* bugs,' said Stephanie, 'Mother.'

'Pardon?' said Stephanie's mother.

Stephanie felt too nauseous to go on. Which was the root of the dialogue any way. For three months, every day or couple of days, being sick. And she was blown up. She had gained three or four more inches round her waist from what her mother crudely called *wind*.

When the doctor examined Stephanie, then summoned the nurse and had Stephanie up on the couch, and then had her down again and informed her that she was four, almost five months pregnant, Stephanie 'laughed in his face'.

'I can't be. I'm on the Pill. And I haven't missed any. I've had my periods.'

'Heavy ones?' asked the doctor drearily.

Stephanie thought this in bad taste, but doctors were.

'I'm always light.'

The doctor explained to Stephanie that the rhythm of the Pill could induce, sometimes, regular showings of blood despite pregnancy.

'But I didn't miss a single tablet!' wailed Stephanie, her voice lifting as, in later life, it would in the house of Iain Web.

'I think you've probably had some sort of stomach upset. That'll do it. Didn't you read the leaflet you were given?'

Stephanie had, but it was long ago. She had not been *sick* – not then. Ever since she had started to be sick she had not attempted sex.

'Diarrhoea will have the same effect. Your contraception's gone straight through, I'm afraid.'

Stephanie sat down. She said, after the nurse had hurriedly brought her a bowl, and she had filled it, 'I want an abortion.'

'My dear girl,' said the doctor, 'it's much too late for that. We can't possibly recommend that now.'

Iain had been eager to marry her. He had done everything correctly. He had even fawned on her father, calling him 'Sir', and partly won him round.

'You could do worse,' the father grudgingly said. 'He's got prospects, a goal, that young man. Too much hair. But they're all like that now. Money in that family.' This was the well-off uncle, who might assist them while Iain went on with his training, and Stephanie, her own training in beauty perforce abandoned, enlarged like a balloon in a one-room flat across from the railway.

It was hot, that summer. Very hot. And Stephanie, staggering under her load, seemed any way to have a built-in furnace. Her back ached until her neck and her head ached. Her feet ached from carrying the dreadful – and full of dread it was – weight of the child.

The child.

The baby.

Iain was 'wonderful'. He came in punctually from college and saw to the meals. He made the bed. He brought her magazines, books from the library. He tried to be cheerful. He *was* cheerful. And – victorious. That was the word. As if, by her pregnancy, he had won some battle.

It was through this, no doubt, his victory via her defeat, her downfall, that Stephanie grew to hate Iain.

It should never have been this way. She was used to comfort. She was used to small-breasted slenderness, to a body that did what she wanted.

Instead she had become a slave, and the sound of the trains going by at all hours of the day and night, was to her the *Vae Victis*, woe to the vanquished.

'You'll see,' said Iain, 'when it's born.'

And Stephanie did see.

Three weeks and two days late, after an eternity of straining and agony, screaming and crying, before an unsympathetic audience, when forth it came, indeed she saw.

A creature, white as salt, tufted with a curl of red hair.

'A girl,' he said, the hated one. 'God, Stephanie. Isn't she

192

fantastic? You know, I'd really like to call her Hester. It was my gran's name.'

'Call her what you want,' said Stephanie, her womb burning within her, as if the white and red-haired thing had set it on fire.

But a month later, Stephanie showed off the baby, now a doll in a pram, in just the feminine way her father approved of.

A month later too, Iain's rich uncle died. He left everything he had, a considerable amount, to a racing stable in Ireland.

Two

Penny, was that her name? Yeah, Penny. She was waiting by the office door at the back of the wine bar. Almost standing on one leg, like a stork.

She didn't look much, not in daylight. Straight fine hair. Very slight. Legs after all, in the short skirt, a bit too thin. Cute face. Big full mouth. He recalled the mouth. She had some talent there.

'Hallo, babe. What's up?'

'Can I see you, Marty, for a minute?'

'Customers OK?'

'Jill's took over my tables.'

'Fine.'

He walked through the office door ahead of her, something he never did with an older woman. But these young girls preferred it. It showed them where they stood.

Inside he sat on the desk, and left her, knowing where she stood, stork-standing.

'What's the problem?' Penny, if she was, looked down. Funny that, these old Victorian gambits of timidity and evasion. 'Sorry, babe. I haven't got all day.'

'When we went out, Marty,' said perhaps-Penny. That was

a laugh. They'd had a drink alone, after the bar shut. 'I thought you took me serious, Marty.'

'Well I did,' said Martin Peecey.

'That was why I didn't say no, Marty.'

'It was lovely,' said Martin. It hadn't been bad. 'I appreciated it. And you had three days off, full pay.'

'I didn't want that,' said Penny-perhaps. 'I thought we was going to have a relationship.'

Martin composed himself. 'There you've got me. I'll be honest, luv. If I was free, it'd be another matter. But you know, I've got a lady. You were smashing to me. But I thought you understood. It could only be just a friendly thing.'

Penny – *was* she? – drew herself up, squared her shoulders, as they used to say. 'We did everything, Marty.'

'That wasn't my fault now, was it, baby?'

Penny looked confused. Big blurred eyes. She'd forgotten. He would have been happy enough to come in her mouth, she was good at that. But she'd said she couldn't. She wanted him inside her elsewhere. She knew what she was doing. No virgin. She had enjoyed it, judging by the row. Everyone knew women had a better time than men in orgasm. You could tell from the racket they made.

Martin Peecey thought he would be wise to be diplomatic. Staff were staff. He had not seen Stephie for a while, not after all that fucking fuss over her hand, but she *was* handy, for this sort of business.

'You know I'm pretty tied up with my lady. But, if you understand the situation, I'd be very glad to see you again. You're a lovely girl. No strings. Nothing wrong with fun. Tonight . . . maybe. What about it?' He had better gild the lily. 'We can go to the Italian. Do you like Italian food?'

'Marty,' said the girl, 'I'm pregnant.'

Martin Peecey felt an incredible shock. It was an immemorial one, passed down through all the ages of the world, this moment, so natural and so unwanted. But he did not believe its farcical truth.

'Come off it.'

'I am. I've been up the doctor's. Five weeks.'

Martin drew himself together, had to, as if bits of himself were trying to fly apart.

'Are you saying it's mine?'

'You didn't use a rubber,' said Penny, prissily. 'All the other boys do.'

'Well those things aren't a hundred per cent, you know. I reckoned you were on the Pill.'

'I can't take the Pill. It makes me bilious.'

Like so many before him, Martin wanted to strike her, this little bitch with milk curds in her mouth, the lowest of the low, with all these unnecessary, unsuitable 'better class' words somehow picked up. This threat. For it was a threat, wasn't it?

'If you're right, I'll see you're OK,' said Martin. He would consult with Kev. Kev knew where to get assistance for all types of difficulty.

'I can't have,' said Penny, 'an abortion.'

Martin was suave, Brylcreemed, suited, sitting on the desk, half of which was his. 'Why's that, then?'

As he said it he saw, like an emblem of fiery steel, the little gold cross in the hollow of her throat.

'I'm a believer,' said Penny. 'And my dad won't hear of it.

Or my brothers. They said come and tell you. You'd have to do the proper thing. 'Cos you was responsible.'

'Yes?' said Martin. But he quaked within. Father, brothers. Insane Catholics or something worse.

Penny looked down again, and a blade of sunlight, squeezed suddenly from the November cloud, pierced the window, and lit over her hair, like a bridal veil.

At the bus-stop, the young girl was writing in a notebook, her bag propped by the post.

For a minute, Stephanie was not sure that this was the right one. How many times had she seen Janey? Not many. And Janey's black hair was very long, but this girl's hair was in short black spikes.

Here was the place, however, where Hesta's bus came after school – the long wall, and down there the shop run by Asians. A scatter of people walking by, and the herds of traffic belching pollution at the dark dull day.

'Have I missed it?'

The girl glanced up. At her look of horror, Stephanie knew, after all, that she was Janey.

'No . . .'

'It's Janey, isn't it?'

'Yes . . .'

'How are you, Janey?'

'OK.'

Stephanie smiled, irritated, despite everything, at Janey's lack of all the social graces. But what could you expect?

'My car's in for repairs,' lied Stephanie. She hid her bandaged hand a little behind her. How much had Janey known about the mousetrap? Perhaps nothing at all. 'I do hope Hesta's written to you.'

Janey said nothing. She was very pale, and picking up her bag, held it between them like a shield.

'Oh, hasn't she? Isn't that just like Hesta. She must have called you then.'

Janey did not speak.

Stephanie fixed Janey with her wine-washed eyes.

'You see, I'm in rather a bad position. What am I supposed to tell her father?'

Janey glanced behind her. The bus was not coming. Even if it were, Stephanie presumably would get on the bus with her.

With an agitated movement, Janey pivoted around. She started to walk. But Stephanie was at once beside her. 'Walking? Yes, a much better idea. Exercise. You ought to get your mother to go on a few walks.'

The black, short-haired head was down.

'You know where she is, don't you?' said Stephanie.

'Mum's at home.'

'I don't mean your bloody mother, you little bitch. I mean Hesta.'

Janey shot her a look then. It was full of animosity. It seemed – dangerous.

Stephanie thought, keeping up with flat-shoed Janey in a proper woman's high-heeled boots, that after all Janey might be a true enemy.

'Go away,' said Janey.

'Now, Janey. I can't do that. My daughter's disappeared. I could go to the police, couldn't I. I could explain that she was with you, and then, she never came back.'

Janey stopped. The road ran on behind her to a pair of tall gates – a park? – the bare trees across the ominous sky.

Traffic roaring.

It was odd, the noises in Stephanie's ears went away, here. The traffic drove them out.

'Look,' said Stephanie, 'you've done something quite serious, you know.'

'No – I haven't—'

'Yes you have.'

'You called me a bitch.'

'So what. Aren't you?'

'*No.*'

'Then tell me where my daughter is.'

Janey's eyes were full of tears.

'She hated you,' said Janey.

It had been mutual, but before Stephanie gripped hold of that, other less real biases rushed in.

'I'm her mother. Don't be silly. Where is she?'

'I won't tell you.'

Janey turned – and ran.

How long ago had Stephanie run? Ten years, surely, and that was for a train. Which she had missed.

Now she galloped after Janey.

They were outside the laws of everyday life, which went on sluggishly all around, ignoring them.

Through those park gates. Up a sort of drive. Huge trees.

Stephanie ran, her feet swerving and hurting from the high heels, her handbag thumping her in the back as Janey's school bag did Janey.

As Stephanie ran, invective poured through her brain. Like sick it escaped her. 'Little cunt—'

A cold lake appeared. A large pond? Swans, cool as ice.

A small boy throwing bread stared round at Stephanie in terror.

She caught Janey in a copse of bare willows. Stephanie slammed her back against a tree.

'*Tell me!*'

Janey fought, as if against a rape. It was. A rape of integrity, such as the Inquisition had perpetrated.

'*No,*' snarled Stephanie, slapping aside Janey's narrow hands. Next Stephanie slapped Janey across the face.

'My mum—'

'Your bloody fat tart of a mother isn't here. Now tell me the *truth.*'

Janey, on her knees. Stephanie crouched over her. This terrible day. The white-black sky.

Janey with her hair cut as if in ancient mourning. Tears like white silk unravelling from her eyes.

'I *won't.*'

'You will. Or I'll get the police. How about that? What will fatty Lulu say? Fiddling her benefit. Questions. That cat – you're not allowed to keep a cat in those flats. Come on. *Tell me.*'

Janey turned her face. No one was near. The world had gone away.

Stephanie, no longer human, said, 'I'll count to five.' She pushed Janey hard enough to bruise. 'One –' she counted on.

At four, Janey told her.

* * *

201

'Hallo, Martin.'

Martin Peecey sprang around. Curiously, seeing Stephanie sitting there, in the electric gloom under the fake tree, his face filled with relief, almost pleasure.

She had not anticipated that. She had realized that Martin Peecey had only been using her.

'Stephie – I've been calling you all afternoon, baby. I was going to drive over – How are you – Christ, you look great.' Martin Peecey sat down. He took hold of Stephanie's sound left hand. 'I've missed you.'

'You must have,' said Stephanie. 'All your calls and the way you hammered on the door. The flowers you sent.'

Martin hung his head. This had worked when he was a little boy. Not much had changed, save he had fatally grown older.

'I've been a rat, Steph. It's this wine bar. You know what Kev's like. Leaves it all to me. I *did* call, Stephie, but you didn't answer. I should've sent you some flowers. But I kept trying to get away, get to see you, and there just hasn't—'

'All right,' said Stephanie, 'Martin.'

'Look, you need another bottle. Hang on. I'll get some. Red – you're drinking red?'

'My doctor said it was better for me.'

'There's lots of iron in red wine,' said Martin. 'Build you up. Little fragile slip of a thing. Little darling. You look lovely, Stephie.'

'No, I don't,' said Stephanie. 'I've got to see someone about my hand.'

'Poor little hand. Does it still hurt?'

'No. Apparently it should.'

Martin Peecey laughed. 'What are they, S and Ms?'

Stephanie shrugged.

Martin Peecey got the wine from the cellar, a bottle of top class Pinot Noir.

He was going to say that Kev would be back in the next half hour, and then they could go back to Stephanie's. Dinner later somewhere special, in central London. And he was going to give himself ten days off, had already arranged it. Since Iain Web could not be at home with her, or she would not be here, he was going to suggest that he take Stephanie somewhere warm.

But when he returned to the table, Stephanie, her yellowish faded tan almost green beneath the papier-mâché tree, pre-empted him.

'I need to get away, Martin. And you can see, I can't drive.'

'Absolutely, babe. No need to drive. I know the perfect place.'

'So do I, Martin.'

And when she told him where they were going, his mouth dropped open.

She did not permit Martin to go back with her. She took a thin cold gratification from putting him off. Tomorrow he could come, with his deep blue car, and take her down to the sea.

Calmed by a sort of acid, uneasy smugness, Stephanie let herself in at the front door of Iain Web's house. She was thinking of Hesta, lost in a run-down resort, Hesta probably more uncomfortable than she had ever known, the cretinous foul little brat, it was possible to be.

Over this hung the spectre of Iain, of course. For Hesta might be with Iain. But Martin would be there. And Martin had said too, after Stephanie filled him in, that there might be some extra help. Someone professional. Kev had contacts.

And if Hesta was alone – then Stephanie could be shot of her for good.

Entering the house, it was like passing from one world to another.

Already, once, everything had given way. That had been the mousetrap. And brave Stephanie had put all together again, as, it seemed, they had not quite been able to do, yet, with her fingers.

Now as she looked through her hallway and saw the strange litter of things all down the stairs, and there, by the door of her sitting room, the smashed pieces of the expensive clock, Stephanie could not think what had occurred – what *new* horrible world she had been thrown into.

The police, when they arrived, surprisingly swiftly, in minutes, were able to spell it out.

The house had been thoroughly burgled, and vandalized for good measure. An expert job, the uniformed man remarked, showing her the marks on the French doors. He sounded almost impressed, half admiring.

Stephanie treated him to a couple of words he was quite used to hearing, and went at last to open a bottle of wine. But the thieves had had those too. She had to wait.

Three

For Mr Peck, after some months without employment, the work was welcome.

The phone call had been, as so often, brief. 'Geegee, something for you. Free?' And, indifferently, 'Brilliant.'

G. G. Peck packed his bag. He did not put much in. A couple of clean shirts, Y-fronts, and socks. The not-much-used but elderly, untidy toothbrush. Aspirin. A half bottle of Bells.

When he looked out of the window of the old terraced house that had been his auntie's, saw the spray-painted and unclever graffiti, the roaming dog from No. 5 that would like to take your arm off, the youths in leather, noses full of powders, heads empty as eggless shells, Peck was glad enough to go. Go anywhere.

Bermuda might have been a change. But he never got Bermuda.

It was by the sea, however.

And through his brain, which was not empty, but staffed by efficient memories, went the childish delights of '50s resorts. Ices and ghost trains. Piers of slot machines. The gaudy, glamorous lights.

Obviously though, this was out of Season. Rotten, the

seaside, then. The glutinous furious sea rabidly salivating at a beach of deadly stones. And all the hotels shut.

The job, well. The usual, in a way. A missing man and a girl. Father and daughter, it turned out. Perhaps a bit of incest. Red hair – probably they would have seen to that. A wig, some dye.

Yet he had the vision of them somehow, these two flaming-red people, against the backdrop of oceanic greyness.

The terraced house was just as Auntie May had left it. Even the cat fur was not hoovered from the settee, the antimacassars fading like the dried flowers in the window.

May had never married. Neither had G. G. Peck. They had had empathy with each other. He could remember her once saying it to him, when they had had a swig or two of whisky: 'All that bed business. Never liked the idea of it. If you don't want children. And there are too many of them, poor little mites, that nobody wants. You keep yerself single if you're happy. I'd rather have me cocoa and me cat, any day.'

He straightened her photograph on the mantelpiece before he left to catch the train. Somehow the photograph always seemed to move. Some subsidence in the foundations very likely, tilting the wall.

Two hundred pounds in advance, that was the best thing. And the ticket paid for, too.

Whistling, Geegee Peck took a taxi to the station. He didn't have to find them, after all. Just look.

End of Part Four

PART FIVE

One

The side door of the house, up against the cliff, was open. That is, it was wide open, propped by a large bluish striped stone that perhaps had come from the beach. To find this, she had had to go up through the garden, where great rocks stared from the terraces, and the bare trees leaned beneath the lighted window with its so-many leaded panes, around under the walls, through into a sort of courtyard, with the cliff literally beetling above.

A granite urn stood in the court, empty. Within it was a brick decorated by a seagull's splash. Just inside the open door burned an oil lamp on a narrow table which, in the flea markets of London, would have fetched, after haggling, over a hundred pounds.

By the lamp lay a notepad from Woolworths. Two words were on it in a clear yet complex writing. *Go up*.

The stair also was narrow, and uncarpeted.

Hesta looked at it, but it turned after the tenth step. There was a hint of further light above.

What time would it be now? The clock had chimed – had it? – no longer, out of Season, with its little tune. One 'clock, probably. It felt like that.

She had not meant to come to the house. But when Phaedra was gone, and after Moses had passed along the cobbles in his fuming ghost car, it seemed to Hesta that to stay where she was would be redundant. She had no intention of going anywhere else. Not back to the house of her mother. Not to the phone box to call her father. Not to Skilt's hotel.

There had always been options before. To skip a class at school and walk in the park, or to leave Stephanie's for Janey and Lulu's flat. To stay here, in the seaside town, instead of all and everything else.

But to the house of the man Phaedra called Mr Hassinger, there was no alternative, not in the end.

She knew this, but not why. *Why*, so often, did not matter.

The stairs were the same as the house – to go up, forward, not back. Presently Hesta climbed them, and came over the final section into a bare room, a kind of annexe, with damaged plaster on the walls as there had been below. Another oil lamp was flickering, this time on an upended crate.

There was a solid wooden door, closed.

Hesta tried the round door-knob, and when the door gave, went into a corridor beyond.

The corridor ran ahead, angling out of sight to the left. The plain plaster walls, here, were smooth, pale grey, and lit by low wattage electric light inside a fixture like a pale upturned saucer. To either side of her now, a door.

The right hand door led into a white bathroom, large, functional, very clean, utterly without ornament. Beside the fitments there were only a wooden cabinet, a broad mirror above the hand-basin, a white soap there, and one in a white dish on the side of the bath. Two white towels hung symmetrically over a rail. There was coconut matting on the floor.

Some impulse made Hesta go to the basin. She activated both taps. Both ran freely, one cold, and one almost immediately hot.

Across from the bathroom, the other door was in fact ajar.

He had been in the pub, the Kissing Crab. He too had watched the murder at the bar. Hassinger. The man in leather with greying blond hair and blue eyes. He had not gone by her up the cliff, along the path. Unless he had moved by some circling route through the bombsite, he could not yet be here.

Hesta pushed the door and walked into the short stroke of the L-shaped room.

An overhead electric light was on, as in the corridor, low light, perhaps only forty watts.

An arched window to the left, uncurtained, black, reflecting the room.

There was a tall cupboard of mahogany, its doors carved, shining dully. On a long white table were a miniature oven with two hobs, the sort of thing glimpsed in the staff room at the Aspens, a coffee-maker, a small fridge.

The floor was tiled black. Reflecting, like the window. In the wall was a water tap, with a galvanized bucket standing under it.

Hesta went across the tiles and entered the long stroke of the L.

There were electric lamps on here, five of them, on long, wooden stands, with tawny shades the colour of old maps.

A red carpet ran along the floor, patterned with blue birds and black roses. It was threadbare in places, and might be extraordinarily valuable.

The two long walls were almost entirely covered by shelves of books, nothing else. On some of these winked ornate gilding. Others were paperbacks held together with tape. At other sections what appeared to be unbound typescripts had been wedged in. The uncurtained window at the room's end went from ceiling to carpet, and had two hundred small round panes.

In the right hand wall, among the books, a fireplace faced in black marble held a fire of coals behind a guard. On the upright of the fireplace hung a sword, its grip bound with savaged strips of leather, the blade notched and buckled. On the top of the deep mantel stood two high-stemmed goblets of blue and amber crystal with contemporary squared cups, and a chipped white mug out of which stuck nails, a hammer, and a tube of Superglue. The books and manuscripts hung heavy over them.

Near to the window was a black table with large carved legs. There were some bottles on the table, a blue plate, a decanter, an apple, a clear glass like those given away with petrol, and something stretched out, a piece of material or a torn painting, held at its four ends, and on one side, by various objects.

A fall of soot dashed down the chimney. The fire flashed.

There were two black chairs, upright, carved, with cushioned backs and seats of a stained and faded ivory silk.

Hesta went all the way to the table.

The picture was of a figure, perhaps female, with a red draped shawl and turban on its head.

The top two corners were held by a coldly sweating can of Diet Coke and another similar can of Sprite.

The two bottom corners each had a plate, one with a block of bitter chocolate on it, and one with a bunch of green grapes.

To one side, the ripped area of the picture was secured by a slender dagger with a golden hilt and silver steel blade.

Hesta said aloud, 'Drink me. Eat me. Kill me?'

And from up the room Hassinger said to her, 'The food and drink are for your refreshment. The dagger is for you to defend yourself with.'

Not turning, Hesta said, 'From you?'

'From whomsoever you may wish.'

He was as she recalled, as if she had known him a long while and seen him often. But, unheard by her keen ears, he had entered, sloughed the coat, sat down by his fire in one of the tall chairs.

Into the fire, that was where he looked. Not at her.

Hesta took up the chocolate, broke its back and snapped off a piece. She ate it. It was very rich, very black, not like chocolate, primal, with only a touch of sweetness. Then a grape. Seedless and juicy, tasting of green living things.

She opened the can of Coke, and drank. Familiarity.

With one hand, she weighed the dagger. She liked it, but put it back, on the edge of the painting which, to her, had no resemblance to herself.

'What do you want?' she said.

'So many things,' said Hassinger. 'And you?'

Hesta said nothing.

After a moment, Hassinger looked up. His eyes were like sea ice. Their coldness seemed to draw her on.

She said, 'The man in the pub. They killed him.'

213

'Yes.'

'Why?'

'An intruder. He came back at the wrong time.'

'Out of Season,' said Hesta.

'That's so. But, you see, Hesta, he would be a source of trouble. His photographs and questions. His attitudes. Did you like him?'

'No.'

'Are you sorry he's dead?'

'No. How do you know my name?'

'How do you know mine?'

'Do I?'

'You do.'

'Someone told me.'

Hassinger smiled. 'Someone told me yours.'

She said, 'You're powerful here. You're well off.'

'You could say that.'

She said, 'But you live over a bombsite.'

Hassinger said, 'A lot of the town was bombed. I own the town, Hesta. I leave that particular bombsite as it is.'

'How can you own the town?' she said.

'I bought it,' he said, simply.

Hesta broke off more of the chocolate, and ate more of the grapes. The combination of tastes was odd but effective.

A wash of tiredness came, but there was only the other chair, the tall, theatrical chair across from his, and twin of his.

'I'd like to sit down.'

'Please.' He rose to his feet, and waited for her to come to the other chair.

214

'It's an antique,' she said.

'Yes. But quite safe.'

She wanted to sit in the chair. The lines of it, its straightness, yet properly accented comforts, appealed to her. She sat. At once she was in exact physical equilibrium. It might have been made for her.

'Is it to your liking?' he said.

'Yes, thank you.'

Hesta lowered and turned her head, towards the fire, as he had done.

In her hair now showers of golden amber embers.

He took both glasses off the mantel, as if the splendour of her hair had prompted him.

'I don't want another drink,' she said, when he handed her the coloured glass, filled with a colourless liquid.

'Then don't drink it, Hesta.'

He sat. Each of them sat. They looked into the fire, which, with his return, was blazing up.

They did this, as people do who have been two or three decades together.

At last, she sipped the drink.

'What is it?'

'Dutch gin.'

When she fell asleep, Hassinger lifted her without effort.

He carried her easily and with care, to a bedroom with a narrow bed and, peeling back the covers, put her inside. One minute he regarded her, her head on the pillow, her body wrapped in the patchwork quilt that had been stitched in Old Street, just for her. Scarlet, gold, orange and indigo, the quilt, with motifs of metal lace.

(In the tiny bathroom that adjoined the room, everything was ready. Joy Joy had come to see to it, and slim black Adèle. The Duchess had irrepressibly put one white seagull feather into the vase of green vitreous on the window-sill.)

Only a minute, regarding her. But he drank Hesta in, to deeper caves than the Geneva could travel down to on its wings of alcoholic light.

It had been, after all, a long, long wait.

Two

During the night, Hesta dreamed she was washing her hair in the puce bathroom at Stephanie's house. Red liquid ran from the hair. Was it dye? Or blood.

The gulls woke her.

She sat up in the strange bed in the unknown bedroom.

The room was steeped in blueness, where daylight shone through a single blue curtain across a window.

Quickly she got up and went to the window, and drew the curtain aside. There was a paved area below, with a cluster of empty terracotta pots. Thick ivy and some other winter creeper rioted up from a low broken wall and tressed across the base of the cliff. The cliff rose sheer, grey, green, white, a massive sculpture only twenty-seven feet from the window. Seagulls were noisily busy on the ledges, flapping their huge demoniacal wings, angel-white breasts catching the early sun.

Hesta looked back, at the room.

The bed, under the glorious quilt, was white.

Black tiled floor, with one blue rug by the bed. Two bedside tables, each having a lamp with a pale china bowl. A black chest with a filled water carafe and glass.

A large bookcase went up one wall. It was empty, but for a scatter of paperbacks. In the corner was a music centre. Ten tapes and three CDs sat on the top.

Hesta went to see. Books and music duplicated those she had collected in her mother's house, but only the things she had liked – Janey's gift of Ravel, a selection of Handel, mediaeval chants for female voices, Numan instrumentals, Chekhov short stories, the Arabian Nights, *Wide Sargasso Sea* by Jean Rhys, some poems by Spike Milligan and Blake.

How did he know?

How do you know my name?

. . . Someone told me.

A door let into a small bathroom. The suite was modern, a faint pastel green, eau de Nil. On the window-ledge was a green vase, perhaps Victorian, with a white plume of feather in it. The Kleenex, paper, and towels were white. Scrupulous cleanliness. Two mirrors.

In a big cupboard were tubes of toothpaste, the brand she had used, not at Stephanie's, but at Lulu's flat, and the melon-scented range of deodorants and soaps and shampoo Hesta favoured, some cold cream and cleansers.

There were also other items, all these gift-wrapped. Talcs and perfumes, a set of nail brushes, a manicure set, little boxes of make-up.

In the bottom of the cupboard were piles of white towels, toilet paper, Kleenex and cotton wool.

'*He's got everything.*'

There was even an electric heater on the wall, as there had been a small electric fire in the bedroom.

On the inside of both bedroom and bathroom doors was a new, shiny bolt.

At the hotel Hesta had washed her hair, as the others did, in Fairy Liquid.

The recalled smell of melon and wet hair reminded her of being at Stephanie's house, and she thought of the dream, but only suds and water ran away.

She had slept in her dress.

You see, Janey, I knew he hadn't touched me, I mean sexually touched. Anyone else, I'd have thought about it, of course. But not this man. You could say, like in one of your stories, that he'd drugged me, something in the chocolate or the Coke. But he hadn't. I fell asleep because I was tired.

You don't believe me, Janey?

Janey said, in Hesta's mind, 'I do believe you, Hesta.'

Outside the room was the pale grey corridor, dark without lights. A door faced the bedroom door. On it was pinned a piece of paper with the writing she had seen last night. *Go where you want.*

She opened the door, and looked in.

This, evidently, was Hassinger's room.

A large, flat bed, white, no pretty quilt. Pale grey walls, coconut matting. A long window, uncurtained, but again a honeycomb of small panes, slightly warped. Through each, an abstract microcosm, indecipherable November colours and shapes conveying nothing.

An upright chair stood by the window, and a cupboard and chest, stripped and painted grey like the walls. Some old books with flaking spines were on the chest. One side table had a beautiful lamp, cool blackened bronze in the shape of a winged being holding up a vessel the shade of a spoiled pearl. And one oddity? A mobile phone lying by the lamp.

Another door led presumably into another bathroom.

Hesta went out. Hassinger's room was how she would have imagined it. Perhaps she might not have guessed the phone or the lamp. Or, she might have done, the lamp at least. She herself was mostly indifferent to beauty (it had been in her mirrors – too frequent for interest?). But Hassinger was not.

The first door after the right turn of the corridor did not open, the second did. She realized, as she re-entered the L-shaped room, that the books shelved over the first door on the inside, while the second door had gone unnoticed the previous night.

She had passed some stairs, too, descending. But another of his writings was Sellotaped to a tread. *Take care. Dereliction below.*

In the kitchen end of the L-shaped room was a packet of rolls, unopened, and in the fridge were butter and margarine, a jar of Fortnum and Mason's marmalade, a carton of fresh cream, a bottle of vodka and one of orange juice, and a packet of coffee.

Another note read: *Eat me, drink me.* And by this note lay a paper seaside boater, with red letters: *Kiss me Quick.* No. *Kill me Quick.*

She picked up the hat and turned it round.

Wet paint that became *We pain.* And *We killed Roy, here.* And *I do like to be Poseidon seaside.*

She sat at a stool by the table and ate her breakfast. Then she filled the galvanized bucket and rinsed her plate and mug. She threw the water down the lavatory in the white bathroom across the passage.

It was all – accustomed. Probably only obvious.

What had they done with the slashed and bled-out body of the photographer? Had Hassinger lent a hand?

When he came back from wherever it was he had gone, what would he do? What would he want? What would he say?

The window in the kitchen also faced the cliff, but here the edifice of stones and chalk and moss was only three or four feet away. A gull stood on the window-sill. She looked at it through the glass.

What does she think now, the leopardess?

She thought of Janey being there, in the room. They had eaten all the rolls, drunk all the coffee.

> When a lynx drinks,
> What does a lynx drink,
> Do you think?

Hesta said, aloud, 'Pink ink.'

The gull waddled along the sill, and jumped off, as if throwing itself to its doom.

It swooped below the window, down into the narrowest part of the courtyard beneath.

She went into the book-lined stroke of the L, and sat down in the chair where she had sat last night.

The fire burned low behind the guard. Skittishly bright November light soaked through all the panes of the window.

What was this like? Like something long ago.

She remembered.

When she was seven, home from school, Stephanie – late, gone shopping – and Iain due to arrive. Daddy. Waiting for him.

My room is marked with an X.

Hallo, my sweetheart.

Would he be home again at Stephanie's house, by now? He must have come and gone. What had Stephanie told him? What lies?

He seemed very far away, but then, he had for years, poor 'Daddy', getting always paler and less substantial, a 'shadow of his former self'.

Hesta had tried to protect him.

Perhaps he had only believed Stephanie, as usual. That must be the case . . . Hesta was on some school trip, had gone away with friends . . . or wouldn't he have come after Hesta, tried to find her?

Waiting for Daddy.

She heard him, this time, coming up from below. Did he make sure of that? Not the footsteps of Iain Web, certainly, so light and unsure. Directed, almost heavy steps, and then the door opening into the kitchen end of the room.

She sat still. She sensed the balance, he in the other part of the room, she here in this part.

And then he walked through.

She looked at him acutely. But he was the same as he had been. Handsome, old, or not so old, blue-eyed. A complete stranger.

'You slept well?' Hassinger said.

'Yes, thank you.'

He had made more coffee, and brought it to the chairs. He sat down facing her. That was how it was meant to be, apparently, these chairs, so regal and yet so comfortable, face to face. For dialogue.

She said, 'What time is it?'

He said, 'About nine. I'm sorry I was out. I had to make a call.'

'Like a doctor,' she said, without considering.

Hassinger nodded.

'Rather like that.'

'What happened to the body?' she asked.

'They give them to the sea,' he said, matter-of-factly. 'And to the gulls, of course.'

'What about the police?'

'What about them?'

'Doesn't anyone ever come looking?'

'Sometimes.'

She drank the coffee. It tasted delicious, better than when she had made it. Janey had been used to say that when someone else made you food or a drink, it always tasted better. But she had been meaning Lulu.

'You watched me, didn't you,' said Hesta, 'for weeks.'

'Yes.'

'And in the pub, the first time, that was you.'

'You are correct.'

'You made yourself look older.'

He smiled. His face was lined, darkened by weather, by years and seasons and thoughts. It was old. And young. His smile – reminded her of Iain again. But why? It was not like Iain's smile, nothing of Hassinger was like Iain Web.

'You put me to bed,' said Hesta.

'It seemed the best choice. To sleep in the chair was unnecessary.'

'And everything was there for me, wasn't it,' she said. 'My books, my shampoo.'

'I hope this was satisfactory. If there's anything you need, this afternoon, in the town—'

'Why am I here?' she said.

'Where do you wish to be?'

'I don't know. But there's a catch.'

'There's always a catch, of course,' he said.

'When I stayed in the town, the first night,' said Hesta slowly, 'I walked into Old Street. There was a baby crying, and a woman – dropped it out of the window. It was killed. It must have been. When I went back, someone had cleared it up. The blood.'

'Yes,' said Hassinger.

'What does *yes* mean?'

'It means that I've seen that too. The woman letting the child fall down on the street. I saw it seventeen years ago. Not everyone sees. A monstrous murder.'

'What is it?'

'The shop in Old Street was a house in the 1800s,' he said. 'You must understand, the woman had had a child before that fell sick in the same way. It cried and screamed on and on, and the doctors could do nothing. Eventually the child died, choking horribly. When the same affliction visited the second child, she was alone, the mother, with no one to help her. She knew the child was in agony and would die in agony, and that nothing could be done. She considered smothering it, but that would take too long, it would agonizingly have to struggle and choke. But when she dropped it on the cobbles, it died in a second. She was a woman with steel in her soul. A loving mother. Remember that.'

'It's a ghost,' said Hesta. 'Like Moses.'

'Not exactly. You'll have seen Moses.'

'Maybe.'

'The frivolous question is whether he'll part the sea, or is it the burning bush that set his car on fire.'

Hesta said, 'What am I expected to do?'

'What you want.'

She did not know what that was.

She said, 'Am I a prisoner?'

'No.'

'I saw them kill that man.'

'You're not a prisoner. No one means you any harm in the town.'

'The dagger,' she said, 'to *defend* myself—'

'From others.'

Stephanie? It was Stephanie who sprang into her mind.

Hesta said, 'I was expected here.'

'Yes.'

'All the things in the bathroom – the gift boxes—'

'Presents. They like to give you presents, Hesta. You should always accept, even if the token's unwanted.'

'*Why?*'

'Because it's kindness, Hesta, and gratitude, and respect. These, if not the token, are worth having.'

'They don't know me.'

'That's true.'

'Why should they be grateful? Or kind? Or – respect me, for Christ's sake?'

There was a sudden violent sound, like insane hammering above them.

She started. He said, 'Gulls on the roof.'

Janey said solemnly in Hesta's mind, 'But under a sphinx, if a lynx drinks, it shrinks.'

Hesta said to Hassinger. 'I'd like to go out.'

'We'll go for lunch,' he said.

The absurd normalcy of his words made her frown.

He said, 'They're ready now. They're waiting. I should be with you. This, however, will provide the answer to your questions.'

She went to the table near the window. The picture there had been rolled up and the apple perhaps eaten. The dagger lay on the blue plate.

Hesta took up the dagger. He observed this. How she moved the weapon in her fingers. Then set it back on the dish.

It was sunny, and the sea sparkled. If you had not felt the cold, it could have been late spring.

Nothing appeared abnormal.

A handful of people strolling on the promenade under the lights that would not go on again until the Season started, greeted them . . . Hassinger, or Mr Hassinger . . . 'Mr Hassinger – a lovely day.' And an elderly man walking two elderly dogs, bowed and tipped his hat. 'Hassinger. Miss Web.'

'They know my name?'

'Yes.'

Pointless to probe. She was not amazed.

When it had twice happened again, she said, 'I prefer Hesta.'

'Tell them. Some of the older ones, though, may like to retain formality.'

Just before they moved into the town from the shore, they passed two lovers having sex. Despite November, they were lying on a red blanket in a shelter, and they were half naked.

Something unusual after all.

A woman drew level. 'Oh, Mr Hassinger. What it is to be young.'

The girl came with a low cry.

As the couple lay still, the woman went closer and pulled the blanket up around them both. 'Don't you get cold now, ducks.'

'Thanks,' said the young man.

To Hassinger, the woman added, 'Me and Bill haven't done it outdoors for twenty years.'

'There's always the summer,' he said.

The restaurant was quite small.

No one else was there. A black girl, whom Hassinger called Adèle, waited on them deftly.

They had prawn cocktails, fish and chips, blackcurrant pie and custard.

As they were drinking the brandies Hassinger had asked for, the Duchess passed the window, wheeling her baby in its pram. The seagull was not today wrapped up, but sitting duck-fashion, its beak poking round the pram hood.

They did not pay for the meal.

Up through the town then, in the diamond air, towards the clock tower.

People in the shops, on the streets, turning and gazing at them. Now and then someone approaching. Shaking Hassinger by the hand. 'Hassinger . . . Miss Web.'

'Hesta,' she said.

'Hesta. That's with an A, isn't it.'

They went into the supermarket. A manager came up and gave Hesta a box of chocolates. She thanked him. He put it in a bag for her. She carried it. It felt peculiar. The sort of thing she had mistakenly bought for Stephanie in childhood, before she grasped that Stephanie was afraid of chocolate.

Everything was almost everyday.

If you had not known. It might have passed.

They went into a pub, not the Crab, and sat at a table. Hassinger drank schnapps and Hesta a glass of Perrier.

A girl advanced and put before Hesta a slim silver ring, the type of ring Hesta wore, but with a tiny emerald in it.

'Hesta, I'd like you to have that. We make jewelry in the shop.'

Hesta picked up the ring. It seemed word had gone round about the use of her name.

Hassinger said, 'Put it on, Hesta. The middle finger, I think.'

It fitted.

'There's a dress in red velvet,' said the girl. 'I'll send it to you. You're a ten, I think.'

Hesta examined the girl's face. She was about twenty-one, tall and strong, practical-looking and prosaic.

'Yes, size ten. Thank you.'

'Thank *you*. Hassinger,' said the girl, 'my brother really rates the new flat. Great to get him down here.'

228

Incomprehensible. Not quite so ordinary. Actually bizarre.

Walking up the street, and people standing there, in the road that had no traffic, beyond a pair of bicycles. A child ran out, put a daffodil into Hassinger's grip, ran away giggling.

It was too late or soon for daffodils. This one was formed of silk.

On a corner, a man came out of a baker's. He was in his forties, in a grey anorak, balding, with spectacles. Two bags hung from his hands, and he was bowed over with them.

'Jim,' said Hassinger.

The man glanced up. His youthful middle-aged face was puffy, the glasses like two enormous tears pushed from his eyes.

'Oh, Mr Hassinger. Is it today? I didn't realize. I'm sorry – '

'This is Hesta.'

'Oh, Miss Web. How nice to meet you.'

Hesta looked at him. She felt a curious sense of recognition.

'Jim lives in the Lane,' said Hassinger. 'He makes excellent tea.'

Hesta, static.

Jim said, 'It's not far, Miss Web.'

All around, watching, the weird mad town full of gulls, ghosts and knives. What was this to be? Was Hassinger the pimp and she the entertainment? Was this the *catch*?

Jim was patient, gazing at her. Middle class, repressed 'manners'.

'It's my father, you see,' he said.

(Phaedra said, 'People want to, Hesta. Tell you things.')

An experiment? Hesta began to walk with Jim along the road, Hassinger left behind, the crowd, watching, the knives of sunlight glinting.

End of the Line

Jim wanted to talk? He was silent.

Hesta reached out and took one of the bags from him. Then, 'Oh no, Miss W—'

'It's too heavy for you.'

The bag was not heavy.

'It's just bread and some sausage rolls. I go for supper with my Mrs Waring and Mrs Potter on Thursdays.'

He had not straightened up.

The Lane slid through the shops. The cottages had been built in the third year of the twentieth century. He unlocked a door.

His hall was barely wide enough to let them pass. Inside the room was a wonderful wallpaper, gold and rose and cream. Jim said, lifting his face a fraction, 'It was a card I once sent my mother. She loved that card. I had colour photo-copies made, lots of them, of the card. Stuck them on the walls.'

She sat in the armchair he offered her. He went bustling to make her a cup of tea.

There were heaps of books, on chairs, on the floor, and a jigsaw, half-accomplished, on a table, depicting a steam train above a field of poppies. A large rodent cage stood open. As Hesta sat waiting for Jim to return, a huge white rat, sleek as satin and with strawberry eyes, rambled over the carpet, went into the cage, used its straw, and came out again.

Jim entered with a teapot clasped in a black cosy that might have been a fisherman's hat.

'It's very kind of you to come round,' he said, laying out the tea things with mild fussy conscientiousness. 'Do you take milk?'

'Yes, thank you.'

Kind. They would be kind. She was *being* kind.

Why the recognition? Why had she gone with him? Experiment. First day at school. College? Growing up.

The rat advanced, and climbed Jim's trouser-leg on to his lap. 'This is Tom,' said Jim. 'Jerry's sunning himself in the garden.' He stroked the rat's head, and the puffy teary face flushed with blissful quietness. 'Smashing pets. They sleep in my bed. I used to be frightened I'd roll over and squash them. But I always wake up. And they're quick. When I had more hair, they used to groom me. Reckon that's why it's gone.'

As Jim poured the tea, presumably – Jerry – darted through the door. He was identical to Tom, although not for Jim.

'He likes a drop of tea, does my Jerry.'

Jim and Jerry shared the cup, while Tom lay draped and seemingly lifeless over Jim's knee.

Is it Lulu? Was she somehow being reminded of Lulu?

In the far corner, behind the rat cage and the books, a red telephone with push buttons was drawn up close, in a coil of wire, to the telephone point in the wall.

Besides this, also on the floor, was a cardboard box. A stack of letters lay inside.

'I see you're looking at it, Miss Hesta. That's the bane of my life.'

'What?'

'The telephone. And – those.'

Hesta said nothing.

She felt nothing.

The leopardess is made of stone.

And against this stony shore the sea could rush, could cast itself down, break open, and be formed anew.

Softness devours. Strength gives back.

Though you never must return the blow, the cheek you turn must be hard enough to hurt at that second blow.

The surgeon who heals, cuts.

The god who grants miracles is displayed in icy marble.

The Asian shop. *That* was the recognition. The woman with her black hair falling loose, the mugger, the attack of ice-cream.

'I said it was my father, Miss Hesta – Hesta, may I?'

'Yes.'

Was the recognition *fathers*?

'I feel so disloyal to tell you. But, I can, of course. Talk to you. I've never said a word against him. Not to Mrs Waring or Mrs Potter – seventy-one and seventy-eight – wonderful old girls – they're my friends from the garden club. And there's Mrs Ellis too, she's ninety-six. I take her out in my little Morris. I prefer the company of women. I loved my mother very much. But Gerald, my pa. Well, he was harsh.

He made her life a bit of a misery, frankly. And mine.'

She said nothing. Her face showed nothing. She listened.

'My mother was only fifty when she died. Never had a day's illness. She was coming back from her office, as she always did, Friday night. She didn't have to work, you understand. It was what he called her *pin money*. But she valued her independence, I think. Brain haemorrhage. It must have been very quick. People thought she was asleep. She went right through, and was found dead at Cockfosters, the end of the line.'

Jerry got into the teacup.

'He does that, when the tea's gone. Look at you, old chap. I don't know.'

Jim sat there, holding a white rat in a cup, but the funniness had melted, because his face, that the rats filled up with light, was sweaty and sickly again, like that of someone with food-poisoning.

'I'll be brief, Hesta. My father's a bastard. Gerald. His name. When I had my mother I was all right. He'd bullied me since I was a lad. More or less forced me into the only job he thought I could cope with, library work, pushed me to take library exams – I used to get so nervous I'd vomit. Never passed, of course. Silly, for a full-grown man. He told me I was useless. Had a nervous breakdown in the finish. He said I should have been in the war, like him. That would have put me right. Made a man of me. My mother used to – well, she protected me. She'd get round him. She understood.'

Jim looked at the rat as if he had forgotten it was Jerry.

'After she died, I had to seek psychiatric help. I came

234

down here on an outing. Well, obviously, I stayed. I've been all right, since then. Till this last year.'

Jim looked at the phone now, the red phone, red for danger.

'I felt I had to keep in touch with him, my father. He's getting on. He kept reminding me of that. Seventy-eight, like Edith, Mrs Potter. He's got arthritis badly. He phones me every night now. Between five and nine. If I'm not here, he phones until I am, and *then* I get it. Where were you? Fine son you are. He writes to me every week. Those are the letters. He wants me to go back to Hampshire and live with him. He bought his retirement house there, you see. I'd have my own room. He says it's my duty.'

Hesta waited.

'Gerald's got plenty of money. He could afford to get some sort of professional help. He doesn't need me. He doesn't – he doesn't *like* me. He told me that often enough. But what can I do? I know what will happen. He'll just grind me away. And my boys – Tom, Jerry – ' panic flooded Jim's face – 'he doesn't like animals. Says they're dirty. He'd never even let Ma have a cat. He's told me straight, get rid of those filthy vermin, they'll give you some disease. I couldn't take them, if I went to him. And he keeps on and on. He can't manage. I'm his son. The letters – there.'

Hesta turned and looked at the box.

Jim put the two rats carefully into his chair and went to the box and took out the top four letters. Three were neatly opened, the fourth had been left sealed.

'It's always the same. This one – I just couldn't look at it. But it sits there, gnawing away at me.'

Jim took a letter from its envelope.

' "Dear James, No news from you, as ever. Your selfishness never ceases to astound me. To think of those years I supported you, your phase, as I call it, of parasitism. And now, when my every movement is intolerable pain, you can't even pick up a pen." '

Jim hung there, in space. He lifted the letter towards the wall that he had papered with the duplicated card his mother had loved.

'He says I've got to face up to my responsibilities. He says I owe it to him. *He* made me have that phone. I didn't want it. He paid for it. He's got a five-bedroomed house that overlooks a golf course. He says I'd be better off there. I wouldn't, Hesta. I'd die. But it's the guilt. The way he goes on. I'll have to—'

Hesta rose.

She walked past Jim towards the door.

When she reached the telephone, she stooped, and ripped out the line from the wall and from its insides.

'Oh God – ' said Jim. He dropped the letters and picked up the rats and held them to his face.

Hesta took all the letters, there were very many, and tore each of them across two or three times. She said, 'Use some scissors. Then they can go in the rats' straw.'

Jim shakily laughed. He said to Tom and Jerry, 'Make wee-wee and poo-poo on Gerald.' The weight was off him. He stood straight.

Hesta took the last, sealed envelope.

'Is there a pen?'

'A Biro somewhere – yes, by my jigsaw.'

Hesta wrote across Jim's name and address NOT KNOWN HERE. RETURN TO SENDER.

Simplistics. Tea cosies. Ice-cream. Knives. (Mousetraps?) What works best.

Three

'From the land, the sea is no different.'

'No?'

'Not safe, as it appears to be. It can come in, devour everything, like a lion. Just as with a ship. I've been under the waves, Hesta.'

'What colour were they then?'

'It was at night. Black. With stars broken inside them.'

'You survived.'

'What do you think?'

Part of the long window could be undone.

They looked down from the house, across the town, to the promenade, the sea, and darkness.

'Where do you come from?' she asked.

'Places where they ask me, from where have I come. And in one of them, the sea is higher than the land.'

'That's possible?'

'Yes.'

She had stayed a long while, on the beach. She walked as far as the pier, and then as the Victoria Hotel, and looked up from below. She thought she glimpsed Catsmeat's golden hair in an upper window. Perhaps not.

The sun set behind her, as she walked back.

Sea grey. Caps of cream like old curtain lace, and filmy greenness extinguishing. Then the cold sky turned a clear hot orange, fading up like smoke into violet. And the sea reflected, a chameleon, lying graciously. The sea was not any such colour, not even when she came in wearing red—

Hesta lingered on the promenade until the last light went.

Reaching the steps up from the town, she climbed to the house. Blackness had settled, but the electric lamps burned in the many panes of the long window, which seemed usual, as if she had returned to it for years.

Warily she entered the – his – their? – room.

Men and women came, he had told her, from the town, to clean this house, and to bring food, to put alcohol and juices into the fridge.

The fire was burning, and two bottles of red wine stood warming on the hearth.

He sat in the other chair, his back to her.

'I did it. What I was supposed to do. I suppose I did.'

'You were a help to him,' said Hassinger, and not seeing his face, she could hear, as before, the foreignness of his accent, and his voice.

'It's rather simple, isn't it?'

'Shouldn't it be?'

'What is *it*?'

He said, 'A sort of ministry, if you like.'

'You said this would answer my questions.'

'It has.'

She walked round the chair and stood looking at him. 'Like a priest?' she said.

'You took the guilt out of his hands,' said Hassinger, 'whatever you did.'

'It wasn't anything to me.'

'That's how you're able to do it. If you had any involvement, any qualms, you'd be no use.'

'And you?' she said.

'The same. Priest and priestess.'

'If I don't want all this.'

'Then you will leave.'

'I don't believe that.'

'Others have done so. Again, if you don't want to stay – you will be useless. You must consent. Be comfortable with it. Or it won't work.'

It was then he rose, massing up over her, so large, tall, solid, and his eyes that she was quite aware might appear terrible, but none of it alien to her. She might have seen him every day. She knew him better – than her father.

Going to the window, he undid the moveable section, and she stood beside him, and they looked down to the ocean as it floated them through the night.

She could always try to catch the train tomorrow.

But as this thought occurred to her, she laughed.

What train? Did it even exist?

'Some of this house is a ruin,' he said, 'but there are a few rooms you might like to see.'

'You mean, now it's my house, too. Is it?'

'Unless you prefer somewhere else. The town's full of accommodation.'

'Or Skilt's.' He said nothing, and Hesta, who had so much the knack of that herself, seemed compelled to speak, as

241

others so often did, in her presence. 'What is Skilt – Phaedra said, the beginning.'

'The guide, perhaps,' Hassinger replied.

'The cheque book,' said Hesta. 'Is that Skilt's money?'

'Mine.'

'And the bombsite – you won't let anyone build on it—'

'No one is permitted to do so.'

'You own it all, you said.'

'I misled. It's been given to me. Let me show you the rest of the house.'

The door that gave from Hassinger's room did not go into another en suite bath.

Coming to the bedroom, she had not halted or wondered. When he had said, *Given to me*, she had not thought – *And me?*

The leopardess tells by signs and scents, and the priestess by the writing on the walls.

The walls in the massive room, which clearly was two or three rooms knocked together, were covered in shelves which held not books, but *things*. Oil lamps glimmered on them all, ready lit, shimmering like water.

The bottles predominated at first. They were black, livid deep green, opaque blue, all crusted by barnacles.

Inside them, the messages.

'You collect messages in bottles,' she said.

'This place collects them. They come here.'

On a table under the shelves stood a huge broken jar, a Nebuchadnezzar. And by it a brown vitreous flask.

He showed her how to look inside with the jeweller's glass.

We are going down.

'It sank?'

242

'She sank. The ship is feminine, like the sea herself.'

'Why?'

He smiled, and there was a fearful attraction in it. But seeing this, she only knew it for himself, an aspect of him. No allure, no threat.

'What stronger power is there? To begin with, everything powerful was female.'

She read, *You who find us, leave us in peace.*

'What does it mean?'

'That he – or she – knew they would be drowned. They didn't want their graves disturbed.'

'How could they think of that, then?'

'Strange thoughts come in the moment of death.'

'How do you know?' she said.

'Because I've imagined death. The ship was the *Titanic*.'

'Then – ' Hesta said, 'they've been discovered. How could they be sure?'

'Sometimes the messages arrive here long after.'

'What do you mean?'

'What do you think I mean?'

'That they communicate – ' she waited, then said, 'after they're dead. That doesn't happen.'

'Of course not, Hesta. And perhaps the dead cosily believe they were never alive.'

She shrugged, and he let her go alone, under the shelves of bottles. There were other tables, with bowls of coins on them. She ran her fingers, one with the gifted ring on it, through these. They had no meaning for her, they were dull and dim. Then a silver coin surfaced against the silver ring. 'What's this?' she called back.

243

'Roman.'

She saw the weathered head of the deity. The coin fell back.

There were bowls of buttons, too. The brass buttons from the navy sleeves of captains. Garnets from some woman's dress, mosaic from a rich man's coat.

Low down on the shelves, here where three oil lamps had been lit together, a statuette, a being in black substance, raised one arm.

'What's *this*?'

But Hassinger had gone away and left her there.

Hesta looked at the statue. She thought of a guiding god, less careful even than on the coin. The Phoenicians had traded with Cornwall, and storm-blown from their course, sunk here, perhaps. Or some Egyptian craft, for hadn't someone said that the Egyptians visited Britain. Or it was Roman like the coin.

Its ugly smeared face was full of smouldering dynamism.

Though he was not ugly, and his features had not been smoothed away, Hassinger . . . was like this.

Had he too been drawn here in a ship, a female ship, a *she*, pulled against the shore. Imagining death. The star-smashed waves.

On an unvaluable plate, roughly painted with fruit, a transister radio stood, leaking water, little sparks cracking along its edges. It was barnacled like the bottles, and the god. It was working, a buzz of sounds came from it. A label on the shelf read: *Batteries recharged indefinitely by the sea.* But she could not detect what came out of it, if it were words, or music, the jargon of the here and now – or something caught

244

in past time. She did not identify the writing on the label as being his.

There was a starfish glittering with gold. Perhaps the gold was real. The label read, *Is there gold at the bottom of the ocean?* Odd, this. The writing was again not his, and yet it looked – similar to a calligraphy she had once known.

A champagne glass, the kind shaped like a saucer on a stem. Barnacled at the rim only. Intact.

Fish, mummified, peculiar in form, the tint of sardines, but one yellow, and one with a horn.

A map drawn on wood. *No place on earth*, the label said. (Again, the handwriting seemed familiar.)

A large egg too big to be real. A genuine fake?

Bones.

Picture frame, very ornate, once gilded, with a new picture, constructed from knots of jet black seaweed and fisher's rope.

Coral, a foot in diameter, in the shape, unmistakably, of a bull.

Glove of leather, with limp fingers, and on one a silver ring, but not like the silver ring she wore tonight. The label said: *All that remains of a woman's hand, flesh, skeleton, washed away.*

And in the corner, here, papers and sketches, artefacts and facts, paintings on the wall, and a gramophone record, *Perhaps from 1910. It plays, but only makes a sound like the sea.*

Hesta looked up. At the paintings.

She saw, past the ancient cartographies and sea-logged photographs, the ships suspended in bottles, the half tiller, the rudder, the rib of a whale, a contemporary colour Xerox, of the very kind Jim had employed to reproduce as wallpaper the card his mother had loved.

The picture was evocative, sea-coloured. A temple drifting on water. Underneath someone had written in a new, round, careful, immature hand, *Showed it to Mr Marks. He said wishy-washy*. And then there were two other lines.

Cast not your peals before a swine
And I mean you, and I mean mine.

And a coiled signature, a snake of a J, with a dot after it that was an Egyptian eye.

Hesta turned. She walked back through the long wide room. By the doorway, Hassinger was trimming the wick of the first lamp.

'Hassinger,' she said. 'Janey's picture's on the wall.'

He straightened. In the oil lamplight, his cold eyes were laved by gold, as if from the depths of the ocean.

'Yes.'

'You know Janey.'

'I have only met her once, in your company.'

Hesta waited. Then she said, 'She did that painting when she was fourteen. I remember. The teacher upset her, Lulu dealt with that. Then Janey wrote the poem.'

Hassinger said, 'I was sent the copy of the picture when she was fourteen.'

'Who – ' Hesta recoiled: '*Lulu*.'

'Yes.'

Hesta said, 'And Lulu told you about me, too.'

'For a long while.'

'The books – even the soap – that's how you know.'

'That's how.'

Hesta said, 'And now tell me why.'

'Janey might have been the one. But she wasn't. That was soon clear.'

'And I am.'

'It seems so.'

'Instead of Janey. A *substitute* for Janey.'

Hassinger stood, filling her eyes. Finally, after several moments of silence, he told her. 'Janey is my daughter.'

· *Tell Tale*

Within a pool of soft electric light, the cat was playing with a catnip mouse. Lulu and Janey watched her with respectful, almost religious attention. The play did not last very long, but the old cat, glossy as a walnut, the colour of a ginger bee, enjoyed it. Play done, she washed her paws, and rolled over.

Janey went to the cat and rubbed her face on the smooth belly.

'She's lovely.'

'She is. Aren't you?' said Lulu, to the cat.

Purring, the cat lay back into sleep.

Outside, a long silver sound, rain fell.

Janey sat on the floor. It was about one in the morning. 'Mum,' said Janey. 'I betrayed Hesta. Didn't I?'

'No. You were forced to say what you did.'

'It was when she said about the cat—'

'I know. Under torture, very few people can hold on. And if you can't, you shouldn't try. They'll get what they want. Cut your losses.'

'But you said she couldn't get us thrown out any way—'

'She can't. And our cat is perfectly safe. But you couldn't know that then.'

248

'Tell tale tit,' said Janey.

Lulu laughed. 'Not at all. Stop worrying. Hesta is quite all right. Stephanie's the one who'll get into trouble. She could have found out where Hesta is in lots of ways.'

'I was frightened,' said Janey, 'you'd go round and kill her.'

'Because she hit you? Yes, it's tempting.' Lulu sat back, her face itself the mask of a great cat. 'But I'll leave it to them.'

Janey said, 'The town? What do you mean?'

'Oh, they'll give her a hard time. I told you how partisan they are. A close-knit community. The run-around, that's what she'll get.'

'I'm sorry to go on,' said Janey. 'I said it all when I came in.'

'Say it as often as you need to,' said Lulu. 'When you do, I'll just remind you that it's all right.'

'You're sure?'

'I'm sure. Perhaps it was meant, for you to tell Stephanie, I mean. Then she can go away quickly and waste lots of time and money, and realize that Hesta really has got free of her for good, and then she'll be, my *God*, a *bad* mother.'

Janey giggled. 'The mother from hell.'

'Exactly.'

'Can we have,' said Janey, 'cheese on toast?'

'Yes, let's. There's a wonderful old horror film at two. *Castle Dracula*. No school tomorrow, yes?'

'*Yes*.'

Like a child of eight or nine, Janey beamed at Lulu.

'We could go to the British Museum,' said Lulu, 'and

Romeo and Juliet's on at the National. Fancy that?'

'*Yeah.*'

'It's that actor you like as Romeo. The one with black hair.'

Janey had never questioned how, without apparent prior notice, Lulu could get the best seats for a play. Maybe she booked up earlier, and kept them for a surprise.

As Janey sliced tomatoes and lettuce heart and cut cheese, she looked at her mother. To Janey, Lulu was the most beautiful woman in the world. Not beautiful as Hesta was, not beautiful as she, Janey, could begin to see that she herself was, but beautiful as – life.

'Tell me—'

'Tell you?'

'About *him*.'

'Ah. Who could that be?'

'My father,' said Janey.

Lulu turned the toasting bread. 'You see,' she said, 'you've never told anyone about him, have you?'

'No, I never have. You said you didn't want me to.'

'Not even Hesta.'

'No.'

'So you're not a tell tale, are you?'

Janey thought. She weighed it, her terrified admission under the willow, tree of tears. This other deeper secret she had kept for ever, and would for ever, unquestioningly, keep.

'I'm not.'

'What shall I say then?'

'About how you met.'

Lulu smiled. 'You know it by heart.'

'Almost. I want to.'

When had it first been told? Rocking Janey at the breast, probably. More requirement then, to speak of it. Polished away by now, any sharp edge that stuck into the heart. Tart, sweet memory.

'It was in that town, at the seaside, of course,' said Lulu. 'When I lived there in the old house.'

'With the long window with two hundred panes of glass,' said Janey.

'That's right. And you could open part of the window, and look out, straight down to the sea. And one summer morning, in the Season, I looked, and I saw this perfect yacht with a white-blue sail, coming in. The sea was all broken by little white dabs of foam, and the wind was blowing, a warm wind. The sail bent like a wing.'

'And that was *his* boat.'

'Yes.'

Janey stood, thinking of it. For her, it had a piquancy, a sadness, that Lulu did not seem to feel. It was like the lament in Purcell's *Dido and Aeneas*. Lulu had lived in the town. She had worked in a shop, she said, and made good money, and rented the house, which, later apparently, had passed to someone to whom it belonged by right of inheritance.

But gazing from her high window to the azure ocean, like Dido perhaps, Lulu had seen her predestined lover sail towards the land.

Later on, she met him. It was in that pub, the Crab, a sort of party, this was how the story presented it, and someone introduced him to her.

'Say his name. How he didn't have a first name.'

251

'Van Hassin.'

Janey repeated the name. 'It was Dutch.'

'Maybe.'

'And the moment you looked at him—'

'The moment I looked at him I fell in love with him.' Lulu turned, and snapped her fingers and laughed. 'Like *that*. And then the other thing happened.'

'But you weren't frightened.'

'Oh no. A doctor had told me years before it might. And another doctor had told me it wouldn't. So, either way.'

Van Hassin had been there, some kind of celebrity at the party, handsome and blond, tall and powerful. And the blue eyes. When Lulu spoke of those it was, even now – did she know this? – as if no one else ever, in the history of the world, had had blue eyes.

Then Lulu's stomach had lurched, and when she went into the ladies', there was blood in her panties. She had not, until that moment, at the age of twenty-eight, menstruated.

Lulu did not tell Janey, had never, could never tell Janey, that in this moment, she knew utter bewilderment, and felt the earth cracking under her.

For Lulu had been by then, for ten years, the priestess of the town. And an essence of her ministry was her celibacy, as she had always understood from those who explained to her her rôle in the beginning.

She knew, crouched there in the little ladies' loo of the Kissing Crab, shut off by its cubicle from the celebration which, after hours, excluded the in-Season visitors, that the priest who had come to serve with her, the man from the sea, was more to her than any man.

A normal biological urge rushed through Lulu, weird as madness, for she had never felt it before. And in sudden acid amusement, where the holiday-makers had scratched on the walls *I luv Mick* and *I luv Darren*, Lulu wrote with a lipstick, *Love makes the world go round, so for God's sake fall in love and keep us moving.*

As she went on with her tale, the antique tale now familiar as any often-vocalized myth, Lulu deftly wove her truths and lies together.

For though she wished her daughter to know the heart of this matter, its clandestine elements must be withheld. To partake of such things Janey had not been formed, she – and they – would keep her safe from them.

'We spent the end of the summer together.'

'What did you do?'

'We walked. Along the cliffs, on the beach. He took me sailing. He said after the summer he'd sell the yacht. We lay and listened to music. I cooked enormous meals. I was quite slim then, but that started to change.'

'And he loved you.'

'Yes, he loved me. He often told me so. He wrote me the poem.'

'Yes, the poem.'

'But after the summer, I knew, I had to acknowledge, that I wanted his child.'

'You'd been careful until then.'

Lulu smiled. She looked under the grill, at the toasting supper. 'There was no chance I could be pregnant. But I wanted to be.'

She did not say to Janey, less a lie than a truth omitted,

that she and Van Hassin had never made love. That, although they had held each other, and kissed each other, these embraces were not sexual.

'We discussed it,' said Lulu. 'I made him see that my paramount need was a child.'

And she did not say to Janey that this had meant she could no longer be what she had been. That, if she were to conceive and carry and bear a child, she was no more the priestess. Even so, there had been no necessity to go away from the town. The town, they of all the world, had grasped and condoned her need. But she had wanted to go. Once she was sure that Janey had lodged inside her, she went.

'Why did you leave him?' said Janey, wistfully. She must mean too, Why did you never stay with him and let me have him also, as a father.

'There were things he had to do. I couldn't be part of them. I couldn't hold him back. I knew that. I'd always known. It was selfish of me to demand a child. But we *are* selfish. How else can anyone survive.'

'I don't mind,' said Janey, 'so long as he didn't hurt you – make you unhappy.'

'Oh, no. He'd never have done that.'

'And he knows about me.'

'Yes, you know he does.'

Janey said, 'Can I see the letter again – the letter and the poem.'

Lulu turned her head. The fall of her arboreal hair, the voluptuousness of her fleshy, lovely face, her eyes. 'Take the food through, and I'll go and get them.'

As she opened the drawer, to which, since they were her

private things, Janey would never have gone, Lulu heard the rain flowing on and on. The noise of moving waters, but not like the ocean.

She brought the letter to Janey, and the poem.

Janey read them, several times over, as her supper cooled beside her.

'I love this bit.'

'About the eyes.'

'*Your* eyes.'

Janey read the lines again:

> *Between your jade eyes and the sea*
> *Is only a little distance.*

Janey raised her head. 'I don't look like him.'

'No. You're more like me – the way I was.'

'It's what I want, to be like you.'

'But you're certainly talented – the way he . . . was.'

'You don't know where he is now?'

Time again for the one concrete lie. The huge lie.

'I don't,' said Lulu. A parody and opposite of the phrase of marital consent.

'In the letter, he says, "Janey is a very beautiful and gifted child." ' She recited it without pride or embarrassment.

'You were. You are.'

Janey put down the two pieces of paper, and began to eat ravenously.

Outside, the rain fell on and on and on, as if to wash the world away.

Lulu thought, And are you, my love, telling her now, just as I've told Janey? Is it tonight?

He would not write to her about it. There had been only

one letter. Like the one personal letter she had sent to him, when Janey was fourteen, with the copy of the painting and the little verse, cranky, quaint and witty, worthy of a Janey who had also written, *Sticks and Stones can break your bones. Words can only break your heart.*

She was too fragile a flower, Janey, to crush with too much knowledge. And she was born for living. To make songs and pictures, perhaps to make children. It was Hesta with her torch of hair, Hesta, *expected*, whose school bag never contained a towel or tampon, whose eyes were those of a leopard. Hesta was the inheritrix. And through her, Janey had been spared.

Twenty minutes into the horror film, after the villagers had warned the travellers to avoid the castle, and as bats circled looming, crumbling towers, the phone rang.

Lulu went to answer. Presently she said, 'It's all right, Janey. It's my obscene caller. I'll take it through into the bedroom.'

'But he never calls after four.'

'I think it's a bit of an emergency.'

In the bedroom, balancing her mug of tea on the bedside table, Lulu asked him what was wrong.

'Sorry to ring you so late – I tried not to—'

'That's all right, darling.'

'I know you said not after four—'

'You've always been a very good boy.'

'I didn't know who else to turn to. It's my mother. She died today.'

'Poor boy,' said Lulu, 'go on.'

'She was everything to me,' said the obscene caller, his voice breaking. And as he talked, the tears burst from him, as the orgasm usually did, and Lulu gently guided him towards the shore, as always she had done.

Four

'So you loved her?' Hesta said. She spoke imperiously, while he poured the warm red wine into the amber and blue glasses.

'I loved her.'

'But you let her go.'

'To be here is my function.'

'That was more important.'

'Yes.'

'Your *ministry*.'

He brought her a glass.

He said, 'You also have a choice.'

'Then I'll leave, too.' She was antagonistic. He had anticipated that. He said nothing. Hesta drank a little wine.

They were standing by the black table, where the painting of the being in red turban and veil lay rolled up. Beyond the window, and through the chimney, rain had begun to fall.

'But *you* broke this law of celibacy, and still stayed,' said Hesta.

'Only technically.'

'Technically? You got her pregnant.'

Hassinger said, 'Intercourse is not essential, Hesta.'

Hesta stared. 'How else? The stork?'

259

Hassinger laughed. He said, 'To tell you the details, Hesta, isn't to proposition you. Be reassured. You must understand that. We, you and I, are not predestined lovers.'

'Like you and Lulu.'

Again he said nothing.

She said, 'I don't want a lover.'

'Of course you don't, Hesta. You're better fitted for this place than I was.'

After that, he told her, succinctly, flatly, what they had done, Lulu and he. That to masturbate, since it need involve no physical partner, was sometimes permissible. That Lulu had then been given the result of this action. That she had inserted it within herself simply by using her finger. They had gone through this procedure four times, before it was successful.

He did not, now, analyse for Hesta the ban upon sexual union, that its unique energies, shored up, augmented individual power. This was an ancient belief, integral to the fact of a priest-king and a priestess-queen, who represented their people before God.

Nor did he recount the anecdote from that one, long letter Lulu had sent him, fourteen, fifteen years later, of how, when first visiting her GP in London, the man had informed her she could not remotely be pregnant, since her hymen was incompletely ruptured.

'A virgin birth,' Lulu had written with obvious glee. 'Is that how she did it, Mary?'

Which between them, Lulu and Hassinger, who had been Van Hassin (his yacht the *Flying Dutchman*? Perhaps saved in fact by the love of a pure woman?), was a joke with ramifications. For to the priests of the town, the miracle of a virgin non-carnally inseminated by God, might be credible, and, in the proper circumstances, perfectly to be believed.

But she was jealous. Did she know it?

And – of what?

Alone in the small room, the quilt pulled round her, all its glow of colours, the little fire switched on, drinking the wine.

Was it Lulu she was jealous of?

Hesta had never felt the pangs of love-desire, described for her everywhere, on film, in music, in literature, by the word of mouth of others. She knew that she had not felt, and did not feel it now. So, not jealous of Lulu. Not jealous of lovers.

Of Janey, then? Janey who, it would seem, had never known her father. Less even of a father, Janey had had, than Hesta. And yet Hassinger *existed*. And Iain, somehow, did not. Not really.

Hesta curled on her side. She thought for a moment, of being a child, Stephanie gone, Iain gone. Hassinger towering over her, and her hand in his. X marks my window of two hundred panes.

Then, in rage, the cool still thinking rage by which she had had to live her life, Hesta closed him out.

Trains *did* run away from this town by the sea.

And if no one would stop her, or even if they tried, she might escape. She trusted her own wisdom, her own self. She had never been able entirely to trust anyone else.

End of Part Five

PART SIX

One

Train journeys in childhood had excited Geegee Peck, especially going to the seaside with Auntie May. Sometimes they had even taken the current cat, in a basket, sneaked it in with the landlady's connivance, good old Mrs Holly, or funny old Miss Ambleforth – both of whom, Geegee was well aware, had been younger then than he was now.

A lot of things were different then. He wouldn't have given you tuppence, let alone the two new shiny holiday half-crowns, for a whisky. No, lemonade for him, and Tizer, and Pepsi Cola. These drinks today, loved by millions, would have made him gag, and although he had treated himself to an alcoholic beverage from a trolley, now they had got here, he was going to treat himself to another.

The station was ramshackle and unswept, no one about, but inside the buffet a woman presided over the counter. He bought a sandwich with a tracery of fatty ham, and a single scotch.

'Rough old day,' said Peck to the woman.

'You're right there.'

'Must be dull down here, out of Season.'

'They come and go,' said the woman.

It was true. Just because the Season stopped, people went on living in a seaside town.

'Visiting my aunt,' said Peck. 'Thought I might see my niece down here. Supposed to be coming down, she is. But you know what these young girls are like.'

'Don't I just,' said the woman.

Geegee described his niece, her bright red hair, her slender youth.

Not a flicker. The woman said, 'If you was to say the Cool Stream Guards had been through here, I expect I wouldn't have noticed.'

Geegee had finished his whisky. Had he drunk it? He should be more careful. There was money *now*, but he ought to keep some back. *Plan for tomorrow*. That always made him laugh. His father had said that. And his father had run off with some barmaid and died two months later in bed with her, so his tomorrow had come rather fast and decidedly unplanned, after all.

'I'll have another,' said Geegee, 'for the cold. Got to go down into the town. Sea-front must be parky.'

'Oh, yes,' said the woman, filling his glass, scrupulously, to the legal mark.

'That's where she is, my aunt.'

'Down the town.'

'That's it.'

'Been here before?' asked the woman. She shot him one long bleak look, straight into the face. It struck Peck as quite odd. People rarely looked at you like that in England, straight on. Unless you had mortally insulted them, or otherwise taken them by surprise.

'No, as a matter of fact. Always meaning to visit. You know how it is.'

'Funny place, down there,' said the woman.

'Oh. How d'you mean?'

'Can't say. Out of Season. Funny place.'

'I always find people more friendly, outside London.'

'Maybe not here.'

'Keep to themselves,' he said.

'You could say that.'

Presently he realized he would not get anything else out of her. He was vaguely reminded of something, some sort of conventional behaviour, but could not think what.

Then she went off into a back room, and he heard her cutting more sad sandwiches for non-existent comers and goers.

Which was odd in itself, because he thought the railway supplied all that, but there you were.

He sat by the window, trying to eke out the second whisky. Beyond the glass, everything was grey and blustered by the wind, gulls and white garbage, uninviting. Staircases of Victorian villas rose to cliffs, and a sky full of rain.

Peck took out his wallet and removed the Polaroid the boy, Peecey, had given him.

It had been taken in a wine bar apparently, and was not very helpful, but better than for the missing man, for there was no photograph of him, for some reason. The wife had not been able to find one.

In the Polaroid, a skinny, smiling, middle-aged woman, with coarse, well-cut hair, sat at a table, with bottles and glasses, and next to her, the girl, who was called Hesta, with an A.

Hesta had rose-red hair, either dyed or tinted. She wa:
pale in her black dress, with the red irises to her eyes tha
Polaroids sometimes gave you in the wrong light.

Peck did not like her face. It was sharp and perhaps cruel
Bored and cold. Peecey had said she was a 'babe', but to
Peck's eyes she was only uncomfortable. He could se
nothing to her but trouble.

He left the photo, raised his glass against the window
stared into the last millimetre of fluid. It was bright red.

Peck's heart stopped. Started again, hurting him. You
bloody fool, it wasn't blood. For God's sake, no. It wa:
something over there, on the other platform, some blood-re
thing, waving.

Lowering his glass, Peck focused on the red, and saw i
was the long, long hair of a pale girl in a black dress.

'Well, I'll be – Christ, I'll be—'

Because it was *the* girl, the red-headed girl in the photo
graph, Hesta with an A.

Peck drained his whisky without noticing, stood up an
walked from the buffet, carrying his bag, astonished.

On the platform, the gulls went on screaming overhead
and he pretended to look up the line for a train.

The girl was just standing there.

He had better go over the bridge, since, if another train di
come, it would possibly be the one she wanted, she would ge
on it, and he would lose her, after this remarkable finding.

Not that he had wanted to find her.

He could see, from the glimpse he had snatched, that sh
was in fact what would have been called a stunner. And tha
only made her aura of trouble worse. More dangerous.

But all this was rubbish, and he now was trotting briskly to the steps, mounting them.

When he was halfway over the bridge, the Hesta girl turned abruptly, and walked off the platform, into the booking hall.

Peck ran then, over the bridge, down the stairs, into the hall – and she had gone.

Outside, he saw her, she was striding quite fast, up the slope of one of those hilly ascending roads with the tall stuccoed houses and big bare trees.

Uphill, of course, it would be. Uphill all the way.

Peck followed at an advantageous distance caused mainly by lack of stamina.

They climbed up, and up, until the road levelled. The houses were yellowed, clambered with ivy, door paint peeling, dim nets in windows. Gulls on roofs, and there one stalking down the gutter – Peck gave it a wide berth.

The girl did not pause. She must be going somewhere specific, some address. There, just ahead, a small hotel with a board, The Lodge. But when she came to the Lodge, the girl went by, and any way, the board said the Lodge was closed.

They crossed into another road, this one, thankfully descending. Smoke came from a few of the chimneys, something you seldom saw nowadays. There were the usual things. A bicycle in a front garden. A cat posed on a balustrade. From a half-open winter window dripped the notes of a song Geegee knew from afternoons in pubs, 'Message in a Bottle'.

The road swung into another road, and the Hesta girl was climbing again, around a monkey puzzle tree, passing which you were supposed to keep silent, and certainly she did,

269

although Peck, struggling after, lugging the case, was grunting a little now. Then down again, and all at once he saw, over the down-flow of walls and gardens, to the lower part, the town, and so to the line of the terrible icy unkind sea.

Something, perhaps only tiredness, made Peck halt. In the cold day he was too warm. The girl was going on, a straight road, he could catch up again, maybe even overtake her. 'Excuse me, miss. I'm looking for the Hollies B and B.'

That sea. My God. How he'd loved it as a boy. But it had been blue, then. Like the sky.

The town seemed dishevelled. From here, he could make out boarded-up shops, deserted, broken-windowed buildings. And a bombsite.

Peck stared. There had been plenty of these in his childhood. They were everywhere. The undressed walls still with dying wallpaper, the sheared-through chimney breasts. And on the wasteland round about, poppies growing, and valerian, the flowers of peace and healing that fill the spaces where violent pluralized death has been.

This bombsite, however, went on and on, not downwards, but around – around in a semi-circle, like a broken ring. He was struck by the look of it, from his high vantage. Its regular form as much as the fact that no one had ever, in almost fifty years, cleared it up.

It was like a moat around a castle. Like a magic circle. Bloody peculiar.

Oh – sod it – sod, *sod*.

The girl had gone from sight.

Blast it. Fool. He had only taken his eyes off her for a moment—

Peck lumbered down the road, he looked in all directions – there was an alley she might have entered, and over there another road that turned off both left and right. Or there were all the houses she might have slipped into.

Peck made a note of the road. Victoria Rise.

He was ashamed of himself, but also glad.

At the bottom of the hill was a pub, and he went in. From a jukebox, or whatever they called them now, the same song was playing as he had heard up the street. 'Message in a Bottle'.

He ordered a double.

The man, in his shirt sleeves, was doing a crossword. Three old codgers sat over racing papers.

'Place called the Hollies B and B. D'you know it?'

'Not me,' said the publican.

'My niece is staying there. Something's come up. You know these young girls. Her mother says to me, you go down and sort it out. She's a lovely girl. Red hair.'

'Oh, yeah,' said the publican. 'Enlargement of adoringly religious feline.'

'Pardon?'

'Ten down. Enlargement of adoringly religious feline.'

'Sorry. No good at clever games.' Peck sighed. The whisky tasted to him more familiar than the moisture of his own mouth. 'Anywhere you can recommend to stay? Apart from the Hollies.'

'All shut,' said the man. 'Out of Season.'

'Down the town, then. By the sea.'

'You don't want to go there,' said the publican.

'Why's that?'

'Funny lot.'

'Oh yes? In what way?'

'They just are. And the shops are useless. My old woman goes into the big shopping centre two miles in. They've got everything there. You wouldn't catch her down *there*.'

He was beginning to get it now, what it sounded like – the woman in the buffet, and this man. The villagers near the haunted house or the château of the vampire. Don't go. They are strange, unfriendly. We can't stay. Avoid that place.

Geegee had finished his whisky. Why didn't they last? When he was twenty-five, he could make a double last a whole hour. He was less fanciful then, too.

'Magnificat,' said the barman, as Peck was going out.

'What – hotel?'

'Ten down.'

Across the ceiling stretched garlands of green with red plaster apples depending from them. Tinsel wove around the windows. And on the bar was a little plastic tree, decorated with silver and gold balls, and with a Father Christmas standing underneath holding a box for cancer research.

'My God,' said Stephanie. She laughed, the way she laughed now, high and sudden and soon over.

'Yeah,' said Martin.

'December the first tomorrow,' said the woman, amiably, at the bar. 'We like to get everything done early. And now the children come in the pub, they enjoy it.'

Outside the wind roared and the black sky raced. The stream of this beat against the village pub like a tide, but they had not reached the coast yet. Martin wanted to stop and eat first. The hotel he had located by phone sounded pretty useless to him. This might be their last decent meal.

Normally, he thought, Stephanie would have loitered in the village, which had quaint timbered shops with very elegant, clinging knitwear, and long scarves in loud, edible colours. Plus a ruined castle tower culturally up on a hill.

But Stephanie was not concerned with the village, the prospect of clothes, or somewhere healthy to eat.

She sat at the table in the pub's dining area, and picked at the place mat, which showed a fallen rose, red for the curtains and the carpet.

'What'll you have, Steph?'

'Just a drink.'

'You'd better eat something, baby.'

'All *right*.' She snapped at him as she had never snapped, not even when she had become angry. It was as if he irritated her now, but obviously that wasn't it. No.

Martin said, 'Take it easy, baby. Look, they do a salad. How about that?'

Stephanie glanced deadly yet brightly at the cold and furious sky. A memory disturbed her. Seventeen, and eating a coffee cake in the house of some friend – some *un*friend – who envied her figure and had led her astray.

Salad, crisp and chill. Salad without dressing.

She had already gained four pounds. That was drinking too much. But she needed a drink. And she had not eaten since . . . lunch yesterday.

'I'll have the vegetable lasagne,' said Stephanie.

'Wow,' said Martin, he grinned – as he thought, charmingly. 'Steady on.'

'Just shut up,' said Stephanie.

'Yeah. OK.'

When the woman had taken their order, he said, 'You're being very cruel to me, Stephie.'

'I've had good teachers,' said Stephanie, 'as it says in some book.'

'I hope we can work this out,' said Martin.

She had refused to sleep with him, although she had agreed that, in the hotel, they could share a room. She said she wanted to track down Iain, and she wanted to find Hesta. Both these aims should be reasonable, but of course they were not. For Stephanie loathed Iain and hated Hesta, and even to get the insurance for Iain's death she would do better to sit tight and do nothing.

Martin's private idea was that Stephanie had gone nuts, the way he had read women could do, pre-menopausally. Some HRT would sort her out, but it was too soon to suggest that, she'd probably throw something at him.

If Iain had vanished, then Iain had fallen off the platform of the rig and drowned. And the Company were hushing it all up it was lousy publicity. As for Hesta, if she had even come to this dump they were headed for (Janey just *might* have lied), no doubt she had moved on by now.

On the other hand, the need to get away from the London area and Penny, with her believer's gold cross and mooted up-the-duffness, had been paramount.

So far as the wine bar knew, he was in Tenerife. And of all the environs on earth, no one would look for brilliant, up-market Martin *here*.

Stephanie ate greedily.

Martin watched her, with vague distaste. When she spilt a drop of sauce on her jacket, she did not see, and when he reached to dab her with the napkin she flinched, snarling, 'I have to do it left-handed. Leave me alone.'

The woman at the bar was about fifty, overweight, but well got up and with black, stylish hair. As she had waited on them with such care, Martin discerned that she appreciated him, for in Martin's universe, no one did a thing for you unless they wanted to use you in some way.

He left Stephie to her coffee with cream – at least she didn't spoon sugar in it – and went to check the route with the older woman.

'Oh, you're going there?'

'Yeah. Bit rough, I should think.'

'Well, it is a bit run-down. Nice in the summer, of course. You get beautiful fish from there.'

'I can see me having to pop back here to you, for a decent steak.'

The woman laughed, as Martin thought flirtatiously, 'We're open eleven to eleven.' Stephanie rattled her cup in the saucer. 'Your wife's poor hand.'

'She's not. Just a friend.'

'How did that happen?'

'She broke her fingers. Not doing too well, her specialist said.'

'Poor girl. The air's very healthy where you're going. I expect it'll do her good. Stay wrapped up, though.'

Martin mentioned the hotel into which, over the phone, he had booked them. 'Any use?'

'Out of Season, a bit slow, I should say. You can't tell. Oh, there's a lovely story about that part of the coast. I've just remembered.'

'Yeah?' asked Martin, getting bored.

But the woman came around the counter with her coffee pot, and went to the table and filled Stephanie's cup again, and added more cream.

'I was just saying, you hear some lovely stories about the town there.'

Stephanie looked up. She was blank, as if the woman was not corporeal, and some other agency had helped her to coffee.

The woman seemed not to notice.

'There was this man – I can't tell you his name – oh, yes. No. It's gone. Just before the First World War. It was all a fishing town then. But he was a sort of – well, like a lord of the manor, you might say. And when all the young boys joined up to fight, he said he'd go too, to take care of them. Mostyn? Was that the name? Seems he got killed. Blown up, burned alive. Awful. When the young lads went home to the town, they had to say how he'd died.'

'Really cheerful stuff,' said Martin. 'Well, I guess—'

'He'd been something of a sight in the town, too, very handsome,' said the woman, as if, now, Martin had faded from the state of being, 'and he had this special foreign car. Of course, in those days, any way, cars were a rarity. Now, what do they call them – Bugatti, that's it. A Bugatti.'

Stephanie drank her second coffee with cream.

The woman said, 'About a year after he died in France, the locals started to see him, driving up and down in his car. And sometimes he'd lift his boater, like in the days when he was alive. But the car was all smoking, as if it had gone through the fire with him.'

'Amazing,' said Martin. 'Actually, we'd better—'

'One night the boats were out,' said the woman. She looked into Martin's face. Smiling. 'There was a storm. They lost one. The old feller was at the wheel, you see, he had a heart attack, and then there's just the boy, all alone on the sea. He starts to cry.'

Outside, the wind rushed. Such a wind, perhaps, that night, and the ocean black as tar, land nowhere. Nothing.

'Then, he sees a light, coming across the water. He thinks it's a ship. But no. It's the Bugatti, driving over the waves, with the headlamps blazing. And there's Moses – that was his name, Moses – Moses sitting there, tipping his hat. And when Moses turns his car around, the boat follows it, as if it was being given a tow. Back to the land. Back to the shore. Beached. The boy's safe. But the Bugatti drives away into the town.'

'Can we have our bill?' asked Martin. He had gone off the fat woman in a big way.

'Yes, my dear. Look, there it is, by your plate. Moses. That was the name. He had bright red hair, they said. It's a lovely story. But he really did live in the town. There's a big old house, all derelict now, I should think. I've seen a photo of him, somewhere, in his blazer and his boater. And the car.'

'Red hair,' said Stephanie.

She stood up. She marched over to the ladies' room and the door slammed left-handed.

'See she keeps warm, now,' said the woman to Martin.

He left a very small tip.

* * *

When Stephanie saw the pink hotel, she laughed one of her new laughs.

Martin made no comment. He drove into the parking lot.

It was about three fifteen in the afternoon, and the black sky merging towards a true darkness. Nothing else stood in the lot but for one enormous and incongruous white vehicle.

Martin got out of the BMW. He gazed across the empty space at the huge white car.

'That's a real classic motor. 1960s. American job. Yeah.'

Stephanie glanced. She was not inspired.

She stood on the parking lot, waiting.

'Look, Steph. Christ, I wonder who drives her. One rich fucker.'

'Martin, I'm cold.'

'You're certainly being cold to me, Stephie. Hang on. I just want to take a look.'

He walked off, towards the white American car poised there, alone, on the lot. And Stephanie took in, as if never before had she seen him, Martin's thinness, his graceless, angular swagger, the over-emphatic shortness of his hair, and when he turned, not looking at her, but at a light which had come on in the back of the ridiculous pink-ice-cream hotel, she saw how his hair receded, and how over-brown his tan was, and the mean narrowness of his unbright little eyes.

Chuck, Neil Bolton's 1958 Pontiac Chieftain, had been standing out quite some while now, in the winter weather. Rain and darkness had fallen on it. Going closer, you saw the smears over the sleek hide of it, and the dullness of its pivotal bronze streaks.

278

Martin Peecey was about thirteen feet away from the car, when the bizarre thing happened.

'*Fucking Christ—*'

Peecey jumped back. Even Stephanie raised her head.

In the last of the shadowy light, out of the two sides of the Pontiac, two vast white wings had sprouted, beating, rushing like a wind – and were about to dash the car upwards into the black sky.

'Hell – Christ –' Martin skidded on something and dropped to one knee.

Stephanie started to laugh again. But now it was an extended laughter, all loose, fluid, bubbling over, letting go.

'All right,' said Martin. 'Fucking seagulls.'

The two white, demoniacally angelic wings had separated in pieces, and soared away. Two streamers of gulls, squawking now, in raucous mirth, twenty or thirty birds; it was these, erupting from the car, that had formed the supernatural illusion.

'Christ, bloody car must be full of *shit*. He's left the windows open. Fucking *moron*.'

Stephanie went on laughing. To Martin she sounded hysterical. And when he saw that it was indeed gull droppings he had knelt in, he hated her.

'Shut up, you bitch. These pants cost me. Filthy fucking birds. Ought to poison them.'

He turned from the mystic Pontiac, no longer interested in it, and getting their bags from the boot of the BMW, herded the woman, giggling still, towards the hotel entrance. Above, the light went out.

On the lot, the Pontiac remained.

Although the exterior had been transcribed by weather, there was no bird excrement or other damage within. The smooth seats, a minute before full of gulls, had not been marked. Only one white feather lying, perfect, on clean leather.

From the window there was a view of the town below, a few small other windows burning, and the lamps greenish along the promenade, with the dead or comatose illuminations curlicued beneath.

Between here, and there, the bombsite.

This Victorian villa also overlooked the station, but the trains stopped at seven, and although they recommenced about six a.m., by then Roger Cover and Ann were awake. They always kept to a routine. They rose, used the bathroom, one after the other, performed their exercises, showered, one after the other, dressed.

As Ann swiftly put on her make-up, Roger Cover made the first entries on his lap-top computer. Then he went downstairs, and Ann made hers. After this, she followed, and they ate breakfast alone together in the small dining room (white toast and black coffee), swallowed their vitamins, and were ready for their day.

On any assignment they proceeded in the same manner.

During the morning they gathered whatever information was required and available. At lunch time, between twelve and one, they returned to their little, normally mediocre and rather dingy hotel, to which they had, at all times, access. Here they ate each a sandwich with a salad garnish, drank a glass of mineral water, and, going up to their room, entered details of everything on their computers.

The afternoon was spent as the morning had been. Unless an unusual amount of information had been received, in which case they dealt with this on the computers.

In the evening, at their hotel, they had dinner. Something light, a poached egg on spinach, a fillet of fish with asparagus, a half bottle of wine, and a pot of Earl Grey tea, without milk or sugar.

Between nine and eleven, they inserted any final imput into the machines, collected messages, and responded to them, did their nightly exercises, performed acts of personal hygiene, showered, lay down, and went to sleep.

Now, Roger Cover and Ann were sitting, each at the end of their individual single beds, paring and filing their nails. Both wore vests, and shorts, his grey and hers blue, the garments in which they exercised. Neither had sweated or was out of breath.

The room was very neat, and the lap-tops also sat, one by each pillow, both still ticking over as data was processed.

On a table by the window, however, a colourful display had been laid out. An angle-poise lamp illuminated some fifty odd postcards, set slightly overlapping, like a game of cards.

They came from many places, for example, India, the Middle East, Czechoslovakia and Romania, the Congo, even, China, and Loch Ness. Not all were contemporary, about half were printed with dates between 1910 and '14, or the 1890s, sepia ones these, or hand-tinted. The scenes too were various. Of châteaux and castles and palaces, mountains, inland waters, bays with ocean, forests, mosques, minarets and churches, ruins, ships, statues.

The messages on the postcards had all been meticulously copied by now. With no need to feign socially acceptable amusement or empathy, Roger Cover and Ann read them without expression or reaction.

Today I caught a whale but let it go. From the top of this tower I could see as far as America.

Sometimes there was a spider drawn in faded gold.

Your loving Daddy. Your Daddy. Daddy.

The burglary which the company had organized at Stephanie's house had brought in almost everything of Iain's and most of the discarded belongings, too, of Hesta, his daughter. The postcards, being of possible relevance, had been laid out, and now, for about five minutes every night, Roger Cover and Ann would study them.

Swam with a mermaid but she would keep singing – made an excuse and hurried off.

In this forest is a unicorn called Bill.

Your hair is red, my hair is, too.

You are Hesta, and your daddy loves you.

Ann had finished her nails just in front of Roger Cover. She went towards the bathroom for her shower.

'Tomorrow it's Sally Maclean?' she said.

'That's right, Ann.'

They seldom spoke; when they did, it was in trivia, or unnecessary questions, unneeded answers.

The wind blew past the guest house, empty of all but for its invisible caretakers, Roger Cover and Ann, and the ghost of Iain Jason Web.

Two

Really, what had he wanted out of life? Not much. Just to live.

Geegee Peck surfaced from a muddled dream of Auntie May and Tiger – the name of all the cats. It had been happy. He was about nine, he had been for a swim. The sea was blue, almost navy. And when he came back, she had bought two ices, and Tiger – who, in real life, had been prudently left asleep in the boarding house – was rolling on the sand.

'Auntie, this teacher, Mr Folks, he said, what do I want to be when I grow up. Johnny said he wanted to drive a bus. And Benjy wanted to go on the stage and tell jokes. But I didn't know.'

As he woke, he wondered if he had ever had this conversation. Adults were always asking kids, then, what they wanted to be. As if, at nine, you knew. Some did, probably. He seemed to recall a little girl who definitely had said, 'I want to be Boudicca.' Which in those days was always pronounced *Bow-der-see-er*.

Geegee got up and looked out, drinking the tap water from his tooth glass.

Horrible day. Not blue, of course. December the first,

wasn't it? The window only showed the back of another building. There were broken windows, and a hoarding with an old advert, all stripped, over which someone had sprayed in red. The image was strange, something Peck remembered post-war as 'Chad'. The head, just eyes and nose, and fingers, all peering over a wall.

This was the same, in fact. But the eyes were drawn in a funny way. Like – like Egyptian eyes on a mummy. Tutankhamun.

Geegee realized he had missed breakfast. The stroppy woman on the desk of the B and B had told him, breakfast ended at eight thirty. It was now ten.

By the time he got down the narrow stair, after a skimpy wash in the hand-basin and the putting on of his shabby stale clothes, there was a gale blowing up the front.

Gulls hurtled past the windows, screaming with terror or high spirits.

Everything had been ripped from the table of the dining room, which last night had chequered cloths and knives and spoons, and teacups reversed in saucers. To his inquiry after a sandwich, then, the woman had said, 'We can't do teas.'

How miserable it looked, the sorrowful rooms that should have thrummed to forks and hungry swallows.

'Like a bacon sarnie? I done some upstairs.'

Peck turned in astonishment.

A pretty girl in jeans and jumper.

'Well, yes. How come?'

'Oh, she's a cunt. But we do it just afore we goes out busking. Come on.'

Upstairs again, and into a tiny room, smelling of damp

and nappies – and glorious bacon. A guitar and a young guy on the bed, he dancing a baby. And a little clandestine gas ring and grill.

They reminded him suddenly of Gary and Shelagh.

But this girl was more pretty, and any way, that was over ten years ago.

The sandwiches were stupendous, laced with marg, tomato sauce and English mustard. He wondered if they had stolen the bacon.

They had instant coffee too, watery but hot.

'How'd you end up here, mate?' the young man asked.

Peck had been told, *they* had ended here on the non-actual charity of the state. To add to the subsistence of benefit, on which they could legally starve, they went to play and sing in this end of the cold winter town. 'We don't go past the pier,' the boy added. 'Bit elitist up there, you get me?'

'Well, I'm looking for my niece,' said Peck. 'She's sixteen. She ran away from home. You know how it is.'

'Too right,' said the girl.

'I've been asking. It's not I want to make her go back. Just tell her mum she's OK. Redhead,' he added, and saw flame like a dart between their young jewelry eyes, a *look*. 'You see, I'll be frank, I'd just like to have a talk with her. Her mum's a bit of a cow. It's me wants to know she's all right. Really attractive. She could've been a model.'

'Fancy her, do you?' asked the young man.

'Me? No. All that went off years ago. Any way, what do you take me for, she's my niece. I'm just plain worried.'

'Redhead,' said the girl. 'No, no one like that.'

They were lying, patently.

Then the girl said, 'Have you seen the Victoria Hotel?'

'Don't think so.'

'Bit further along. This side of the pier.'

'You mean, try there?' Peck asked.

'Could do.'

The baby made a joyful burbling noise, and Peck looked at it, again surprised.

After they had all gone down, and the boy and girl had gone off with their guitar and their baby, Peck stood by the rail, looking out on the savage sea.

It ran full tilt towards the land, and leapt against it. The stones made a sound of breakage and the sea exploded. Then it was dragged away, but at once prepared again to charge.

The kindness of the couple in the B and B had shaken Peck, just a little. And the lying. They had seen or known a red-haired girl.

He thought about Gary, and Shelagh.

Geegee had been a lot younger then himself, working on the local paper. That, in the end, had been all he could think of to do. And they had kept him making tea as it seemed for years, but finally he got the funerals, too, the weddings, and he learned to smoke and drink liquor and sit about and mourn.

He used to be concerned for the people he interviewed, that was the silly thing. If they'd made the right choice, would be happy, if they were unlucky. He felt sorry for them.

One day, when he was nearly forty, the best reporter fell ill – or, as it turned out, a jealous husband had stabbed him in the carpark of the Pig and Parrot. Peck got sent instead.

The headline had already been handed to him, *Alien*

Abduction – Close Encounters of the Third Division Kind.

Truthfully, it was an amateur football club, and Gary only played on weekends. After that he went into the showers with the others – they had lost – and later on the showers were empty, and Gary was nowhere to be found.

It was Shelagh who said it must have been aliens. She had explained to Geegee, Gary was gentle and loving. He had married her when he got her in the family way, and they had been here in the bedsit for two years, and he did everything he could, and held down his job in the factory. And on the day in question, having stayed in with the baby because it was so cold, she had prepared his favourite tea – fried eggs and beans on toast, what they could afford. And he never came back to her, back to their child.

She was a lovely girl, and crying, and Peck had been so sorry, because at once he had known. It had all abruptly been too much for Gary. Gary was honourable, and he had done what he should. And maybe he even loved her, loved the child the way Shelagh insisted. And in the photo of the three of them, Gary had looked proud, and glad – and so very young. He was only twenty.

Instinctively Peck discarded the idea of an alien abduction. He went looking instead in Gary's teenage haunts, the coffee-bars, the illicitly drunk-in pubs, even the earlier things – the former school, the previous terraced house, where Gary had lived with his mother.

Peck found Gary eventually on a swing, in a playground.

Geegee sat down on the next swing, and complained about the way you could never get them to go, once you were over fourteen.

At which Gary showed Peck how to make a swing go to the roof of the world.

When they stopped, their bones misplaced, laughing and high as kites, Peck talked to Gary about Shelagh.

They moved on to the local afterwards, talked on, until closing time. And then they went to Peck's place, which, then, had been a one-roomed bedsit like Gary and Shelagh's own.

They talked and drank, and in the morning Gary was sick four times in the sink, but they had worked it out.

'I loves her,' Gary said, 'I loves her like I want to die. And him. I loves him. He's part of *me*.'

He was too young for it all, but having become a child again, now he had aged. He cried so much for Shelagh after the sickness passed, Peck phoned her from the call-box, and left them alone in his room, among the scattered dirty socks and empty bottles.

The story never got written. Instead Peck became what, in certain books, they called a Private Dick. Which said everything, perhaps.

Peck left the raging sea, and under the blown-about shouting gulls, walked down until he spotted the Victoria. Much boarded up, it had the unmistakable signs of squattage.

On the steps outside, a thin girl sat with a littler girl, about seven, by her side. Both stared at him. In the child's lap was, of all creatures, a tortoise.

'Hallo,' said Geegee. 'Shouldn't he be hibernating?'

'It's a she. It's Poppy,' said the child.

'Excuse me, Poppy.'

'She don't,' said the child.

She wore a thick jersey and a coat, and her hair was shining, newly washed. She held the tortoise like a careful gift, or a prized toy. Yet, not like that. Like her heart on her sleeve.

The thin girl said, 'Bad weather.'

'It is,' said Peck.

'Bad storm,' said the girl. She added, 'Tonight. Around eleven.'

Peck said, 'You heard it on the news.'

'That's it,' said Phaedra, who had just come from the fishing boats, with a large cod as reward for her warning.

From the side of the hotel, a man was walking, in a big black coat. He was enormous, broad and tall, about six five, with a shaved head. At Peck he did not look, but only at the child on the step. A fair-sized matching black dog padded behind him.

The girl on the step stood up, but the child stayed where she was.

The big bald man had stopped, shifting his weight. Only the dog came on. It put its head into the child's lap, then licked the shell of the tortoise named Poppy.

The man and the child laughed simultaneously.

'Hi, Susan,' said the child. 'My name's Susan, too.'

'I know,' he said. He seemed nervous, pleased. Embarrassed and excited. He came to the steps and reached down and shook the child's hand. Then she got up, holding her tortoise conscientiously. They walked off down the promenade in the howling gale, the dog padding behind like a Praetorian guard.

'She's seven,' said Phaedra, 'and he's thirty-two. They'll

have to wait at least nine years. Sixteen and forty-one. Cradle-snatching, eh?'

Peck could not follow this.

'I'm trying,' he said, 'to locate my niece. I'm very worried.'

'You must be,' said Phaedra. There was a beauty to her face, which came now in violent flashes, like the bursts of the predicted storm. It confused him. One minute she appeared thin and ordinary, though nice enough, then tall, and clad like a witch-queen in an old film, the wind blowing her weak tendrils of tresses into a mane, lambent-eyed.

'Redhead,' said Peck.

'Cor,' said Phaedra. 'I did that once. Half me hair fell out.'

And then they both turned, for a smart black car was inappropriately cruising down the vacant road, the wind streaming over it, and spray from the sea flying up on its right hand side.

It pulled up at the kerb. A man and a woman got out. They wore ultra-fashionable macs, his grey and hers blue, and carried briefcases.

She moved forward at once, open-faced, and gay in the former sense.

'What an awful day!'

'Right,' said Phaedra.

'We're looking for Skilt,' said the young woman.

Behind her the man was jovial. 'Mr MacQuenna.'

Peck slid aside. He leant on the railings by the hotel. The young girl that he did not know was called Phaedra, replied, 'Yeah, Skilt said. I'll take you up.'

And she led them round to the side entrance, while

something kept Geegee Peck from pursuing. And the sea boiled on the edge of the earth.

In the doorless doorway, after Phaedra was gone, Ann rapped on the frame.

Skilt turned from his shrimp-netted window. In Skilt's scarred hand, a Spam sandwich.

'Thought you'd come by,' said Skilt. He bit another chunk from the sandwich.

'The office reached you. That's fine,' said Roger Cover.

'All the offices,' Skilt swallowed the food, 'do that.'

Ann said, 'It's nice, the way you've done your room.'

'Do you think so?'

'And isn't that ballroom impressive? I stayed in an hotel like that when I was fifteen.'

'Where you lost your cherry,' Skilt said, 'perhaps.'

Ann lowered her eyes. It might have been modesty, or total incomprehension. Did Ann have a cherry? Or did her legs meet there, like the groin of a store mannequin?

'How do you want to play this?' Skilt asked. He had moved to the table, where lay today a black bottle of red vermouth, another sandwich on a paper plate, the seagull feather, the stones, a Greek play in the original Greek. No syringe.

'However is convenient, Mr MacQuenna,' said Roger Cover. 'But first – just a formality – would you be kind enough to strip?'

'Ah, the formality. Always that.'

'We have to be sure,' said Roger Cover, 'that it *is* you.'

Skilt said, 'I'll leave my shoes on, if you don't mind. The floor's got splinters.'

'Anything that helps, Mr MacQuenna.'

They stood impassive as Skilt sloughed a jersey, unbuttoned the blue shirt, undid the trousers, rolled down the plain black underpants, and left everything lying around his ankles. A narrow white body. Unlike the chipped front teeth and rimmed fingers, no scar.

Ann said, reading from a print-out, 'Sally Janet Erika Maclean. Born 1950—'

' 'Forty-nine,' said Skilt, level as an unmined airstrip.

'I'm sorry.' Ann made a quick note. 'Thank you. I'll see that's rectified.'

'Excellent,' said Roger Cover. 'Do put your things back on. It's quite chilly.'

Sally Janet Erika Skilt Maclean pulled up Sally Janet Erika Skilt Maclean-MacQuenna's nether garments, and did up the shirt. There lingered on the cold air the after-image nevertheless, although perhaps not for Roger Cover and Ann who had already known.

Skilt, naked, was thin and hard, with unusually small fallen breasts that did not, dressed, show, and the unweaponed loins of a female, that the slightly padded underpants disguised. Skilt was a woman, physically.

'You'll know the story in Ovid,' said Skilt, biting once again into the sandwich.

'Ovid?'

'Successful writer. Quite some time ago.'

'Oh yes. Greek . . . Roman?'

'A girl turned into a man by Neptune or Poseidon, the sea god. No, I'm not justifying it.'

'Of course not, Mr MacQuenna.'

Ann read, from the print-out, 'The hotel, formerly called the Victoria. Unofficial sanctuary or academy for potential psychics and healers. You know, my mother attends a faith healer. She swears by him.'

'Fuck and shit by the faith healer,' said Skilt, softly.

Roger Cover laughed jollily. 'We're taking a great deal of your time, Mr MacQuenna. I expect you can guess what we need to know.'

'The girl is here. Hesta Web. She's the one.'

'Ah,' said Roger Cover. 'The – priestess. That's right?'

'That's right. With Van Hassin.'

'Could you spell that,' said Ann. 'I have him down as H.A.S.S.I.N.G.E.R.'

'It's him.'

'Just the same.'

Skilt spelled the old name that Hassinger had altered.

'And the father, Iain?' asked Roger Cover.

'No.'

'Can you be sure?'

'Yes,' said Skilt. 'Iain Web isn't here. Never has been. There's a sort of detective – Gregory Peck, or something like that.'

'Yes, we have him on file. I think he was below,' said Roger Cover. 'No problems there.'

'And the mother has arrived.'

'I gather,' said Roger Cover, 'that will be taken care of. She's of no interest to us.'

'But *we* interest you. Your Company.'

'Of course you do, Mr MacQuenna. But as you know, everyone leaves you all alone.'

'Like in all the other places,' said Skilt, 'all over the world.'

'*Other* places?'

Skilt said, 'Can I tempt you to some vermouth? Belgian. Quite old. Washed up last week.'

'It sounds lovely,' said Roger Cover, 'but I mustn't. Not on duty. You know what it's like.'

'I'm a G and T girl,' said Ann, with a giggle.

'Gorgeous and Tits,' said Skilt. And Ann giggled at greater volume.

'By the way,' said Roger Cover, as they turned towards the dark stair, 'the Christmas thing – that's on, I assume.'

'Oh yes,' said Skilt. 'Why don't you come down?'

'Never mix business with pleasure.'

Skilt started on the second sandwich, as their footsteps died down the dodgy staircase.

His Face

The man and woman had eaten their light dinner, drunk their
single glasses of wine and their cups of tea. They had entered
any extra information they had gathered in the town, very
much what would have been expected, on their computers.

Now they were packing their spare and efficient bags,
each at the end of their individual beds. Processing, the
computers ticked on.

'We'll be in London about ten?' asked the woman.

'That's right, Ann. Ten or ten thirty.'

Her computer made a strange new sound. A sort of low
twitter, the noise of a brooding, thoughtful bird.

Ann turned.

She had closed the incoming channel.

And yet, something was coming in.

Words appeared on the screen.

*Giles Sullivan. 1890 to 1917. Birthplace unknown.
Resident of the town sometime after 1910.*

'Look,' said Ann.

'Yes,' said Roger Cover.

*Called by the nickname MOSES. A reference to his red
hair and its central part: 'Parting the Red Sea'.*

Ann read out slowly and distinctly, 'During the First World War, served as an officer. Ordered to cross an open stretch of Flanders countryside, Moses held his troops back. He insisted on the presence of concealed enemy guns. When the men were forced to move forward, Moses alone went ahead. He proved his assertion by directly drawing fire. He was killed instantly, by a shell, his body dismembered and incinerated by the blast. There were no other casualties, as the advance was halted until the gun position had been taken out.'

Ann stopped.

Further words came up on the computer screen.

Roger Cover read, 'According to local legend, Sullivan's car in England naturally combusted at the same approximate time as his death, and was reduced to cinders.'

The screen blanked out.

Roger Cover said, smiling, 'Where was Moses when the lights went out?'

'In the dark,' said Ann.

On the screen, something else appeared.

It was a face, a kind of face. Black, fraying off at crown and chin. Three burning white holes in its blackness – eyes, nose? As if a bulb blazed inside . . .

Then the screen flamed blind white. Went out.

There was the smell – of burning.

'It's all right, Ann. Remember, we were warned. You backed up all my data. I backed up your data. Nothing's lost.'

Roger Cover's computer twittered.

On to the screen rose two lines of words.

Adam and Eve and Moses went down to the river to bathe –

Where they drowned their youngest son, Dave.

Roger Cover's screen flamed bright white. Went out.

'It's all right, Ann. Nothing we can do. We were warned.'

Ann said, quietly, 'Adam and Eve and Moses.'

'Yes, Ann. A version of a childish rhyme.'

'*Their* son Dave.'

'Yes, Ann.'

'Two fathers and one mother,' said Ann.

Roger Cover laughed. 'Very *good*.'

When the lights go out.

When the lights go out, the face of the sun, and the moon and all the stars, are clearly to be seen.

And when the lights of falsehood and reason go out, to be seen is His Face, the Face of God.

Three

Hesta had come down the garden, to the brick wall at its end. On the way, she had examined the leaning, ancient, winter-bare trees. At the foot of one, fifteen metres high, perhaps, was a little plaque, which read, *Jesus wants me for a Hornbeam*.

Below the wall, where she now sat, the Norman church, where, on Sundays, bells rang for two minutes, morning and evening. Then the town. The promenade. The ocean.

Yesterday, she had crossed through the bombsite. She had gone to the station, and waited for the train to London. It arrived, and went without her. For a while she lingered on the platform, considering this.

Then she walked on, up the heights of the town.

No one stopped her, although she believed she had been followed, by a little brown man in an impoverished raincoat, part of the way.

She had proved to herself two things:

She could leave, if she wished.

She did not wish to leave.

Going through the town alone, today, though hailed by some people, smiled on, and, in the café where she went for hot chocolate, brought also an éclair she did not want, both free, Hesta found them all more easy, found she could ignore their eyes and looks. He had explained to her – Hassinger – that simply by being in their midst, she brought them a kind of gladness. Even if she never came out of the house, they understood she was there. 'It's enough,' he said.

She knew by now to bite a large piece from the unwanted éclair, and say that she had liked it. Outside, down the street, she threw it to a gull. The gull certainly liked it.

Did the gulls stare at her, too?

She had passed the Duchess on the promenade.

'Hallo, dear. It's stopped raining. Look at all those stones thrown up here. A bad storm last night. Out to sea.'

'Yes.'

Baby stood up in the pram, glaring about in a military way.

It was all a joke, was it not? This place. What Hesta represented.

A small black child on a bike went by, 'Hi, Hesta.' She raised her hand.

The air was beautiful, coldly soft and purified by thunder and rain.

She had walked to the edge of the sea.

Anything might be out there . . .

But her rage – had it gone, or was it only transmuted into emotionless and thoughtful questions?

'If I stay,' she had said this morning, 'what happens?'

'Not a great deal. You know it, any way.'

'I help them if they ask. I live my own life?'

'Of course.'

300

'But no sex, no babies.'

'You want sex and babies.'

Hesta replied, 'Like a hole in the head.'

Hassinger grinned. (Janey's father.) 'They brought your red dress.'

Hesta went to see. The dress was on a satin hanger in her little room. Crimson velvet, long sleeves, and a long skirt that would reach her ankles. For the waist, a crimson velvet belt with a buckle of complex silver, from the same jewelry and clothes shop. The buckle intrigued her the most. A beast skull – sheep? wolf? – clasped in leaves. How had it been fashioned?

Returning to the outer room, she watched him. (Janey's father.) Eventually she said: 'I'd like to see how they make the jewelry.'

'They'll show you. It's very fine work.'

'Is that what Lulu did here? Something like that?'

'No. She sold books and records.'

Hesta had gazed at him, expressionless. Thinking of Janey, who was his child.

'The red dress is a present,' she said.

'And for Christmas,' he said.

'Oh. Christmas.'

'A festival here,' he said.

He was not being sarcastic.

Hesta said, 'What does that mean?'

'To bring luck to the town,' he said. 'And the boats.'

'Supposing I'm not here, at Christmas.'

'Then you won't be here.'

'But I'm the substitute – for Janey.'

'Or, in another form,' he said, 'you are what Janey migh
have been.'

'What happens at the Christmas festival?' said Hesta. Sh
had her back to one of the walls of books.

Hassinger stood by the table. He said, 'They carry fir
around the boats. The boats get blessed.'

'How?'

'I touch them. The timbers.'

'You and I?' (Janey's father and I.)

'I. You, if you care to. They'd be pleased, if you do.'

'If I'm here.'

'If you are.'

'What else?'

'One boat goes a short distance out to sea, to represent th
rest. It's very cold. Sometimes there's ice on the beach.'

'It sounds very innocent,' said Hesta.

'It is innocent. Innocent in the original meaning.'

'Something else, then,' she said.

Hassinger unrolled the piece of the painting, on the ebon
table, held it flat with both hands.

'Is that,' she said, 'supposed to be me?'

'Possibly.'

She came over, and they looked down at it, the pale blu
of face, the – perhaps – throat and breast of a woman. Th
scorch of the red hair.

'Or who?'

'There's a tradition of red hair here,' said Hassinger.

'And murder,' said Hesta.

Hassinger straightened and looked full at her. She tende
to forget, between, the power that could emanate from hi

302

as if at the flick of a switch. A cool and radiant force which came also – at a flicked switch? – from herself.

'Sacrifice,' said Hassinger, 'is the word you want.'

Waking, he felt fantastic. He lay there, luxuriating in it, and grew rather perplexed, because why the hell was it he felt so great, down here in this dump, with bloody mad Stephanie?

Perhaps the air here was as healthy as they said. He had slept a lot yesterday. So had she. Into the morning, again after lunch, early to bed. No frolics, of course, she on her side of the mattress, brittle-hard as a stick of refrigerated rock, but not sweet, or sticky.

The room, though, that had been a surprise. The receptionist explaining they could have a suite, for the price of an ordinary single, it being out of Season. (Martin Peecey had reasoned the receptionist liked the look of him. Unluckily for her, she was a non-event.) But he had charmed away, and they got the suite.

'Well, Steph. What do you think?'

'It's all right,' said Stephanie.

But the suite was not all right. It was – grandiose. Plum velvet with warm bronze, swags of bronzy tassels, huge gilt mirrors, sitting room, bedroom, a bed the size of the QE2 and an epic bathroom of apparently real marble and gold-plated taps. There were chandeliers aloft, and squares of Victorian stained glass in the windows that Kev would have given his expensively capped eye teeth to chivy out.

After the magnificence of the suite, the food in the empty and run-down-looking dining room had not amazed quite so much.

Peecey had now dined twice on, and otherwise noted such creations as, Sole Véronique, Steak aux Poivres, Vegetables Africaine, Duck Alsace in brandy, Salmon with purée of lemon and grapefruit, and a Marsala mayonnaise. The wines on offer had knocked the wine bar list into a dustbin, and when he had tasted of them, Martin Peecey raised his eyes to heaven in appreciation.

Meanwhile, there was also another menu, which purported to be 'lite'. The waitress explained, they were trying this one on their winter guests, out of Season.

But Martin Peecey seriously doubted the second menu was lite, as he watched Stephanie tucking into her orders from it, mushroom fritters, chicken breasts in sauce, strawberry pie. Sensibly he had not said anything about that.

As Peecey rolled over, he grasped that Stephanie was not in bed, and that on his wrist, just by his costly watch, something insectile must have bitten him.

He scratched, but it did not really itch.

'Bloody mosquitoes—'

Mosquitoes, at this time of year? But it could happen. Central heating – which, also to his astonishment, worked perfectly in the pink hotel – gave them an extended life span. Better try to find some repellent in the godawful town.

Despite the heating, there was a draught.

Peecey squinted. The thick forest of velvet curtain parted a crack by the French windows. Which seemed to be ajar.

'Stephanie – are you completely off your trolley?'

Having flung the curtains back, standing there naked, tanned all over by his London sun-bed, cock-sure but phallically limp, he beheld her. She was in her tiny cerise bikini, lying

304

ut on the long wicker chair on their private terrace, among
e empty urns, with only the sea visible, cold as a witch's tit,
rashing and spuming beyond the high balcony rail.

'Oh. Martin.'

'Have you gone fucking loopy, or what? It's less than
inus fifty degrees out here.'

'No, Martin, That sounds more like Antarctica.'

'Stephanie. It's *cold*. But you're – what are you doing –
unbathing?'

'I'm warm.'

He thought, right, it was her age. Hot flushes. Bit early –
ut there you go.

'You'll catch the 'flu, Stephie.'

She laughed. Quietly.

'Yes. I expect you're right.'

She rose, and he walked off into the bathroom to relieve
is bladder.

When he turned from that, and gazed into the gilt mirror
ver the double marble basin, he saw she had written him a
ft-handed message in her lipstick on the glass, which read:
ARTIN PEECEY, LEMON SQUEEZY.

here was an elderly woman in a brown coat at the bar. She
t on a stool, and a maroon pram was drawn up beside her.
he had taken from the pram a gull, which now itself sat on
e bar-top, preening.

They had a budgie too, bright green. It was singing on one
the figureheads.

'Like another, dear?' asked the large woman, who had
id, 'Call me Joy, dear.'

'Just a small one, Joy,' said Geegee (Graeme Gregory)
'Rough old day.'

'That's right,' said Joy Joy. She filled his glass with a tripl
Bells.

'Steady on.'

'It's all right, dear. You have it on the house. You've bee
here a long while.'

'Supposed to meet my sister's boy.' Geegee took the glass
'Missing relative, you know.'

'Yes, I heard you'd been looking. Blonde young lady, isn
it?'

'Well, she was a redhead when my sister last saw her. She
very worried – my sister.'

'A mother suffers,' said Joy Joy.

The Duchess cackled. 'My boy's always good.' Sh
nodded at the gull. 'Do you like birds, Lord Visitor?'

'Yes,' said Peck. 'But I've never seen a pet gull before.'

'Bravest birds in the world,' said the Duchess. 'Pigeon:
too. Had a racing pigeon in here in the summer,' she addec
'Walked in and sat down.'

'Some of the trippers were laughing at it,' said Joy Joy
'exhausted, poor thing. They said to me, Fetch some pastr
quick. Its wings was all right. Just too tired to fly. Com
across the Channel, seemingly. We got it right, any how. Ver
fond of it, the owner.'

The seagull went close to the Duchess and she poure
some of her drink into the clean ashtray no one had used. Th
gull siphoned this up.

Peck laughed.

He liked the pub. Normally it might have been difficul

hanging around for Peecey, who had said they would meet here at twelve, over an hour ago. But this was restful. No loud bad music, no flashing machines. Something that sounded like an ancient radio station, although it could not be, was playing a selection of Ivor Novello.

May had enjoyed Novello. And Strauss too. As a boy of fourteen or fifteen, he had been nervous of her choices, but once, coming to her door one Saturday evening thirty years later, near to the evening she died, he had heard the strains of 'We'll Gather Lilacs', and the beauty of the melody had pierced him through, making him cry, there on the doorstep.

'Cheer up, dear,' said Joy tenderly. 'Though you know, I never say, Cheer up it may never happen. Usually it has. We had an Asian visitor in once, looked very down in the mouth. And this young lout, another visitor, doesn't know him, shouts at him, Cheer up, it may never happen. And the visitor answers, My wife died on the coach coming down today. I've got to make arrangements in half an hour. And then he punched the young fella in the mouth. Broke two teeth.'

'When he did that, I laughed my head off,' said the Duchess. Peck picked up abruptly how educated her voice was. She'd called him *Lord*—

'Lives up near the church now,' said Joy. 'The older man, the Asian. Mr Petal. Like a flower.'

Martin Peecey burst into the Kissing Crab.

Peck was struck at once by Peecey's radiance. He looked better than he had in London.

'Corner seat,' said Peecey. 'You've got a drink?' He ordered a glass of red wine, brought it over. 'Well, then, Peck.'

'Nothing, I'm afraid. I haven't been idle. And I might have a couple of leads. But nothing definite, yet. I'm sorry.'

Martin Peecey scanned him.

'Kev said you were all right.'

'I do my best.'

'You look like a loser to me,' said Martin Peecey.

Peck shrugged. 'Sticks and stones, Mr Peecey.'

'I think Kev was having a joke, yes? At my expense? Look, I want some news. I'll give you until tomorrow. Then you'll have found her, or you'll know where she's gone, or you're fired. Fair?'

'Mr Peecey, I'm afraid this isn't a BBC TV series. It's real life. People are often hard to dig out, when they don't want to be.'

'OK, OK.'

Despite the harsh words, it was all quite easy-going. Martin was having a sort of game, perhaps. He looked happy, or high. Both? He said, 'This wine is OK. The drink *is* good here. Weird. Place like this.'

Peck remembered Tizer on the beach. Auntie May's first cup of tea after the train. 'Tastes *good*, here.' But they had never come – *here*.

The whisky was pleasing, too. If he had the time to notice.

Peecey downed his wine. 'Have to get back. Keep an eye on her.' That would be the girl's mother, presumably. Why hadn't she come to see Peck as well? Too nervous? 'If you get anything, call me. If *she* answers, say it's a wrong number.' Yes, it must be that. Protecting her.

'All right, Mr Peecey.'

'Failing that, I'll meet you here – three days. Same time.'

'One thirty.'

'Twelve,' said Martin Peecey.

'Ah,' said Geegee. It was one thirty, nearer quarter to two, but the customer was always right.

When Peecey was gone, Geegee made himself also go out into the raw wild air. He stood at the rail for a while, watching the sea. It never tired. It always changed. Was always constant.

There had been no leads at the squat. None he would follow.

As he strolled about the town, along by the shops, many of which were shut (half day?), up by the clock tower which seemed to chime the hour, but not consistently, something occurred to him, some oddity, and he could not think what it was.

Not until he had gone to the promenade's end, and was peering away at the curling wall of limestone cliffs, thatched with vivid winter grass, pocked with holes, where seagulls with black skulls flew in and out, everything ultimately dimmed by mist, did it, inappropriately, come to him.

There were always the jibes, with some cause, worse and worse through the years, how the stores did it, the pubs, everywhere, earlier and earlier. But not in this town. It had no Christmas decorations, though December had begun. Not anywhere that he had seen. Not the shops, not the pubs. Not a wisp of tinsel or sniff of holly. No reindeer. And in the windows of the flats and houses, no trees or cotton wool snow.

Now why was that?

* * *

309

When she had the surge of anger, Stephanie fought to hold on to it. She did not know why. Perhaps, the reassurance of habit.

Martin had gone out, not telling her what for or where. That was so like him.

Well, she did not need to crouch here in this stupid sugarmouse pink and vanilla hotel.

She too would go out.

Let it be.

When she put on her fawn suede skirt, it was uncomfortably tight at the waist. Sometimes this happened before a period. And since the trouble started, *they* were all over the place. The skirt was in a very small size. She did up the zip around a safety pin and put on a loose cream and orange silk top.

In the mirror of the large ornate dressing-table, she took in her face. She had a strange new fresh clear colour.

The time on the balcony had obviously done her no harm, although probably it *was* too cold . . . Why had she *done* that? To annoy Martin, without doubt, snoring and supine in the bed.

Something had bitten him, so he declared, after he had stamped from the bathroom, and told her writing on a mirror was like some inebriated kid-stuff at the wine bar.

'*Poor* Martin, poor *baby*, oochy coo, diddums den.'

'You're a bitch.'

'Yes-ums, nasty bitchums to *poor* baby Marty bitey *ooh*!'

Stephanie, you look terrific.

Her tan had faded away, but this brightness seemed to

310

have come instead. She could recall the look, after playing games at school on a frosty day.

But a bitch. Was she?

'Bitch,' said Stephanie, pausing in putting on her eye make-up. 'You're a bitch.'

She did not laugh at this.

As she was brushing her hair, Stephanie congratulated herself on how adept she was becoming with her left hand. But then she recollected her peculiar dream.

Someone had been in the room.

In the dream, she was not afraid, more amused. Through a veil she glimpsed a tall thin figure bending, bending, like a sapling. Male or female? It had not concerned her. And then a silvery glitter. What was that? Martin's arm up in the air, held there as if after some victory, but Martin asleep and mildly snoring.

She had meant to say, 'What are you doing?' But actually, she was not bothered, and only turned over and sank back into the lovely death of sleep.

Stephanie forgot her dream. She thought for a moment about death. If there was nothing after you died, and probably there was not, there was still nothing to be frightened of. It would be like a deep and dreamless sleep. A for ever of comfort and serenity. A for ever without anger, pain or fear.

Two tears spilled from Stephanie's eyes, not spoiling her waterproof mascara.

She observed their gracious fall.

You're beautiful, Stephanie. And you look so young.

When she went downstairs, the woman behind the desk signalled to her. 'Miss Hope. A letter for you.'

311

For a second, Stephanie did not recognize her maiden name, under which she had checked in. Then she started. Everything gushed back, almost bowling her over. Why she had come here. Looking for *them*. For Hesta. And for Iain. She began to tremble.

'But –' she said, as if to ward this off.

The woman was already rummaging in her cubby.

Stephanie turned blindly, cornered. She saw, unseeing, a lounge led off from the uncarpeted foyer, with dingy large sofas and tables with gilded legs. A man was sitting there with a coffee pot on a tray.

'Here you are, Miss Hope.'

'Thank you,' she said, and took the letter.

She walked away from the desk, holding the letter in front of her.

It was plain, a white envelope, her name written in a mannered yet very legible handwriting, the sort of writing they had tried to teach her at school, redundant now. No one used it. Except for whoever it was who had written to Stephanie Web, née Hope.

About five yards from the desk, standing in the middle of space (where had the carpet gone? To the cleaners? Those curtains in the lounge over there, pallid from years of sun, and cobwebs), she realized she was going to find it difficult to undo the envelope, any way, one-handed.

Better wait until Martin—

To hell with Martin.

The nail on the smallest finger on her right hand, free of bandaging, and very strong, slit through the envelope's top.

A single sheet of thick white paper, written all over in the

312

dark blue antique script of the 1960s.

Stephanie read it.

Dear Miss Hope, or Mrs Web, should you so prefer,

The Company for which your husband, Iain Web, formerly worked, has been investigating you and to some extent your daughter – a procedure which involved the burglary of your house – due to the curious circumstances surrounding Mr Web's disappearance.

Which are these:

At approximately 4.09 a.m. on that Sunday morning, all the lights of the rig failed. The blackout lasted some sixty seconds, at which time emergency power took over. Contrary to what you have been told, a helicopter was at this very moment coming in to make a night landing on the rig platform. When the lights went out, the pilot held his craft in the sky. He was not unduly alarmed. Such stations are of necessity well prepared with emergency back-up.

While he waited, however, the pilot, hanging quite low above the platform, saw something else happen below. What he saw, or so he has claimed, was Iain Web leaving the installation. The obstacle to this statement is, that the pilot has said he saw Iain Web 'walk away from the rig'. Despite intensive interrogation, involving some use of drugs, and even in the light of his inevitable loss of employment, the pilot has refused, so far, to go back on these words. There was and is no indication of any abnormality in his physical or mental condition.

Thus, Iain Web apparently jumped from the platform of the drilling rig at about 4.10 a.m. on Sunday morning, and walked away across the sea.

Yours most sincerely.

There was no signature.

Stephanie threw back her head to laugh. Or was it to scream? Nothing came from her throat but a miniature squeak.

The letter from the unknown – *well-wisher?* – dropped to the floor and lay there like a dead white leaf.

'Excuse me.' The voice was cultured and gentle; male. 'You seem upset. Let me take you to a chair.'

She was aware then of an electric warmth, which guided her, so carefully, over space, and into something else which held her up.

'Have this.'

'No—'

'I insist. You've had a shock.'

The brandy seared her mouth, went down like lightning.

Iain . . . Iain walking on water.

The laughter came after all.

'I've just found out I'm married to Jesus Christ.'

The man chuckled. 'One or two women have had this experience. They discovered it was a deception.'

'Walking on water –' said Stephanie. She thought *Shut up*.

'Ah, but that's not the essential of a messiah. Christ, it's true, was also a magician, able to perform miracles. It's his teachings which make him Christ, and his superhuman capacity for love.'

Stephanie whispered, 'This is ridiculous.'

'So if your husband walks on water,' said the man, 'he's only a magician. Nothing to worry about.'

Her eyes refocused.

He was an old man, in his seventies, very straight, and elegantly dressed, but like an actor, and flavoured by 1940. His tough brown skin had formed into a hundred carved wrinkles, as a beach formed under waves. He smelled clean and expensive.

There was a hot-house rose, saffron yellow, in his buttonhole.

Stephanie took him in with contemptuous brevity.

But she must be polite. 'You're right. I had a shock. A poison pen letter.'

'Surely not? Although loveliness can attract discord.'

Stephanie marvelled, as her senses came back. A dirty old man! And straight out of her youth. She could see them now, wealthy men some of them, like this one, actorly, casual, at the school gates, not doing anything, smiling and bowing. And all the girls tittering. Think of those horrible gnarled paws on your nice firm white flesh – ugh!

'Can I help you to another brandy?'

A decanter was with the coffee on the table, cut glass like the accent.

'No. Thank you.'

Stephanie got up.

So did he. Cut glass, old-fashioned manners, or was he daring to think—

'You were kind,' she said, grudgingly.

'And you,' said the old man, 'are wonderfully lovely, my dear young woman. How can I let you go?'

315

A wave tumbled through the air and hit her. It was warm, pulsing, and covered her, filled her. It must be the brandy. But, my God, she was blushing.

Who had ever said that to her? None of her lovers. Not even Iain in the beginning.

Dirty old man. And she, a firm white blushing girl of fourteen.

'I'm afraid you'll have to.'

'On one condition.' She wavered there, revolted, stirred, bemused, the dead leaf on the floor forgotten. 'That you'll have some lunch with me.'

'I can't.'

'You can.'

'I'm married,' reminded Stephanie, amazing herself afresh, for she did not need to make an excuse.

He said, the old, old man, 'You would have to be, my beautiful girl. Who could resist you? Just a little lunch.' And he reached across and took her hand.

The electricity that shot through her was like – not even the little snorts of cocaine she had sometimes had. Not even like her first taste of alcohol or sex. And yet, sex was the closest. This spinning tingling fire, this *ardour*. And all from this withered-up stick, this ancient mariner with a shave and hair-cut.

'I –' said Stephanie, breathless. And in her loins came a warm golden rush. She wanted – God – she wanted to—

'That's so kind,' he said. 'May I call you Stephanie? An appealing name. My own, is Courtney Aims.'

To Martin Peecey's peeved inquiry, the woman on the desk

was vague. Yes, she thought Miss Hope had gone out. She didn't know where. The time? About one – or was it two? She couldn't be sure. So sorry.

Nothing lay on the floor by the desk, or near it. No carpet, envelope or paper.

Martin went up again to the suite.

If she wanted to play soppy bloody games, he'd let her.

The bed wasn't made yet. Tacky.

He phoned Kev. The call cheered him. Apparently the pregnant Penny had got extremely drunk at Kev's private party, and either miscarried or come on.

'Could be back a bit sooner, in that case,' asserted Martin Peecey.

What was there to stay for?

Food, wine, air—

London was his scene.

Yeah, pay off that Dick, Peck, and leave the silly bitch here on her own. Maybe she would meet Iain after all, and he'd thump some reality into her. Not that he had the guts.

Someone knocked as Martin was putting down the phone.

He went and jerked the door open. And thought again, of giving the arrival a mouthful.

She was about sixteen, with long, long, *long* flaxen wavy hair, tied in a loose blue ribbon. She had on a perfect hotel maid uniform, little short black dress, black stockings, *legs*, little white apron. What a way to dress a girl. But in her case, it was criminal.

'Well, hi,' said Martin.

Wicked face. Dark big eyes, black lashes, ripe mouth, white teeth. She smiled, lowered her eyes, looked up at him again.

'I'm here to do the room.'

'Oh, right. Come in, babe. Big bed to make.'

'I'm strong,' she said.

'I bet you are.'

She brushed against him as she passed, slowly. It was deliberate. 'I bet you are, too.'

You make me feel so young – she felt so young, Stephanie. Fourteen. Too young for this.

And excited, vulnerable, frightened, desperately eager. And beautiful. And, a virgin?

They lunched in Courtney Aims' rooms at the hotel, it seemed he had another suite. The velvet here was a rich autumnal brown.

What did they talk about? Fragmented, their speech. She did ask him, if the collectable American car on the parking lot was his. He said it was not, but a present to the town, which, soon, they would give to the sea. That made no sense. Nor, really, the comment he had made on some woman, called Catherine, later, Miss Lawrence, a very wonderful woman, now dead, who had promised to send a postcard, it transpired, if she could. Crazy. But was Stephanie truly listening?

On finest china, a prawn salad with a cucumber dressing, and some smoked fish – local? – with creamed celery, and a mosaic of tiny fried potatoes. He insisted she eat a piece of the apple tart. There was champagne – but *pink* champagne.

She did not eat all that much, although it was delicious. Could not eat, her heart in her mouth. Because every now and then, their fingers brushed together, and she would be flooded, the sea cave of her body, with the most dazzling lust.

She had stopped caring. So what, he was old. She would be old one day, although it was hard to believe it. And any way, a handsome man. And moneyed. And his manners, so exquisite. What her father would have called a 'gentleman'.

In the end, she was sitting on his lap, and she was swooning against him, even though, when he kissed her, they were the most decorous, closed-mouth kisses, but his hands, touching her waist, her hip – oh God, his *hands* –

'Can I make love to you, Stephanie?'

'Yes.'

The bed was quite large, although not so large as the bed in the other suite, where even now Martin might be, and served him right.

Marty, I've met this elderly man who makes your pathetic performance quite redundant.

Aims undressed her, and at his gentle touches, Stephanie writhed and moaned. 'Oh – hurry – hurry—'

He did not himself undress. Well, he was old – Oh hurry, hurry, darling—

As he palmed and stroked her breasts, Stephanie rose and fell, sensation on sensation, almost spasming, almost coming just from this.

He lay along her now, melting her body into his – in his elegant historical clothes. He tongued her breast and fingered her other breast, almost there – almost – He must be a healer. Oh, yes, yes—

Would he enter her now? She could hardly stand another minute, and yet, if he were to stop—

'Dear girl,' said Mr Aims, his face so kind and calm above her.

And then, to the incandescent accompaniment of his tongue and his fingers upon her, his other hand stole into her sexual centre.

Stephanie made terrible noises, like cries and shrieks of utmost agony. But never, never in her life of arid lovers, struggling to orgasm against great odds, never had she known – never known – this tumultuous ecstasy.

Up and up he bore her, on the electric flutterings of his much-praised hands, up into the firmament, until she lay screaming, shrieking, a gull stretched on wings of flame, and stars broke over her in showers, and she floated free, among the silent suns, to lovely, deep and dreamless sleep.

End of Part Six

PART SEVEN

One

'Deck the walls with boughs of holly,' sang Joy Joy, decking them, 'fa la la-la la, it is such fun. But please don't tell Uncle Solly, fa la la-la la, what we have done.'

On 18 December, the snow had fallen, lightly, frosting the town. After this, a great coldness came on. The sky lifted and turned an immaculate blue. The edges of the sea froze.

Each day was the same, icy, blue, with a sheer, glacial atmosphere. The sea seemed almost immobile, a darker blue than the sky, ribbed with bands of mysterious unreflected shadow.

At night, stars stood out thickly, and planets – Jupiter, perhaps, Mars, and Venus at dawn and dusk – flashing in enormous brilliance. Christmas stars on the tree of darkness.

The budgie flew about the holly, green as an expensive decoration.

Upstairs, Peck at a window, elbows on the sill, marvelling. Lovely day. Fine night. Shame May wasn't here. They could have had a walk. She never minded the snow or ice, and broke her hip in tepid impartial weather, coming back with the last dead Tiger, put to sleep at the vet's. He had buried Tiger by the others, in the garden. Auntie May was cremated a month later, and he was the only mourner.

But no use thinking of it now. Or of how she'd have liked this weather, and the gin and It or the whisky she'd have had, after the walk.

Martin Peecey had not come to his second arranged meeting. Geegee had heard no more of him, and was not that surprised. Trying to phone the pink hotel, Geegee found Mr Peecey was always 'out'. Some of the two hundred pounds was left, however, and it seemed a pity to go back to London, where apparently the snow was dirtily thick and the sky filthy with smog just like in the 1950s, or worse. The big shot at the wine bar had not contacted Peck, either. Peck was, after all, officially still looking for the girl with red hair. He had not seen her again, and doubted he ever would.

In fact, it was rather strange, the way the money had lasted. Of course, he had by now almost made an arrangement to take a bit out of the bank down here. But he didn't really seem to need it. He felt he must have spent well over what he had brought with him, yet there was a sort of float of around fifty that always seemed to be there. Mind you, Joy Joy put everything but his drinks on the slate.

The pub was grand. He liked the pub.

He had helped Joy Joy and Ted with some of the decorations, after hours. The room was cheap, and comfortable, with a big electric fire, and a clean bathroom just down the hall, where, every five or six days, he had a hot bath. Joy Joy's breakfasts of ham and eggs, fried bread and potatoes, were like nothing he had eaten for twenty or more years. And if he wanted, she would always make him a sandwich at night.

Christmas tomorrow, wasn't it?

It would be good, to live here. Sell May's house maybe . . . But the bottom had fallen from the house market, he wouldn't get much, what with the damp and the bad roof, and the antiquated lavatory, and the bloody awful area. And what would he do here? There was no work, unless you had some trade. Too old to change, any way. Any way, no plans for Tomorrow, remember Dad and the barmaid. Just a holiday, then.

Joy Joy had put some holly too over his bed, with a scarlet bow in it.

Up and down the town, the shops had on now their festive wreaths. Overnight it had happened, between the 21st and the 23rd. Real or plastic trees with magenta and cherry balls, paper-chains and dangling coloured paper explosions of gold and aquamarine, balloons, tinsel and spangles.

In the windows of the flats and houses, at last the cotton wool and reindeer, the holly and the ivy, and the white-eyed mistletoe.

Someone had written, on a wall beside the bombsite: *On the first day of Christmas I called the RSPCA to rescue a partridge stuck in my pear tree.*

Bells rang like knives in icing sugar air intense as vodka.

The Duchess had decked the *pram* in garlands of silver. A brooch of red berries was pinned in her hat.

By night, under the full white ice of a moon, Adèle and the Duchess and Joy and many others, their feet in socks and boots, the Duchess in her hat, ran otherwise bare as bones along the shore.

Who saw that? One or two.

(Peck had turned on his comfy bed. Heard their wild high voices, thought of gulls.)

Martin Peecey – always 'out' – had been lying on his back Stephanie forgotten, with a slender girl in only an apron and stockings, riding on his body, flicking him with the soft prickly switch of her long, long, *long* hair – champagne on the tray, champagne for free, acquired by this nymph, and caviare – And 'Oh Christ – yes—'

By day the buskers and the tramps, and a thieving of things to which no attention was paid. The addicts with their new fix, better than the other stuff, coke, crack, the clean syringes and bottles of green mud, and the orange in the stocking and the apple, and the tiny flask of rum and the small white bear for the baby. Oh, Christ, yes.

Phaedra freezing by low water, in her two vast jerseys and her fisherman's hat. 'Cold innit? Still as a mill-pond that sea. In the fisherman's caff, toasted in swarthy tea. And outside half the tail-wag dogs from the winching sheds, prowling round her over the frosted cakes of the stones.

Susan and Susan and Susan's mum drinking coffee in the café under the blue-faced clock tower, while the black dog stared across at the sixteenth-century pub, watching the ghosts that only he could see, the drinkers celebrating for ever in the moments before the siren and the bomb came down on them.

Oh I do like to be beside the seaside.

Jim, at Mrs Potter's, elevenses with his other older ladies, and Tom and Jerry the rats, running about through the cups, Edith giving them butter off the hot scones.

Through the alleys and the lanes, along the promenade

around the huge thews of the cliffs, borne over the upper airs, the angelic squawking gulls. And one white *snow* white evacuation, just falling clear of the winching gear that was lowering careful as a cradle, the American car, Chuck, down on to the beach of stones.

Oh I do like to be beside the seaside.

Oh, Christ, yes.

'Oh – Christ –' said Bish-Op, jagged, unemotional with getting it right. 'Oh, Christ, Sk-ilt.'

'Yes.'

'Can't, Skilt.'

'Can, Bish-Op. Decay will go with you.'

'Course I will,' said Decay, already enormously dressed in her black coat and her berry-red scarf. 'Phaedra'll come over, once she gets back.'

'It's not – I – just – No.'

Skilt leaned against the plastered wall of his room. 'Can't make you.' Bish-Op looked unsure.

In the doorway, Decay, and behind her, crowded against the storeroom of furniture, Bod, and Brillo eating Kenno-Meat from a tin with a plastic fork.

Bod said, 'Only thing is, Bish—'

'Only thing is,' said Skilt, 'it would be a shame if she had to go up to the hospital.'

'Meself,' said Bod, 'like, if I could, I think I would.'

Bish-Op dropped his head. His hair had been growing, short fur silk across the crown, the long tail at his neck.

He said, murmuring, so they must strain to catch it, 'This is like my, like my mother. Just try, darling.'

'No it ain't,' snapped Decay. She came into the room and put her arm around Bish-Op firmly. 'She just wanted you to be brainy so she could show off – ain't he triffic, *my* son. But this ain't *that*. She's scared, that girl. I seen her. Scared and in pain, and pretty soon they've gotta get a doctor.'

'Hesta,' said Bish-Op.

'Hesta will go,' said Skilt.

'Maybe,' said Brillo.

'Look here, Bish-Op,' said Decay, 'we'll walk along to Mr Hassinger's. See if she is.'

'That's – over *there*.'

'Well, Phaedra's *there*. You've bin *there*. Go on,' Decay said. 'There's Skilt's book. Do it.'

'It's I – when I want –'

Skilt got up and pushed the book, which was a paperback of nursery rhymes, forward on his table.

'You want to,' said Skilt, 'hit me. I'm pushing you. Like Mummy. So do it, Raymond.'

Raymond Bishop raised his head. His eyes were very wide and suddenly the paperback shot off the table and slapped Skilt full across the mouth.

Bod and Brillo stamped and catcalled.

The book dropped down. Skilt said, 'So.' A trickle of blood ran from his lip.

Decay took Bish-Op's arms and heaved him into his coat.

'What you got ter think is, *she* wanted you to do what you couldn't do. Skilt wants you to do what you can do. Different. See?'

328

Wearing Red

They had gone their separate ways, through December. Sometimes the mobile phone in his room had sounded. He had answered it, and frequently gone out.

She had got up early – seven, even six, roamed the town, eaten when hungry (always welcomed), stood, sat, walked by the sea for hours, come back, slept in the small bedroom.

They had been civil, quite friendly, and said nothing of any importance. Too many important things were said before.

Once, she had mentioned TV, and so a colour set appeared in her room. There was also a video machine, and a few films to go with it – of course, the ones she had liked when watching with Lulu and Janey.

Things in the bathroom were always replaced, including her make-up. (Never any sanitary protection.) Always food, drinks of various sorts, alcohol.

A bowl of apples on the table.

A pineapple.

She tried on the red dress, a flawless fit, but did not show him.

He would read before the fire. If she spoke, he spoke in turn, it seemed, for as long as she wished. But saying . . . nothing?

Sometimes sitting, studying him. What did she see?

The thick longish hair, grey to blond. As if he had been born grey, grown blond with age. The eyes, faded in firelight, suddenly startlingly blue. Winter eyes, not summer. Or not now. The unfashionable, uncareful clothes that described his largeness, his strength, his laziness, his quietude, and the abrupt animal movements that sometimes galvanized his frame – a young man pretending to be sixty. A man of seventy, eighty, who had not correctly deteriorated.

Handsome. Harsh. Intelligent. Sexy. *Wanton*. Controlled. The lips, flickering with amusements, or pain. Perhaps?

Hassinger reading.

No first name as, now, she had no second name: free of her web.

Here with him – but who was he?

Janey's father.

Once she said, 'What book is it?'

'Very old,' he said. He read to her three paragraphs she did not understand, of such beauty that she got up, cold, too hot, and went into the rest of the house, the other upper rooms he had shown her, neglected, but possibly to be renovated – her own sitting room? – *not* the store behind his priestly bed, the chamber of bottled messages and oceanic things, and Janey's picture on the wall, kept as a secret treasure.

On the wall. Where the writing was.

WET PAINT

Hesta: a Janey substitute. Just add water.

Close to ten, today, 24 December (she had slept late), the mobile phone sounded. Hassinger was out.

She walked into his room – bed made, unassailably couth,

like her own – and took the phone up.

'Hallo.'

'Is that Hesta?'

'Yes.'

'Please would you come?'

'What is it?' she said.

'Corinne's in labour. I'm her midwife, Carol.' She had become aware, in return for hers, they tended to give her their first names only. 'It started eight last night. We're not doing too well.'

'Get a doctor,' said Hesta.

'You see, Hesta, she's terrified of hospitals. Her sister died in one of an overdose two years ago. I don't want to recommend that unless I must. And any way, I'm not sure they can – it's not simple.'

'What can *I* do?' said Hesta. Her voice sounded like a lost little girl's, a little girl of six, without a mother, running to a stranger – Help me, I'm lost, what can I do?

'All right,' Hesta said. 'Give me your address.' The priestess.

Out in the transparent blue gemstone of the day, whiteness on roofs and railings, steps, edges of the road. The sea below, stilled by freezing. A crochet of ice against the beach, High Tyde – with a Y. Ancient English Ocean.

Full fathom five—

Mother and father have I none.

She walked through the side alleys, along by the Lane, where Jim lived with the white rats, behind some gardens with bare trees, and came to the address above a shut shop which, in Season, sold curios.

In the doorway, huddled together, were Decay and Bish-Op, his dark eyes large and red-rimmed.

'We walked up,' said Decay, 'but you wasn't there yet.'

'There's a woman having a baby,' said Hesta, blankly.

'Dead scared,' said Decay. 'And so's Bish-Op here. Phaedra's down the boats, y'see. With all them dogs. Two followed her back last time. Ate a whole tin of pilchards.'

Hesta reached out, but Decay rang the bell before her. They heard someone run downstairs.

It must be Carol, the woman opening the door.

'Oh, hallo. Thank you. Come straight up.'

She had a uniform on, presumably the proper uniform of midwifery, and her face was creased with the same worry repeated over and over.

Bish-Op slunk upstairs, Decay, Hesta last.

Inside the flat, the girl was on her bed, and at her movements, the plastic rustled under the sheet. The heating was on and the window open, and there was a smell of blood and urine and disinfectant and struggle – a hospital smell that after all could not quite be avoided.

The girl, exhausted, terrified, her hair black with sweat, turned her head and stared at Hesta.

And what *was* Hesta supposed to do?

There was a sheet too, over the girl's lower body. Over the hump of her body and her raised-up quivering legs.

Hesta went forward.

'Corinne.'

'It's the pain,' panted the girl, explaining. 'I'm frightened it's going to tear me in half. And it won't come out.'

Carol said, cheerfully, 'Of course it won't. Of course it will.'

The leopardess looked down into the face of human anguish. For a moment she looked at Corinne, and then the greater pain came in and Corinne was no longer human at all. She screamed and thrashed, a being of the primal swamp.

Decay said, 'We could hear her outside.'

Bish-Op made a faint noise.

Hesta thought, Why is he here?

There was blood, more blood, on the sheet, where the legs were.

Hesta thought, This will never happen to me.

She thought, But it happened to Lulu.

She thought, And to Stephanie.

'Can't you give her nothing?' asked Decay of Carol.

'I've given her all I can.'

'That gas stuff,' said Decay.

'It doesn't work, not for her. I'd better,' said Carol – she seemed suddenly to realize she was in a room full of adolescents. 'I'd better call the—'

'Don't!' screamed Corinne. She seized Hesta's hand. 'Don't let them make me go—'

'All right,' said Hesta. 'You needn't go.'

Corinne, out of all her torment, gazed at Hesta. Her face was full of love. Just as Hassinger had said. Then all of her was contorted again, her body thrusting and screaming in another constipated agony.

Bish-Op – there must be a reason why he was here. Hesta said, 'Bish-Op–' She did not know why she spoke.

But he said, 'Yes,'

Then he moved to the foot of the bed.

His sad eyes settled on the bloody sheet. The scar under

the left eye was blue from the cold outside.

'Don't look,' said Bish-Op. He pushed off the sheet.

Hesta said sternly to the girl, 'Look at me.'

Corinne looked up at her. Corinne hung from Hesta like a star from a moon. Hesta thought, I did this to Stephanie. No wonder she hates me.

Corinne said, 'Will it be all right?'

'Yes,' Hesta said. She focused on Corinne. Holding her up in buffeting dangerous space. Hesta could feel her own strength, a strong muscular grip. She said, 'It's cold outside. The snow's still on the roofs. It's Christmas tomorrow. All this will be over then.' The girl nodded, half insane, following every word, lying loose in Hesta's mental grip. And then Corinne's eyes widened and went black, seemed to go all black without any white, and from her mouth came a long pale wailing note.

Hesta turned, and saw the baby ejecting, head first, clothed in crimson, disgusting, filthy, and miraculous, sliding down as if without impediment, and falling on to the lower sheet in a puddle of blood and slime that glittered like jewelry, and stank, and after it the cord, silver, dancing, a snake.

Corinne's nails had gone through the skin of Hesta's wrist. Blood for blood.

It was a girl, and she had come in wearing red.

Bish-Op sat on the floor. Decay was rubbing the back of his neck.

Carol was bustling. Washing up after the meal of emotion, horror, labour and pain.

Gaps, between everything.

Corinne held the baby now, staring at it, caressing it, not hating it after all. It was clean, and wound in silvery white like a trendy Christmas present, but something one had wanted.

'Oh, Hesta,' said Corinne. 'Thank you for being here. Oh, you'll never know how you helped me. And Mr Bishop. Oh thank you.'

Bish-Op laughed. All his face seemed blue at last.

Decay glanced at everyone, exasperated, pleased, an unwed mother with all these talented children to care for.

Hesta could not feel her body.

As the baby spilled from the tunnel of the girl's flesh, Hesta seemed to have been loosened from her own.

She walked to the door. Without feet or legs.

Downstairs, outside, was Phaedra tiny and far off, just about to ring the bell, and turning back once, she did not know why, Hesta saw Phaedra and Bish-Op, the door standing open, kissing, passionate lovers, in the cold and frosty morning. And the baby was crying in the room above, a cute little toy bleating sound. Not at all like the crying baby which was a ghost, and that had once been dropped on the cobbles of Old Street.

Two

Would he be there?

She wanted him to be there. But did not know why. Was it anger?

She must have walked back to the house, but did not remember it. All those panes in the window. Stand outside and count them. How difficult. She could not do it.

Hesta went up, and through the corridor, and through the shorter stroke of the L, where there was coffee being made but she could not smell it, and a gull on the window ledge, but it could have been anything, a gargoyle, a winged dog.

Or a baby. The Duchess called the gull in the pram, Baby. She fed it milk and gin and blood.

In the long stroke of the L, all the books gleamed at amber firelight, and blue gemlight through the window. And the carpet was red and blue, and the ivory silk on the chairs so blond and the ebony table so brunette. The decanter *sparkled*. Russet apples and purple-ruby grapes, and a smoked vitreous chemist's bottle with a yellow lily in it – a still life. What a beautiful room.

And the man standing there, just taking a book from the shelf, at home, relaxed, turning to see her now.

'What's wrong, Hesta?'

'What's wrong,' she said.

He stood, waiting.

She stood, waiting.

'I heard that someone asked for your help,' he said.

'Mine, and Bish-Op's. The guy from the Victoria. He made a baby get born by telekinesis, like the glass he put in the air in the pub. I suppose, if you can lift something up without touching it, you can pull something out the same way. But he did it very well. She wasn't damaged. Either of them.'

'Yes, he's very gifted,' said Hassinger.

He did not look so far off as the others, or the room. He seemed to be poised in space, but quite near.

Hesta went past him and took the lily out of the bottle and laid it down carefully. Then she showed Hassinger the bottle. 'Is there a message in it?' she asked.

'No, Hesta.'

'Here's the message from the bottle then,' said Hesta. And she flung it at him. At his face.

What was the message? A spray of water like diamonds. Violence and pain, from the room over the shop, from all the rooms, from the room behind her eyes. Hesta heard herself at a small distance shouting and shouting until her voice cracked – red dress – put on so they can kill me – sacrifice – I don't care – I mean nothing – they mean nothing—

Hassinger held her arms. His breath was warmly cool on the moisture in her eyes.

'The red dress is for killing. But you're not the sacrifice.'

'Priest-kings die for their people,' she shouted.

'If they must. If they're able to. Moses did so, for example. I could do so. There must be consent. Always that. In that kind of sacrifice. If you weren't willing, it's of no value.'

'*Kill me Quick.*'

'A joke on a hat.'

'The photographer wasn't willing.'

'Not that kind of sacrifice.'

'Let go of me,' she said, her voice roughened and falling, for he was holding her against him.

'In a moment.'

'Let *go*.'

'Hesta,' he said, 'this isn't a sexual embrace.'

She thought of Bish-Op and Phaedra on the stair.

'You had sex with Lulu.'

'I told you about that. There was no sex.'

'You *loved* Lulu.'

'But not,' Hassinger said, 'in a sexual way.'

'Because you're the *priest*.'

'Because I don't have those feelings for women.'

She pulled away then. She stood there grimacing at him, noticing herself come back into her own body, tingling and hurting like circulation running back into a limb. 'You're *gay*?'

'Not significantly. I'm homosexual. Sexually I desire men. But I no longer indulge in that very great pleasure, and never will again, because I accept the celibacy of my rôle here.'

She shook herself, and as she did so, he walked away and picked up the bottle she had thrown, and which he had merely stepped aside from. It had broken neatly in two pieces. She felt sorry for it, as if she had slaughtered a defenceless harmless living thing, broken its spine, and, like a child, she began to cry bitterly.

'I can remember,' he said, as she cried to him how she had killed the bottle, 'Lulu doing just that. She dropped a little china cat she had, the night before she left. She cried for an hour. But I mended it. I can mend the bottle, Hesta. It will only be an honourable scar. And the lily, faithless thing, will drink from anything.'

Hesta bit at her hands, wrists, at the marks of Corinne's nails. She cursed herself for being such a fool, such a stupid *cunt*. He rocked her in his arms, which were safe since he did not want to rape her.

'In any case,' he said, 'there's another reason.'

She recalled Iain, picking her up when she had tripped and gone down in the hard grazing street; she was about five, probably. He held her gently. Daddy, Daddy—

This man was warm. He too held her gently. Did he care for her in the way he cared for Lulu?

What other reason?

'You're mine.'

But she was no one's.

'You also resemble someone who was once of great interest to me.'

Nonsense now.

Who?

'My last lover. The lover I should never have taken and never meant to take, since I knew I would be coming here.'

'A man,' said Hesta.

340

'Obviously, a man. A young man. Only nineteen or twenty.'

She was sitting in the chair now, comfortable but upright, and in her hands a mug of coffee, steaming, chocolaty. And Hassinger sat across from her, in the other chair, placed for dialogue.

'How can I be yours?' she said. 'What do you mean? *Janey's* yours.'

'Janey is my daughter.' He looked at her, his winter eyes, a lightning flash, up then down. He was mending the bottle with Superglue. This was funny. This man, this room – and Superglue. He set the bottle down. 'So, there's Janey. But Hesta, it isn't as simple as that. Things to do with the town seldom are.'

She was ashamed she had cried, in front of him. Of course, it was not the bottle. She had seen a baby being born, that was all. And probably Bish-Op's being there was a coincidence. Nothing supernatural had happened. Only Superglue happened.

And they were mad, here. So she could be the priestess. And they murdered people. But they would not murder her. She had not, not really, thought they would.

'After Lulu left me,' he said, 'she spent some time searching for my lover. My male lover. She was curious, she wanted not to be quite alone. She told me this, in the one very personal letter that she sent to me, years after. But before that personal letter, Lulu had already written to me many times. About you.'

'You said.'

'You see, Hesta, once Lulu had located this lover of mine,

and learned what had happened, Janey was about ten. And Lulu made certain that Janey would, in her turn, make contact with the daughter my lover had subsequently had.'

Hesta raised her head. She stared at Hassinger. 'You're saying—'

'And one day,' said Hassinger, 'my lover brought his daughter up the stairs to Lulu's flat. Because my lover's daughter, Hesta, had been asked to tea by Lulu's daughter, Janey.'

'My father was your lover.'

Hassinger said nothing. He sat, gazing now into the amber fire.

'*My father was your lover.*'

'He was. You're very like him, the way he was then. On the island they used to call him "the god". Young and golden, and the red hair, very long, in the English way. A beautiful temptation. He didn't know what was happening to him. It was easy, therefore, to have him.'

'Were you – in love with him?'

'What a woman's question,' Hassinger said, smiling. 'But you want to be sure. If I hadn't been expected here, I would have stayed for him, for your father, Jason. But then, too, I think he would have resisted that. He didn't want to be what he was.'

'And Janey—'

'She doesn't know any of this,' said Hassinger. 'Lulu only placed her in your junior school. But the moment the two of you met, you became friends. Better than Lulu could have planned. There's a reason perhaps also for that.'

Hesta shook only her head now. 'None of this makes any sense.'

Hassinger sat back, facing her.

He began to tell her about the island off the coast of Greece, late in the summer.

The colour of the sea, that was like turquoise, or the deep blue on the packets of cigarettes that Iain Jason Web had, in those days, still smoked. The olive-green olive trees, with their ripening fruits, the trees of tangerines, and the pineapples, husked like the fir cones of Dionysos, on the ground. And the villa, which straightforward Latin name for house, in Greek, meant something bawdy, and its view down to the bay, and how the village, having only seventy-three people in it, trod its own grapes, milked its own goats. The sweet savage air with its smoulderings of thyme, wild mint, and tamarisk. The crystal light.

And out of all this (as the yacht idled below on the corundum that was water, ready for sailing away), from the olive trees in their flush of gilded gossamer, Jason came walking with his name of the Ancient Greeks, his hair of fire, the knapsack on his back.

Hassinger had needed – or pretended to need – to improve his English. Iain, fascinated by one casual meeting, by a drink of real lemonade from the villa kitchen, had been so unguarded a prize.

A dinner then, in the wide cool room with its open terrace, music of cicadas and vines. A lot of local wine, potent not only from soil and rock, but from the living skin which had crushed the grapes.

An instinctive, inventive and charming lover, Jason, when with another man.

But in the morning, recrimination, terror – and panic, that old god-given state of the islands. A necessity to dissuade. He had never, as Apollo enjoined one to do, known himself. And now, he did, Iain Jason Web. Now he knew. To regain him was harder, the second time.

They had six uneven days.

After that, the arguments, that was, the railing of Jason against himself, and eventually against the man who had opened his eyes, his loins, and his spirit.

Hassinger had let him rail. On and on. Over and over.

Once, in the garden of the house, under the lemon trees, fierce sex, guttural and acid, a tearing.

And after that the swim in the bay below, to calm down, down there, in the sapphire sea.

'I know what it is,' Jason had said, threshing the water, 'you treat me like some fucking girl.'

'Do I?'

'Some silly little bint. An easy lay.'

'You were. They're the best. Unless you prefer assault.'

'You're so good with words. Big *man*. You fucking bastard A *girl*. You think I'm a *girl*.'

A fight then, Iain lashing out. Hassinger fending him off without too much difficulty. Too much *physical* difficulty Until at last, Hassinger struck him.

'He went under,' Hassinger said, in the quiet room, in the English winter. 'I waited for him to surface. When he didn't I dived to find him.' Hassinger's eyes were old. But so eyes become, even the eyes of youth, with such memory. ' couldn't find him, Hesta. I swam around for thirty minutes longer, searching. I thought I had killed him.'

She sat imperious, the red-haired girl, sat in Iain's beauty and hair, and said nothing.

344

Hassinger said, 'Hell on earth isn't only a phrase. You find versions of it in many languages. Two days later, I heard he had been seen, leaving the island on the boat. Then I knew he lived. But he left everything behind in the house. His things, even his clothes. He must have stolen clothes, or begged them from the village. So then, as intended, I came here.'

'And loved Lulu.'

'I loved Lulu. In my mind, I love her still. But never sexually. I loved your father, Hesta, with a carnal and devouring love. He was all that could have kept me from this place. And as it turned out, I was all that kept Lulu from it, and sent her away.'

'And she traced – Iain. And found out. About me.'

'And your mother,' said Hassinger.

Hesta turned her shoulder, just a fraction.

'Stephanie,' she said.

Hassinger said, 'I have something to put to you now, Hesta, which you won't be able to believe. But I shall tell you. Please listen to me.'

'If it's about Stephanie—'

'Your father was a virgin,' said Hassinger. 'He'd never – what shall I say, he had never made love with a man, or a woman. I imagine that he could only bring himself to have sex with your mother because of a desperation to prove to himself that he was heterosexual. Which, by inclination, he was not.'

'Yes.' Hesta met his eyes coldly again. 'Yes, I can believe that.'

'That isn't what you need to try to believe. I can show you

one of Lulu's earlier letters to me. I think you were about twelve. In it, Lulu makes a point of describing how she cares for you, and how this is because, in so many ways, you remind her of me.'

Hesta blinked. 'You.'

'I filled your father,' said Hassinger, 'with my seed. And after an interval of abstinence, Hesta, he filled your mother with his own.'

'That's—'

Hassinger chose the word. '*Weird*. Like the town. Yes? I fucked him, and my seed passed through him when he fucked her. Stephanie was only the vessel, like the Nebuchadnezzar, the jar that held your picture. I broke it to get you out. Two fathers, Hesta. And no mother. Only a precious jar to carry you.'

'That's biologically impossible.'

'Of course,' he said. 'But look in a mirror. You're like Iain, but not like Stephanie. And who else do you resemble?'

'But this—'

'Who else?'

'It can't—'

'Who else.'

'You,' she said. 'You.'

He stood up, and behind him the room towered, and he was winged by books, all golden, and his head touched the ceiling.

Looking up at him, she knew him, as she had known Janey for a sister from the first moment of meeting. Hassinger was her father, her true father. Father and daughter. Priest and priestess. Hassinger and Hesta.

And she need never shield him, or lie to him or for him. She need never be afraid. She need never rage. Home is where the hurt is, but no more.

It felt like blood running out of her, but was only all her life. She stood up, also, watching him. And in that second she felt pride, such pride, since he was hers, and she his. Even though it could not have happened. But it had.

Three

Sometime after three, Geegee Peck came into the Crab from his walk, looking forward to a drink, and the toasted sandwich Joy Joy would offer him.

The sun was going towards the curve of the sea, and the sky had been like stained glass, dove blue, turning rosy yellow in the west. Snow and frost still drew in the shapes of things, the tiles on roofs, the pinkened coils of the stones along the beach. Not bleak, the sea so calm, like a painting.

'Day after Boxing Day,' Geegee said to Joy, 'I'll have to get off then.'

'We'll be sorry to see you go.'

'Sorry *to* go. One of those things, I'm afraid.'

He could not, even at the cheap rate they had given him, afford to stay longer. He thought of the melancholy house in the London suburb, where sometimes, in his sleep, he had thought he felt the weight of one of the cats on his bed, but reaching out, never found it.

Christmas tomorrow.

Joy and Ted had asked him down to their Christmas dinner, but he had made some excuse about visiting a friend a couple of miles inland. It would mean wandering about for

349

a few hours in the cold, a dismal prospect, but he couldn't face their family gathering. There would be two grandchildren, a happily divorced daughter, and a son and his wife, all local, all related. And Geegee?

Joy brought him a toasted cheese sandwich with lettuce, pickle and crisps, and a double Bells, on the house, for Christmas Eve. She had put ice in the whisky, she always did, and he had stopped trying to prevent her. The ice added an extra flavour to the drink and he had come to like it a lot. Must be the water here.

As he sat in the lighted bar, the oil lamps and holly wreaths around him, and nearby the three-foot balm-scented pine tree, garbed in oranges and golden rain, Peck tallied his accounts.

Despite the floating fifty pounds, it didn't look too good. What did?

Well, he'd worry back in London.

Not here.

Here had been a real holiday. And although probably that Kevin character would turn very nasty over Peck's lack of discoveries, it was worth it.

'I wish we could stay, Auntie.'

Yes, that was him, nine, ten years old, in the seaside town, and May shaking her head in her flowery hat. They couldn't.

'But why not?'

'I got to get back, Graeme. And you've got to get back to your school.'

Horrible meaningless enforced responsibilities.

He could recall her, in her last days, propped in her bed which she had, with unusual vehemence, insisted on being

350

conveyed from the hospital, and the nurse he had found the money for saying, outraged and admiring, 'A proper tyrant, your aunt, Mr Peck.'

Poor old May, with her sad collapsed face, dying of the drifting banes of a snapped hip.

'You know, Graeme, I sometimes think we get it all wrong in this world.'

'How do you mean, dear?'

'I think we were meant to have a happy time here, really. Just enjoy ourselves, and be kind to each other. But we waste it all, don't we, muck it all up. Perhaps it's better on the other side.'

Not believing in any other side, Geegee had gently said, 'I'm sure it is.'

'Go on, you fraud,' said Auntie May, 'You don't think there's anything. But you know, I've seen all me cats. They'll come back, to show me they were all right, bless 'em.'

Outside, the sea sky deepened and darkened.

Peck looked up. The Crab was full and he had not noticed. A big blond handsome chap, late forties, early fifties, was shouldering over to the table in a frosty leather coat.

'May I sit here?'

'Be my guest.'

The man sat.

Peck felt himself become shy. It surprised him. Though almost anyone could frighten him, by this hour of his life, very few could impress. But the man in leathers was – impressive.

He had never found the girl's father, either, that man with red hair. It wasn't this one, any way, even bleached. The father had been nondescript, physically slight, not up to much, a 'wimp', as Kevin had expressed it.

Odd, to think of that now. As if, somehow, the blond man had reminded him.

'I see you have the ice made from brandy in your drink.'

Peck started at the renewal of the voice. Foreign? Something.

'Ah – do I?'

'White brandy from the smugglers' caves in the cliffs below the town. Joy puts it in the ice trays.'

'No wonder my whisky tastes special,' said Peck.

'Have another. On me.'

'Why would you do that?' asked Peck.

'It's Christmas tomorrow.'

The man smiled at Peck, and just then, Joy Joy came up, with the lime-green budgie, like a rare flower, on her shoulder, chirruping.

'Good evening, Mr Hassinger. Let me top you both up.'

And the glass of the man called Hassinger was filled full from a jug, and Peck's glass filled full from the Bells bottle.

No payment. Joy Joy going blithely away through the crowd. Men and women, and a child here and there, and the figureheads at the walls, making the crowd larger.

Peck wanted to go on talking to the man called Hassinger. So he said, 'I've been hearing about those caves. I heard a mermaid was seen there.' He grinned.

'There's a notice on the cliff,' said Hassinger. 'A warning. Rockfalls. Also, when the tide come in, it floods the caves. There's a high tide tonight.'

'I might take a walk down there tomorrow, at low water.'

'It would be safe enough then,' said Hassinger.

He must be an actor, the charisma that came off him was ‌lpable. That would explain, too, the familiar look to the ‌ce. Or that might only be the phenomenon Peck had read ‌ once, the way very attractive people often seemed known, ‌ if you had been looking for them, or met them previously ‌ frequently the cause of so-called love at first sight, ‌parently.

'Better see as much of the place as I can,' said Peck. 'Back ‌ London day after Boxing Day. Not that I was here on ‌liday. Came here looking for someone. Young cousin gone ‌issing. Girl with red hair.'

Hassinger – was he a German – no, he looked more Dutch ‌he eyes very blue, very pale. And yet, Peck found himself ‌nking of the bad Polaroid of the girl called Hesta, with an ‌ the other eyes that had gone red like a fox's.

'She may have come to the coast to see her father,' said ‌ck.

Hassinger seemed to be waiting.

Peck, abruptly nervous, almost what May would have ‌lled 'fluttery', downed his drink. For once, it affected him, ‌ way it would have when he was seventeen.

And as this occurred, Hassinger said, 'You must mean Iain ‌eb. Iain and Hesta.'

Peck swallowed air now.

'You know them?'

'Do you?' said Hassinger.

The room tilted a little.

In Peck's mind there swam, easily and at peace, all the ‌es he had found, Gary for Shelagh, and Reginald and

353

Elizabeth and Sean, and the rest, all the rest, who had wante to be found.

And further off, only partly to be seen, the ones he had l go, the ones he had colluded with and hidden from pursuer Mr Brand's wife who had fled with her lover, and the sist of evil Beverley Spriggs, and the little girl taken by h mother, and Connie, who had become a whore but wa cheerful, and saving up to buy a maisonette.

'Mr Hassinger, I'm what's laughingly called a Private Ey Her mother's boyfriend, and the mother, perhaps, they hir me. And some manager in a wine bar. But to be honest, didn't think much of them. Don't tell me anything else. Whe I get back I'm going to say that I couldn't find anything ou Between ourselves, I did spot the girl, in fact, I think so. B then, I'm a drunken old fart, so what do I know.'

'Mr Peck,' said Hassinger, who presumably had got Peck name from Joy and Ted. That was all. *Mr Peck.*

Peck felt well up in him, up from the very depths of a Pe that Geegee would never normally have grasped to be a pa of himself, an aching wish to confide in Hassinger. 'We frankly, I've got to get back. Try to look on the bright sid That's what my aunt used to say. She was good at that, too mean, not like the ones who preach at you and can't bloo do it themselves. I've done my best. I learnt a lot from he

'She sounds a fine woman.'

'She was. Indeed she was. The thing is, just before I g this job, the detective, that's me, found out something abo himself.'

Hassinger sat, listening.

Peck thought, Why not say? Talking to a stranger—

'Funny, really, staying in this pub. The Kissing Crab. I only worked it out a while ago.'

Hassinger waited. Then he said, 'How long have you got?'

'They don't know. Not long. I'm supposed to get in to hospital and have some things done to me. But I didn't fancy it. I've put it off. And of course, you can't do that. Can't wait. Not with cancer.'

Hassinger said nothing. From him radiated the cool still calmness, massive, like the sea, a silence that took and bore up. It is not always possible to swim. Lie back, the water carries what gives in.

Peck said, 'There's very little pain. Which is a bit of luck. And the drink keeps it off. Especially here. But I'd better get on with it, hadn't I. Go back and face up to it. I don't want to upset anyone here. Nice people.'

Hassinger listened.

'There's a wonderful old car down on the beach,' said Peck. 'Pontiac, I think. I can remember seeing a couple in my twenties. What it's doing there, God knows. I thought I was dreaming when I saw it. Cleaned and polished, and with holly and streamers all over it.'

Joy must have come, unseen, and Peck felt a moment of alarm that she had heard his confession, but there she was, laughing at the bar, and the budgerigar on her head, and she was too kind a woman to be laughing, at once and quite like that, if she had overhead. But the glass was full again.

'Forget I said all that, will you,' said Peck.

'Yes, Mr Peck. Of course.'

Hassinger reached across, and Peck realized they were to shake hands. He shook Hassinger's hand. The touch was full

355

of power, not healing, as in some TV film it might had been, but – emptying. That was it. As if Hassinger, like the sea, had taken away the sourness and the creeping horror.

It would come back. But not now. Not yet. Not here.

The girl walked across the room, her delicate pallor glowing against the plum drapes.

Martin Peecey watched her.

'Come back to bed, baby.'

She turned, smiling at him. 'What's it worth, Marty?'

'Come and see.'

'Naughty Marty.'

She drew the curtains closed and glided over to him. She looked only fourteen. Breasts like buds. No surplus of anything but the hair that poured from her head, like Christmas tinsel, to the backs of her knees.

He had dispensed with her apron and her stockings by now. He wanted only her skin and her bones. For the first time, he wondered, vaguely, if he loved her. He had never loved anyone. (Love was a myth.)

Coming, her mouth clamped to his, her slight weight forcing him under, drowned, all was rainbow, and then dark. And in the dark she lay, feeding him oysters, which it seemed could be got here, like everything else under the sun, and the pink champagne.

'There's a party tonight.'

'Oh, yeah.'

'Want to go?'

'Just stay with you, baby.'

'To please me.'

'I'd do anything.'

'Pretty Marty.'

He laughed. Embarrassed. Tickled.

But he was 'pretty'. He must be. The incredible hotel where, for the first time in his life, everyone seemed genuinely to like him, to want to give him the best. The sauna opened just for him, and for her. The swimming pool. The amazing cuisine. Every service.

Sometimes, through a veil, he recollected Stephanie. But she did not matter, and any way, she had gone. Left him here. Stupid bitch. But why not? Why not let her have some fun. He was.

They showered together, the girl and he.

He did not know her name. Had she ever told him? When he began to make small plans, London, the wine bar, she and he – they were like dreams. But it was all like a dream. A creamy dream. Delights of the flesh. All melting and melding into one perfect and seamless endless hour, where night and day were only moths against the blind.

He did not know, for who had told him, that into his arm, that first night, when he and Stephanie lay drugged in the excellent suite, someone had injected the essence of the sea, to cleanse his blood.

He did not know, how could he, that into every morsel of his food and sip of wine, the sea had entered.

Now the sea was in his veins.

The drug of the sea, the weeds of the sea, gathered from the shore, from under the pier, from the rocks that stepped into the water.

Martin Peecey was not himself.

Looking in the mirror, after the shower, after she had shampooed his hair and body, laved him with unguents, kissed him with her lips and tongue, he saw only his own face, Stephanie's graffiti wiped away.

He was a prince among men. Lean and mellow as marble, his hair silken, his eyes grown larger as if with seeing.

'Pretty Martin.'

'Men aren't pretty, baby.' So soft, his reprimand.

She wound the serpents of her moon-pale arms about his neck. 'Are you happy, Marty?'

'Yes.' He meant it.

He was happier than he had ever been.

Four

Hesta stood by the dilapidated wall at the base of the garden, and looked down across the town. She wore the red dress, and over that, the red velvet cloak that had been brought about five this afternoon. Five was a red hour, for Hesta saw numbers and letters in colour, which Janey had said was called sinesthesia. But the world was black, and only the lights of windows and Christmas trees and stars, interposed. Ten now, a shadow hour, and next eleven, hour like silvery parchment, with the tide beginning to come in. Midnight, the hour of gold, would be high tide tonight. The moment of the birth of gods.

A man was walking along the promenade.

She could see him, distantly.

He walked alone, for no one else was out in the town.

She was waiting for the lights. Hassinger, her father, had told her, and she had come down to see. This was childhood's end.

As Peck walked along to the end of the promenade, something made him turn, and look up, to the pillars of the cliffs above the town. A curious house with one long lighted window stood high up. Who lived there? It must once have been a wealthy house, but appeared less certain now. There could even have been squatters in it.

Turning away, he stared out into the dark that was the sea.

There was no one in the town. They had all gone away, leaving only their lights behind them. This was how it felt, but actually, obviously, it was he who was to go away. When the bell tolls, you are alone.

He went down the steps carefully, they were slippery, to the beach. The moon was behind the land. The cliffs showed palely black, full of grotesque faces and carvings made by weather and time.

A girl said, nearby, 'You've been really quiet today.' Peck jumped. No one was there. A trick of the silence, or the whisky-induced hissing in his ears.

Joy Joy had given him a bottle, put it on the table in his room above the bar, with a green bow. *Happy Xmas, Mr Peck*, said the label with a teddy bear.

Geegee picked up the bottle and held it to him, chucked the painted teddy under the chin. A little item lay next to the bottle, done up in a piece of shiny white paper. He did not unwrap it, but put it in his pocket.

Then he went and had a bath, cut his nails, shaved. He scrubbed his teeth with the straggly toothbrush. Back in the room, he put on clean underwear, dressed.

After this, he shoved everything in his bag, did it up, and pushed it under the bed.

His money, the fifty-two pounds that were still left, and what he had cashed from the cheque yesterday, he put on the table. It would more than cover what he owed.

Standing here now, in the cold, under the architecture of the cliffs, the strangest thing happened.

For the world changed colour.

Every vein and hollow of the rocks was pink and mauve and violet and silver-yellow. And the frills on the sea were touched with gold and green. The sky gleamed.

Peck looked back up at the promenade from which he had descended.

The lights had come on.

How like this place to do that. To activate the illuminations on Christmas Eve.

With innocent wonder for a moment, Geegee took in the line of the esplanade, outlined in garnets and topaz and emerald and amethyst, the seahorses with peridot manes, and manes of diamond embers, the fish made of lapis lazuli, the sapphire dolphin and boats of opal with fiery sails.

'Oh Auntie, look, look!'

And down on the beach, between this spot and the long, now lighted pier, a blaze of white, which he realized was the headlamps of the American car, that must also have been switched on, burning out like a lighthouse to sea.

He was glad he had seen all this. It was another facet he remembered, of any seaside, those glamorous lights, everything illuminated, so that the darkest night was bright, was turned into day.

At eleven, the clock struck.

When they were walking down the stair to the town, a gull flew from the cliff and Hassinger, raising his arm, let it perch there.

361

He smoothed the feathers of its head with one finger.

'Can I?'

'Yes.'

Hesta stroked the gull with her left hand.

The gull looked at her. What did it see?

She lifted her right hand slowly, the hand with the dagger in it. The gull craned its neck. Perhaps it thought she offered food. It flew up suddenly, the vast wings skimming the crown of her hair.

But they went on, downwards, to the end of the steps.

The windows of the Norman church were alight, and beyond, many of the decorative windows in the shops and flats. They moved into Old Street, walking over the cobbles, across which light fell like gilded oil, and at the end, the promenade opened, left and right, and the illuminations were on, as she had seen from the wall of the garden.

He stopped her.

'How are you?'

'Fine.'

'Are you afraid?'

'Yes.'

'That's as it should be.'

'But you told me how to do it,' she said. 'Did Lulu – did she do it?'

'Yes, Hesta.'

Hesta said, 'Janey couldn't.'

'I know.'

'I thought perhaps,' Hesta paused, and below, on the beach, she heard them now, all of them, waiting there, moving, murmuring a little, as the sea did, coming in. 'I

362

thought Lulu might have given me the mousetrap, deliberately.'

'I don't know. It's possible.'

The sea breathed.

They went on to an area where steps led down towards the stones.

Going to the party on the beach, Martin was in his best, his flesh-colour loose suit with the white French T-shirt that cost eighty-nine pounds. And the girl, she looked lovely, ace, in her little short white strapless dress, and he marvelled how she did not seem to feel the cold, but perhaps the metres of her silken hair kept her warm, and even he needed no coat, full of champagne, and feeling great.

The lights were on. Maybe it was summer.

That must be it. Late summer, or October maybe, and quite mild.

The moon was rising.

It was as if he had forgotten about the moon, seen it last in childhood, but it had come back.

A big party. A rave.

Thousands of people on the beach.

'You're the star, Marty.'

He was. They were shaking his hand. Patting his back. Passing bottles, laughing. Like birthdays. When he was a kid.

It was warm enough here, the warmth of life.

They had torches, too, as if from some historical film . . .
The vivid red of the flames and the liquid ribs of sea reflecting, roses and sparkle from the lights, and wine from the torches, and women kissed him, and some of them were OK.

His mother had iced the moon for him.

We killed Roy, here. Christmas 1925

First they carried the flaming torches round the boats, and on every hull, a bottle was smashed, whatever the boat liked – vodka, gin, whisky, geneva, absinthe, brandy, advocaat. Two of the boats, *Stella* and the *Black Girl*, preferred modern drinks, Malibu, White Lady ready mixed. One was teetotal, and for her, the *Tippy*, they brought a pricey non-alcoholic wine.

They tied red ribbons, such as had been tied with the first nails, to the masts, and turned on the radios, which, with the static of the freezing night, produced a compendium of noises, voices apparently speaking English or African dialects, or tongues from antique lands, or outer space.

On the car too, they broke a bottle of Jim Bean, and tied red ribbons in the holly over the bonnet.

Then the wire let her down slowly over the wooden slides, down into the rising, bobbing sea.

'That car,' said Martin, as the Pontiac coasted out, her movement not that of a boat, 'she's a classic—'

Chuck forged into the inky swell, and drank up, through her open windows, the thirst-quenching ocean.

Her headlamps beamed cheerfully through a curtain of water.

She sank without resistance, and golden bubbles rose in her wake.

It was the big boat, painted black, standing down against the edge, where the world gave way to chaos. Her sail was up, a sail that was white. Her radio had caught a pulse of classical music from Thailand, or that was how it sounded.

Mr Rutherford had gone up by the engine. He wore his demob suit, the suit they had given him in 1945, when, drunk with freedom, he had staggered off the ship under the White Cliffs of Dover, white, as he had said, from all them bloody bluebirds flying over.

The suit was a freak, for it was beautiful, donated by a Jewish tailor. Black as the dark which had almost come, wool, double-breasted, and streamlined, with turn-ups, and the hand-set sleeves of Savile Row.

Porky Arthur Rutherford had not suited the suit, then. But time makes a man, not war. Now, grown thin with his ninety years, and one inch shorter, he looked like a king. And where the material shone a little, it was only like satin. Within, a pristine blue shirt, and the tie his sister had sent him for Christmas, retrieved early from the packaging. She always said, Arthur had a special Do, some Christmases. And he liked the ties she chose.

In the stern was Flin, eighteen years of age, a part-time weight-lifter, slimly muscular and delectable, covered in hidden love bites, with rainy Irish eyes. He wore the latest suit from the catalogue, only just paid for, in shade 'Natural', three-button, single-breasted, but with turn-ups, also, though of a man-made fibre. Beneath, the striped waistcoat and black T-shirt.

At the waist of the boat, the priest in his rich man's suit, pale like the young man's, his greying fair hair tied back.

And the priestess in her long red dress.

As Martin was helped up the ladder into the boat, he felt the thrill of childish freshness, the adventure. He was going somewhere. He was on his way.

There was a sort of plank, or raft, and this was where he came to stand.

And looking up, with the bottle of pink champagne in his hand, as the young man, careful and friendly, stripped him, Martin saw a girl so beautiful that even *his* girl, left below on the stones, went from his mind.

'Hesta?' said Martin.

He had always known she was for him.

Her face was so serious, and something new was in it, something he had never seen before in her. He took it for attraction.

'Hesta, you look brilliant.'

Naked now. How marvellous the night felt. He could taste the stars.

Hesta reached out, and with her left hand, held his right hand.

He had always known, for her he would be the first.

The boat was moving now, bumping down over the slides, and the wire singing from the winch.

To look back, was to behold them all, all the town, standing on the shore, and in their eyes the jewels of the lights.

So we set off, and leave the world behind, upon the sea of night.

In fact, it had not been difficult to get up into the cave. Never difficult, no doubt. The smugglers with their casks of brandy, rum and other merry-making substances, climbing here. The sea presumably had not come in so far, at that time. Unless they had used the wash of the ocean to send the excise men to their doom.

Peck sat, at ease, on the rock. The floor sloped back, and already the sea, lapping at the cave mouth, was spilling through in long, piscean trickles.

The moon was up. *All* the lights were on.

Joy Joy's whisky was very strong, something from Belgium, it seemed to be, and even without the magical ice, it had worked its spell.

What a boon booze was. Good luck to it.

He was not frightened. The man in leather seemed to have taken all that. Not frightened, not anything. Warm and comfortable. Not a worry in the world.

Geegee recollected a rhyme from somewhere, the epitaph for a toilet: *The trouble you see with the WC is it's rubble you see.* And laughed aloud. But no demon stood up in the gloom to remind him that he was a stupid sod, dying alone in a cave. Instead the cave took his laugh, and doubled it. Company.

Half the whisky gone. Timing spot on. When the water came, he might not even feel it.

It had been the hospital that upset him, like May, knowing they could do nothing, and lying there.

Not a thing pushed at him now, to think of it, the going out like a light. What happens when the lights go out? He could just recall May saying, 'Of course, it's not for us to know. If we knew, we'd never put up with all this, would we?'

The sea was round him now. But the sea was warm. A hot bath. Soak away your aches and pains.

Then the hard thing in his pocket shifted, and absently, he took it out. It was already wet, and the shiny Christmas paper flaked away. Joy Joy and Ted had given him, as an extra present, car keys. But the Belgian whisky, under the ocean for a hundred and twelve years, told Peck he need not bother about that. So he held the keys in his right hand, and tipped the whisky into his mouth as the water tipped down into the cave.

A little less than a quarter of a mile from shore, they cut the engine. The black boat sat upon the black sea, her one lamp piercing down into it. The sounds and musics faded from her radio.

Looking towards the land, Hesta saw tiny creatures caught in the arc of lights. The lights were all an entity, the fires and the electricity, the colours, and the human things contained within. The curve of the earth, pressed to the curve of the sea, seemed quite small.

Martin's face against the far-off radiance was a young face, that had forgotten its wearer.

It was compassion he had glimpsed in hers.

'Martin,' she said.

He smiled, happily. Sure and safe.

'Baby,' he said.

'Close your eyes.'

Martin closed his eyes, and Hesta kissed him on the lips. And holding him lightly, with the dagger like a razor, she slashed open both the veins of his neck.

Flin caught him, and the rare pale suit was splashed like butcher's apron. The blood burst up. It hit Hesta's cheek, and all down her dress. It covered the boat, the sail.

Martin's eyes did not open. His smiling mouth did not change.

When he was dead, Flin and Arthur Rutherford laid him

on the raft and, taking it up, Flin carrying most of the weight, dropped it over the side.

The raft landed, and Martin lay straight, upon it, exact. It had been excellently done.

Hassinger gave Hesta the moistened cloth, with which she wiped her cheek and hand.

Silence after this, on the face of these waters. On the lilting black boat, the fire-lit shore, on the raft and the dead, and on the moon-span of the enormous sky.

Not a breath. Not a sound.

And then, the sky breaking, altered into a tempest made of wings.

The gulls, flying as it seemed from the back of the moon. White wings black, and black heads white. Eyes like torches brought from shore, like electric bulbs. Beaks a duplicate dagger.

There was no sky. Only the wings. And the noise of the wings.

They fell on him, on the dead, and tore his body in pieces. The sea was feathered with them. Their beaks were scarlet, as they ate.

The water spun round and round, and seemed, although perhaps it was not, to be all red. But above, the moon was white.

And the girl, white-faced above her red. But red on white with hair.

On the shore, a sort of roaring, a sort of dancing under the light. Moving as the sea moves, although the land remains without emotion.

After the sea had come in through Peck, he opened his eyes and he saw the mermaid. She was trim, but not young, her long grey hair covering her decorously, her tail strong and flexible and silvery as a sardine. She had her hat on, too, and behind her, Tiger was swimming, playing about with his tail which was also, perhaps tantalizingly, that of a large and limber fish.

'We'll go and have a cup of tea with a drop of something in it.'

'Auntie May,' he said, 'you can't drink a cup of anything under the sea.'

'You'd be surprised, Graeme, what you can do, down here.'

Is it over? Has it begun? Am I myself? Or another? The ocean whispers to the land, and the land, little by little, goes back into the waves.

Long after the lights had been switched off, along the promenade, and in all the flats and houses, in the dark, Hesta found herself standing on the cobbles of Old Street. No one was with her, and on her dress the blood had caked stiff. She knew, washing her hair at three or four a.m., the blood would run out of it.

She had been answered. To this answer there now needed to be formed no further question.

Know yourself. What is best, eventually, is always that.

And standing in the dark, presently she heard the car, the throaty thrum-thrum of the Bugatti, and Moses drove towards her, slowly, down the street.

Debonair Giles Sullivan of the parted red hair he was no

longer. Now a Moses burnt black, a countenance between that of an ancient man and a seagull, gramophone needles for teeth, a straw boater, and the black car smoking, close as a sarcophagus, round his body.

But raising his hand, seeming to pull a cord, the lights flash on in his eyes, and inside the vacant bone where once his nose had been.

And Moses tips his boater, politely, to the young girl wearing red. She sees this quite clearly. The courtesy of the dead. And up from under the boater, after all, the red of fire, hair of fire, fire of hair, a conflagration, and the ashes and sparks flying off into the night, until the boater is set on again.

After which the car drives by, or through her, soft as the snow which once again begins to fall. And as the noisy motor vanishes from hearing, Hesta goes up the steps towards her father's house, her home, where the unquestionably welcoming light burns on in all two hundred panes.

End of Part Seven

Sea-Change

April weather blew along the shore. The Duchess waddled behind her pram, and Baby sat inside robed in a shawl. This was their last outing, for a while, since the Season began again tomorrow. The first visitors had booked into the hotel, the B and Bs. Tomorrow night, the illuminations would be switched on. The funfair would be opened. Already, on the salty wind, a faint premonition of hamburger.

Down on the beach, the sea also blew a bright grey wind, trimmed with yellow lace, that broke to white velvet. Clouds set sail, and from the blue patches behind, spangles of rain went scattering.

The little girl was dancing along the stones.

'Be careful,' Adèle cried, to her new daughter.

A plump child, tall, with a white clear skin and long light hair. 'I will – I will –' Bending now to take up a stone with a dark blue pattern. 'Look – it's like eyes—'

'So it is.'

From the promenade, Hesta watched them.

In half an hour at the jewelry shop, Hesta would sit down and begin, working from her drawings, upon the twists of dull silver and the small polished agates and ambers. Making

welry interested her, even the polishing, some of which she
d at home, in her sitting room of pale gold walls. She liked
e way she had the knack, already, of taking something
nformed, and forming it to its own unarguable and unique
ape.

But the letter from Janey, brought this morning, which had
rrived care of the post office by the station, was in her hand.
t the railing, she had read it again.

The London flats were to be pulled down, and Lulu had
id she did not any way like the pressure on Janey at the
hool, all the fuss about exams. 'We're off somewhere, don't
now where. Mum says it's great, like your town, but not. So
cited, Hesta, I couldn't sleep. We told the cat. You always
ould. But she doesn't mind travel. Mac's driving us. Mum
nt her new number to her obscene caller.'

Near the end, Janey mentioned Lulu had suggested
irecting the letter via the seaside post office, so it would
ach Hesta. 'I hope it does. I hope you're really OK.'

There was a watercolour in with the letter, which had
urneyed in a stiff-backed eight by ten envelope. The
ainting showed Hesta herself in a herb-green mediaeval
ress, standing by an ice-green ocean. This Hesta was even
ore slender and had even more hair of an even more
ntastic red. Yet, it was so like Hesta, she had stayed some
me with the picture in silence.

Janey had signed her work with her J, and the Egyptian
ye.

Under that it said, *I miss you. Always love.*

But the letter ended, 'Yours very truly insane, Jane.' And
ext to that was a tiny perfect cartoon of the cat.

There had come to be talk, too, of cats in the town. Catsmeat (appropriately) had told Hesta he had seen the ghostly car, not Moses' Bugatti, but this white American job with fins. There was seaweed on it, but inside it sat, it seemed, a sort of Bogart and Bacall, a private eye from an American early film, very suave, with just the right hat, and a smart young woman with luxurious silver hair in an elegant 1930s style. Her hat had a veil.

Otherwise, the car was full of cats. You could just see them, jumping about and playing. And they purred. You could hear the purring, for the car itself made no noise.

Down on the beach, Adèle's adopted daughter laughed, waving at the gulls. Adèle gave the child bread. The child fed the gulls, fearless, delighted. Her hair was blown. Like the sea, it had a lot of grey in it.

The Duchess had gone towards the pier.

Hesta walked down the steps, on to the windy beach.

The sea was loud. It crashed – a thousand goblets shattered – to the stones and was sluiced away, and galloped in again.

'Mummy –' the child, startled to see Hesta approaching, drew back against the black girl.

Adèle, only slightly taller, shielded the child.

'It's all right, Stephanie.'

Hesta stopped, looking at the woman who had carried her and given her birth. Stephanie appeared very well. Her face only a little puckered now by concern. The dryness and the sharp lines had gone, perhaps on the morning she woke up from her dreamless sleep, and was ten again.

'How is she?'

'She's doing great. Aren't you, Stephanie?'

'Yes.' Stephanie eyeing Hesta, unsure.

Did she remember anything? No, it was only a natural nease at the presence of another, unknown, adult.

What does she think, the leopardess, seeing this? Hesta imply inclines her head.

'Do you like the gulls, Stephanie?'

'Oh yes. And we've got a pussy, and a dog.'

Stephanie beamed. The adult was not so terrible after all. There's a circus,' announced Stephanie.

Adèle said, 'That's the new white car, did you hear? It ounds like a circus – horses and tigers – like that.' She uffled Stephanie's hair. Stephanie looked pleased. 'She likes im's rats, too.'

Hesta turned her head, just a fraction. It might have been nything. Nothing.

But Stephanie, free of restraint, went suddenly dancing on long the beach in her plimsoles, punching at the wind with oth hands, under the armada of the clouds.

'Her hand looks OK.'

'The boy – Bish-Op – reset it. She screamed, of course. It nust have hurt. But she's doing well now.'

'She used not to like animals,' said Hesta.

'She's silly over them. She has the dog and the cat in bed. Von't go to sleep until they come in. And we've got a quirrel runs over from the park. She feeds him.'

'Thank you,' Hesta said. 'Thank you.'

She turned from Adèle, and from the prancing ten-year-old vho was almost thirty-seven years of age. Stephanie knew he odd name of the purring ghost car: G.G. May and Tigers.

Hesta walked away over the shore. She watched the waves

She had noted already, something was coming in Something long and pale, yet oddly colourful at one point wriggling and turning. Adèle had not seen. And now Adèle and the child were a hundred yards off. That was definitely for the best.

Hesta stood. She waited.

He swam to her feet, a little at a time, in and in, and knocked at last against her boot. Like a fish of wood disjointed and broken, pale so pale. She did not need to bend down.

Her other father had been in the sea for long enough tha most of his face had washed away. A few ribbons stayed fluttering, not gruesome, gently. And a rag of his pyrotechnic hair which, never in her life, had Hesta noticed as being so vividly and appeasingly red.

His face was a skull, purified and laughing, and his teeth must have been first class, for there was not a single filling and not one missing.

Where those pearls that were in his eyes?

Perhaps . . .

In spite of everything, she leaned to be sure. Yes, she could see pearls.

Full fathom five. Rich and strange.

What had he come to tell her?

After a minute, she saw how his pelvis had rotated in the remnants of his jeans, and out of the back pocket, half an inch of glossy postcard protruded.

She had no fear of touching him, and in the end did not actually, touch him at all.

The postcard showed nothing absolute any more, only a aint of exquisite colour, indescribable, near to invisible.

On the back, the writing after all was not that of Iain Jason Web.

Hesta did not recognize the signature, which was just lecipherable as Catherine Lawrence. Nor the two words of he message that remained:

Heavenly here.